ECHOES

Phil.

Copyright © Phil Oddy 2024

All rights reserved. No portion of this book may be reproduced, copied, distributed or adapted in any way, with the exception of certain activities permitted by applicable copyright laws, such as brief quotations in the context of a review or academic work. For permission to publish, distribute or otherwise reproduce this work, please contact the author at phil@philoddy.com.

This book is a work of fiction. Names, characters, places and incidents are either a product of the author's imagination or are used fictitiously. Any resemblance to actual people living or dead, events or locales is entirely coincidental.

Front cover designed by Getcovers

ECHOES

Entanglement Book I

Phil Oddy

Part One

CHAPTER 1

I was not supposed to be on this train. This trip was too important, with too much on the line for me to be entrusted with it. A new contract in a new territory that could set TrakcD Solutions up with a source of revenue for years to come was at stake. Why would they choose a junior salesman with my lack of sales ability to head this one up?

Apart from the fact that my dad owned the company, I supposed.

I didn't want to be a software salesman. I just kind of fell into it, never having had a plan of my own and, well, I refer you to my earlier statement about my dad owning the company. It was an easy option. It wasn't a good idea, but it was easy, so it's what I did.

I wasn't even very good at it. I hardly ever made a sale.

The train sped on into the night. I closed my eyes and sank into the rhythm of the wheels on the track.

> *Duh-dum, duh-dum.*
> *Duh-dum, duh-dum.*
> *Can't-make a-sale.*
> *Can't-make a-sale.*

Phil Oddy

My mind drifted.

I hadn't been the first choice, anyway. I'd been getting tea, avoiding work, when Crispy Burton had cornered me in the break room.

Crispy Burton had a sales call in Trinity the following day.

Crispy Burton had found that, because of "extenuating circumstances", he could not attend. This was, he believed, "an opportunity for you, Estrel. Maybe even a golden ticket to the senior sales team…".

Crispy Burton was an excellent example of why I didn't want to join the senior sales team. He was a man of a certain type, in advanced middle age, with an inflated opinion of himself.

It was impossible for Crispy Burton to believe that I wouldn't want to follow in his footsteps. Which he was sure I would, "if you play your cards right and bring home the bacon, rah?".

Something like that. I wasn't sure he actually said "rah", but it was illustrative of who Crispy Burton was, if the name Crispy wasn't enough for you.

Regardless, it was a bit of a blur, and I hadn't meant to say "yes". No, I hadn't wanted to say "yes", but I did. I wasn't good at saying "no".

So there I was, an eleven hour train ride from home, arriving in a strange city, under-motivated and under-prepared.

I should have said "no". I didn't think I would enjoy being a senior salesman - I didn't enjoy being a junior salesman - but everyone else thought I would. It wasn't just Crispy Burton. My dad thought I would, expected I would.

That was it, then. I had to pretend that I would.

Echoes

I woke up as the announcement finished. I glanced at my watch. It was almost seven. We were due into Trinity any minute.

I hoped the announcement had been to tell us we were approaching our destination, rather than to apologise for the late running of the service. I must have dozed off after breakfast. Despite having drunk enough coffee to stimulate an elephant, it wasn't doing its job, palpitations apart. The pounding of my heart made me feel distant and out of sync.

The carriage wasn't busy. I had two comfortable leather seats to myself and the two opposite me were also empty. My bag was on the wide table between them. Someone had cleared away my breakfast things while I'd been asleep.

I yawned and stretched. My legs had enough space, and I had a cushion for my head. This was travelling in style. Very comfortable. Who wouldn't take the opportunity for a nap?

I looked out of the misted window. We were travelling over a bridge, a viaduct across a vast valley, the slopes thick with trees. At the bottom of the canyon, the Triton wound its way from its source in the Proctean Mountains, flowing through the city ahead and into the Middle Sea.

I hadn't been to Trinity before, but I'd done my research. At least, I'd looked it up on my Com before I set off. I hadn't had long. I'd only found out that I was coming yesterday.

I loosened my neck-tie and ran a finger around the collar. The air-con was blowing a concentrated jet of cold air past my left ear, which wasn't doing a lot for me. I felt clammy. It was making my breakfast stir in my stomach unpleasantly. I tried to sigh out a wave of nausea but gagged, almost bringing up my breakfast anyway.

After I'd failed to say "no" to Crispy Burton, I'd barely had time to get home to shower and throw a bag together before the car came to take me to the station. The office had booked the overnight to Trinity for me. I just had to turn up and go with the flow. That was the one thing I was good at.

I glanced down at the seat next to me. The book I'd taken from the lounge sat unopened, judging me. I thought I'd read on the train, but hadn't, instead spending my time endlessly scrolling my Com, running down the battery until it was into single figures. I hadn't picked up a spare pack for it. When I got to my destination, I hoped I'd be able to find a new one.

Through the glass partition that divided the carriages, I saw someone moving. Their shaven head and azure robe marked them out as a Cleric, one of the Devoted.

The Devoted were known outside Trinity, but we sophisticated Ashuanans tended to view them as more of a superstitious cult than an actual religion. It was interesting to see one of their order up close. He looked serene.

I was about to look away, but the shot of déjà vu I got when the man looked up and locked eyes with me took me by surprise. I froze. It was so familiar that I felt I was looking at my own brother.

He was… I reached for the bubble of the memory, but it floated from my grasp and then burst in the air, disappearing in front of me. The man looked away, and the moment broke. I found myself breathless.

To distract myself from the rush of awkwardness, I rummaged through my brown leather courier bag, open on the table in front of me. I wasn't looking for anything; it was just something to do.

I found an apple and some wax-paper wrapped sandwiches I'd bought before I got on the train, filling undetermined. I decided not to unwrap them as it looked like they were mayonnaise based and already leaking out.

There was also a bundle of waterproofs wrapped around

a bar of mint cake and a crumpled receipt, which I uncrumpled. It was for a pair of hiking boots, from a store I didn't recognise the name of.

I couldn't remember ever owning any hiking boots. A vague memory of stopping to buy them drifted by, but that couldn't be real. I had stopped nowhere.

A dream then? That was silly. I couldn't have used the bag in a long time. I must have owned some boots, left the receipt there from a previous trip. My tablet had worked its way to the bottom of the bag, and it was out of battery.

That was more of a problem than my Com. I needed it for the sales presentation. Buying a spare pack had become a priority. I checked the pockets on the front and found my toothbrush and a change of underwear, so I hadn't been completely useless when packing.

The train reached the end of the bridge and approached the city walls. We were still high above ground level; the track sat on top of a towering embankment.

Trinity. I closed my eyes and blew out. It was going to be fine. This trip could be a big deal for me, but that was only a problem if I let it be. The train slid into a tunnel through the walls, a formidable perimeter some ten metres deep. Momentary darkness.

In the blackness, in the half second, I thought I heard someone whisper my name. I turned to the window, in the voice's direction, but all I could see was my reflection.

I blinked. Not my reflection, not my face, but one that I recognised. An older face, an echo from a dream. Then the automatic fluorescent lights flooded the carriage and my features resolved, putting me back where I should have been in the glass.

I shook my head. My mirror image shook his head back. There was enough to deal with without conjuring ghosts. I jiggled my leg nervously, watching the power cables snaking along the walls as we sped past.

The train burst out of the tunnel. The carriage lights clicked back off, but the light was different on this side of the wall.

We remained high above street level, which was cast deep in shadow by the high-rise blocks that sprouted from the ground. They shot up to the top of the city walls, as if even they needed to find some cleaner air. At this level there was some, although the soot and grime coating the drying sheets that billowed from the balconies left no doubt that "cleaner" didn't mean "clean".

The train slowed to crawl its way into the station, past windows, some of which were not boarded up. I scrolled past intimate snapshots of other people's lives.

A couple entwined, asleep, on a single bed, their twisted bedcovers just about preserving their modesty; a billboard, paper peeling, stuttering to advertise billboard space; a mother feeding her infant in its highchair with a plastic spoon, scraping the corners of the bowl to ensure they got every morsel that she couldn't afford to feed herself; a billboard, paper peeling, faded slogans replaced with the words "Fuck Chaguartay" spray painted across them; a rooftop garden, green shrubs defying the air quality, a brother and his toddling sister playing hide and seek precariously close to the edge; a window with "Fuck Chaguartay" spray painted across it; beyond that, the dismal trash of a tweak palace, balloons and pipes and syringes and bodies strewn where they had fallen; an old woman drinking tea in her rocking chair amongst the chintz and clutter of her refuge from the world she found herself in; a woman, sheets pulled up to her neck, reviewing the credits transferred to her Com, which would have been scant recompense for the services she had just rendered, even if she hadn't found them to be short; an old man tending to his roses on his balcony, breathing deeply the poisonous air as if it were fresh from the Northern Exposure, a defiant gesture that would soon confine him to his bed...

I had to fill in some details myself, but life, not necessarily pretty, not necessarily happy, passed my window. Trinity, it seemed, was teeming with it.

I stood up as the train crawled into the station. The Cleric remained seated in the next carriage.

I walked down the aisle to the doors. They were heavy old-fashioned things and, once the platform had slid into view and the train had hissed to a stop, I had to stick my arm through the window and open them from the outside.

No one else got out of the other carriages onto the deserted platform. The train's engines coughed out a noxious gust of exhaust, and the train pulled away. I looked for a way out.

The only sign was the one declaring the station I had arrived at to be "Trinity - Bridge". There was a coffee booth - shuttered - despite being, surely, close to prime commuter time. I must have got in just ahead of the rush.

A "Vote Chaguartay" billboard towered over the opposite platform, casting a long shadow over the spot where I stood. There was something that might have been a public toilet at the far end of the long platform; a repeated pattern of high lampposts and metal benches, painted green, ran along its length. There was nothing else.

I followed the yellow line that showed a safe distance to stand from the edge of the platform. Maybe this wasn't the main terminus, I thought, although I knew it was. The lack of people was unnerving me. The lack of exits, even more so.

I pulled my Com out of my jacket pocket. It was a reflex action - I wasn't sure what I was going to do with it. As I flicked the screen on, it turned out that the answer was nothing, because it immediately told me it was now fully out of battery. It turned itself off. I nearly threw it onto the track with my frustrated gesture.

I could finally see a wide flight of concrete steps leading down underneath the platform. Past that was only the toilet, which seemed as good a sign as any that this was the way out.

I descended into a wide, gleaming lobby. Surfaces shone back at me, marbled, but whether they really were marble was something I wouldn't claim to have any expertise to determine.

As with the platform above, there was little in the way of ornament or decoration. Sheer walls and clean angles surrounded me, apart from immediately opposite the stairs, where large, ornate gold gates, carved with vines and gargoyles and other bendy but, to me at least, unidentifiable things, stood towering over a narrow entrance. Or an exit. No one was coming in.

Set into the wall to my right was a window, breaking up the marble, with a small counter in front of it. Below that was a logo I recognised, the insignia of Trinity Administration. My appointment was with Trinity Administration, so this reassured me I was in the right place. Behind the window there was a face. I approached the window, bending my neck to see inside.

'Good morning,' said The Face.

'H-hi.' I rarely stammered. I put my hand on my leather bag, which I'd slung across my shoulder. I felt nervous. As I should. I didn't know what I was doing. 'Erm, I have an appointment?'

'Welcome to Trinity. I hope your journey was a pleasant and relaxing one.'

'Thank you,' I replied, stepping up to the counter.

Echoes

I had to crane my neck even farther down to see him and so that he could see me.

The Face swept a pile of papers, which seemed to include a comic and his breakfast of what looked to be rice and fried fish, out of the way. He tapped furiously at a keyboard in front of him.

'We, at Trinity Administration, hope that your stay will be pleasant and mutually profitable.'

I nodded. I hoped for similar things. The Face nodded back, so I assumed this exchange was going well.

'I just need to ask a few questions. Administrative questions, if you like.'

He smiled, as if he'd made a joke. I didn't feel that he had, so I didn't feel the need to respond. The Face looked a bit annoyed, but ploughed on.

'Name?'

'Estrel,' I said. 'Estrel Beck.'

'Purpose of visit?'

'Ah,' I felt, even as I began to answer this, that I was about to offer too much information. 'Well, I'm here from TrakcD Solutions. I have an appointment with…'

I realised that I'd forgotten the name of the person I had an appointment with.

'… with your transport department. It won't be in my name though, it's probably booked for a Crispy Burton. My name is Estrel Beck…'

'You said that.' The Face remained deadpan. 'What's a Crispy… Burton?'

'Oh, no.' I could feel my face flush. It was way too much information. I needed to summarise. 'Crispy Burton is a sales manager. For TrakcD Solutions. I'm here instead of him. I'm sorry for the confusion.'

'Ah,' said The Face, suggesting he understood, although

he continued to look baffled. 'It's OK, I just need Business or Leisure. I'm not trying to pry.'

'Oh.'

I realised the logo had thrown me. My appointment was with Trinity Administration. However, Trinity Administration - which I understood to be some kind of publicly owned utility-provider-cum-public-transport-operator - also ran the railways. What I'd assumed to be a reception desk was nothing more than an information kiosk. Or left luggage. 'Business,' I said, simply.

The Face nodded and tapped at his screen. This seemed to be more in line with the information he was expecting to gather.

'And will you be staying long?'

'Just for the day,' I said. 'I have a train back home booked for this evening.'

The Face nodded again, tapped some more at his screen, then pulled a lever under the desk. This caused a deep drawer to slide out of the wall next to me.

'Do you have any baggage that you'd like me to look after for you? You may place any items in the drawer and I will ensure that they are ready for you on departure.'

OK, I'd found Left Luggage, then. I considered my bag. I should have properly unpacked it before I set off. I was pretty sure that I wasn't going to need the waterproof gear for a day in the city. It would be good to lighten the load.

I reached in and retrieved my tablet, then slid the strap of the bag over my head and placed it in the drawer. I could always come back for the sandwiches. The meeting probably wouldn't take more than a few hours. I was thinking of spending the afternoon sightseeing. Or finding a bar and sampling the local produce.

'Thank you.' The Face smiled. 'If you place your Com on

the contact pad, I will upload your receipt. You will need to present that at Tunnel Terminus when you come to collect your belongings.'

Fortunately, this Com model had a small backup battery so that I could still use it for credit transactions even after it had given up the ghost. I placed it face down on the pad.

'Tunnel Terminus? I'm not familiar…'

'You're at Bridge Terminus, sir.' The Face explained, as the contact pad beeped to show the transaction had been successful.

With a jolt, the drawer retracted and my bag vanished from view.

'Incoming traffic arrives at Bridge, but to depart Trinity you'll need to catch outgoing transport from Tunnel.'

'That's… not very convenient.'

If I sounded annoyed, it was because I was. There had been no mention when I'd got the booking confirmation that I'd be arriving and departing from different points.

'Can I get my bag back?'

'No, sir.' The Face was, apparently, astonished at this question. 'Your bag is already en route to its destination.'

He surreptitiously pressed a button on the desk in front of him, and there was a loud whirring and grinding that reverberated around my feet. If I'd had to guess, that was my bag, only just starting on its journey to its destination. Panic grabbed my groin.

'You just stole my bag!' I said indignantly.

The sinking feeling was eerily familiar.

'I just gave you a receipt,' countered The Face.

He had me there, but I still had a horrible feeling that I was being taken for a ride. However, it wasn't like there was anything of value in the bag. I had my tablet in my hand and I could always buy some more over-dressed sandwiches. And…

damn it, my toothbrush!

I cupped my hand over my mouth and huffed. The warm gust that came back had only a hint of onion. It could have been worse. I would have to buy a toothbrush as well. I needed to check the TrakcD expenses policy before I bankrupted myself on this trip.

'Will that be all, sir?'

I gave him the most scornful stare I could muster. I suspected it didn't hit the spot, because The Face's response was to shrug and take his breakfast back out.

'How do I get to the Administration building?'

'Through the gates, you can't miss it,' mumbled The Face through a mouthful of rice and fish.

I wanted to say something more, but the words wouldn't come. I turned and walked through the overly elaborate gates, out onto the street.

The Trinity Administration building was a windowless concrete block. It was indeed hard to miss being, as it was, directly opposite the Bridge station entrance.

It towered over the multi lane carriageway, the TransWay, which was criss-crossed with roads and tramlines, TransPods streaming past at alarming speed. It had the Trinity Administration logo stamped across its middle.

It gave it the look of a tombstone. I must have scrolled past a picture of it yesterday. It was very familiar, now I was looking at it.

The streaming traffic was mesmerising, but I realised I needed to be on the other side of it. There was very little station-side: a wide plaza with a mosaic tile pavement; a couple of rows of unwell looking trees; a concrete bunker selling newspapers and concrete benches scattered, apparently at random.

Echoes

There were very few people, apart from those huddled under blankets, and they looked like they lived there. There were, however, crowds of pigeons flowing around the square, like an avian army re-enacting a battle.

On the other side of the newspaper bunker, which I noticed now was shuttered and covered in "Vive La Resistance" graffiti, a wide metal staircase rose to meet the overhead PedWay, which ran the length of the main carriageway.

I picked my way through the massing pigeons toward the steps. They seemed determined not to let me leave, and I didn't want to kick or step on any of them, so it was a slow, meandering path I took.

It required a lot of attention to be directed towards the ground, so it was only a chance glance up that helped me avoid the man hurrying the other way.

He, too, was focused on the birds at our feet, was roughly my height, and wore a grey hooded top under a long black leather coat. His hood and his collar were both up, so I couldn't see his face, but his voice was low and full of gravel.

'Sorry.'

He brushed against my shoulder, having seen me at the last possible moment. His voice seemed reminiscent of someone, not a familiar someone, but neither did he seem completely alien. I opened my mouth to reply, but he spoke again before I had the chance.

'Mind the bird crap.'

I chuckled. He hurried on and I continued to dodge the pigeons, but within five paces my foot buried itself in an enormous pile of pigeon excrement.

I looked around. The man was gone. I lifted my foot gingerly, with an unpleasant sucking sound, and added some way of cleaning my shoe to the mental shopping list I was building.

I checked my watch. It wasn't quite half past. I still had time.

In fact, I managed to scrape most of the poo off on the bottom step. I probably should have felt guiltier for what I left behind for someone else to tread in, but I didn't, at least not until I caught the beady eye peering at me from between the fifth and sixth steps.

I jumped back in surprise. Whoever was lurking there cackled.

'Piggens get yer?' the figure asked.

'Mm-hm,' I nodded.

I wanted to steer clear of a conversation I'd struggle to get out of.

'They runs amok, thems do,' continued the figure.

I couldn't discern much about them. The voice implied old age. All I could see was a bundle of rags, and the aforementioned beady eye. The stench was a heady cocktail with notes of urine, ethanol and cabbage. It made me take a step back.

A cluster of pigeons flapped away a small distance, feathers brushing my leg and, I could swear, one beak taking a swipe at my ankle.

'You're new?'

'Just arrived,' I said, wondering if it would be easier to walk another five hundred metres to the next staircase than to ascend this one, with my personal troll hiding underneath it.

'Few come to Trinity these days,' said the bundle. 'Even fewer leave.'

They cackled again.

'There was that guy,' I said, waving behind me to reference the man in the hoodie. 'He looked like he was headed for the station.'

'He comes, he goes,' replied the bundle cryptically.

I nodded slowly.

'Well,' I said, 'I'd better be getting on.'

I needed to find something to clean my shoe with. A glob of spit shot out from the bundle, landing by my shoe. There was another cackle.

That one got to me. Maybe it was the all-night train journey, or nerves about the meeting, or the number of bizarre things that had already happened this morning, but his laugh echoed through my head, leaving me dizzy and disoriented.

'Welcome to Trinity,' muttered the bundle, settling down again behind the steps, no doubt lurking for the next unsuspecting visitor.

I looked around, seeing no one. Why was I doing this? Was it worth it?

Is this what I got because I lacked the guts to do something with my life?

CHAPTER 2

I took the stairs way too fast in my haste to get away. I made it to the top, but only just, and with my head spinning and my chest heaving from exertion. It hurt to breathe.

I put my left hand on the rail and leant against it. My arm gave way, and I stumbled. Unable to grab the rail with my right hand without dropping my tablet, which was tucked under my arm, I fell against it instead.

Fortunately, the PedWay was as deserted as the square and no one witnessed me lurching around like someone who took his morning coffee with a shot of rum. Trinity may have been teeming with life, but it seemed to be kept behind closed doors.

Far below me, TransPods whizzed past, appearing to move faster from up here. I hadn't realised how high the PedWay was; it was literally a dizzying height. Now my head swam with vertigo rather than exertion.

I breathed, straightened up and took a few steps across the walkway, towards where the opposite staircase ran down to the other side of the carriageway. The PedWay itself stretched to my left and right, gentle curves in each direction so that the path was an undulating wave rather than a straight line. There were more of those concrete benches that the Trinity urban planners seemed so fond of dotted along its length. All of them were empty.

I took a moment, high above the speeding traffic, to collect myself. With a presentation to give, a sale to make, I needed to prepare, psych myself up. This, by which I meant selling things, despite being my job, wasn't exactly my forte.

I pictured myself stepping into the foyer of the building opposite, my persona switching, my usual worries and neuroses dropping away. It was a technique I'd read about. It didn't feel like it was working. I didn't think that successful salespeople needed to rely this much on techniques they'd read about in books.

Still, I would sell nothing by being myself. I needed to sit and read through the list I'd made of responses to likely questions. That meant charging my tablet.

Whistles sounded from all directions, making me jump. I could hear people, footsteps, indistinct murmurs of conversation, a sudden, excited yelp.

A breathless man in a boilersuit appeared at the top of the staircase in front of me, turning and rushing along the walkway to my left. I quickened my pace and hastened to the top of the steps.

The flood of workers flowing up towards me was torrential, and I had to step to one side to avoid being swept up or knocked over. I watched the blank faces pass, a sea of people with nothing on their mind but getting away and getting home.

A woman, bent and thin, her head covered in a way that made me suspect she was losing her hair, tripped in front of me. Instinctively, I shot out my free hand and grabbed her by the elbow, breaking her fall and, nearly, her arm. It felt thin and brittle.

Her head snapped up with a ferocity that scared me, but she stared at me with a gratitude that hit me hard in the gut. She regained her balance, and I released her back into the stream. As it swept her away, I barely heard her whispered thanks. Her eyes were so young.

I looked up. The crowd of people had dwindled now. I picked my way down the steps, dodging the pockets of people as I had dodged the pigeons ten minutes earlier. No one looked at me, no one was going my way. I reached the bottom and scuttled into the first open café door.

The smell of frying meat hit me within two steps of crossing the threshold. Café Konoroz, which was the name emblazoned on the plastic menus and paper napkins, was an unpretentious place, by which I meant it contained an assortment of mismatched, wobbly looking furniture with every surface coated in a layer of grease.

The counter, which was unmanned, was stainless steel and banked on either side by giant heat lamps, keeping the pre-prepared offerings warm for longer than was probably advisable. I poked at something grey and greasy in a paper bag at the far end. It looked disgusting, but it smelled amazing.

'What can I get you, governor?' said a voice from beyond. I looked up and saw the head of a man who was grinning widely from behind a grill at the back. He had a strong Ashuanan accent. 'You want some *akar*? I'm making it fresh!'

I thought that if I wanted anything, then it should be something fresh. I wasn't hungry, though.

'Can I get some tea?' I asked. 'And I need to charge this?'

I held up my tablet.

'Take a seat, my man,' said the cook. 'I'll send the boy over.'

Phil Oddy

I turned around and surveyed my options, which were plentiful given there weren't any other customers. I took a wooden stool near the window, as all four of its legs appeared to be the same length. It wasn't the right height for the table next to it and, when I leaned on that, it tilted away. I sat up straighter and waited for the boy.

The Boy, when he arrived, must have been in his mid-thirties at least, which made him older than me. He had a pencil tucked behind his greying temple, which he plucked out with a flourish. He licked the leaded end and then pulled a face.

'What can I get you, governor?' he asked in a very similar accent to the other guy.

'Tea,' I said again.

'Oh yes,' he chuckled, like he knew he wasn't nailing this job. 'You needed this too?'

He produced a battery pack from beneath his apron and handed it to me. I thanked him and swapped it for the one clipped to my tablet.

'You don't have another one, do you?'

I handed the spent battery back to him. I pulled my Com from my jacket pocket and waggled it by way of explanation.

'Sorry,' he shrugged. 'We only have one. I'll go get your tea…'

I put my Com back in my pocket and booted up the tablet as he clattered around behind the counter, putting my spent battery on to charge, putting together a tray with a cup and a kettle and several spoons.

People continued to stream past the window, now in both directions, rivers of people winding past each other. No one was coming inside. The Boy was back at the table, placing a milk jug and sugar bowl in front of me.

He set the cup on the edge of the table and poured a golden

liquid from an unnecessary height into it. I pulled away my tablet so that it didn't get splashed.

'You're not from Trinity, my friend,' he said.

I shook my head.

'I've come from Ashuana.'

'But forgive me, you are not *Ashuaniste*?'

'Well spotted,' I laugh. 'My family is from Øp. I'm… not really from any of those places. I'm not really from anywhere.'

'You just arrived?'

'Yeah.' I nodded. 'Feeling a bit disorientated.'

The Boy pouted his lips and bounced his head in a typical Ashuanan display of agreement.

'This is an… unusual place. Everyone is an outsider.'

'Everyone I've met so far,' I agreed. 'Everyone seems very busy?'

'Is changeover hour.' He proffered a mobile contact pad. 'It is dangerous to be lat*e*.'

'Dangerous?' I asked, confused, using my dead Com to pay.

'Is not possible to work and be late. These people. They sombies. They…'

He trailed off, losing the word.

'Sombies?' It didn't sound like dialect.

The Boy chuckled.

'Papa. His name for the workers. He says "sonambulaires". They walk and they sleep.'

'Ah, "sombies", I get it.'

The Boy nodded vigorously, grinning at me. I sensed we'd made a connection.

'No one comes in here for breakfast?' I looked around the empty cafe.

'The sombies do not need to eat. They have their pills, to replace meat.'

'Pills?'

'Little haffhaff to keep them going, keep them awake,' he explained, without explaining anything. I'd heard, though.

Trinity had a drug problem, the problem being the industrial scale production of synthetic stimulants. They were appearing on the streets of Ashuanan cities, finding its audience in the less affluent youth for whom its low price tag was compensation for the brevity of their buzz and the roughness of their comedown.

'Papa says it's in the water, though. He says no one stands a chance, if the government is drugging the water. I tell him we drink the same water but... You can't tell an old man that he's wrong.'

The door swung open and someone walked in. They filled the doorway, casting the counter in shadow. The Boy started and then nodded to them.

'I ask you to excuse me,' he said. 'We have a regular client.'

'That's fine, I'll just...'

I waved a hand at my tablet, but he was already moving away, clapping a hand on the newcomer's shoulder. The man behind the grill was laughing as they approached.

'Clar! The saviour of Konoroz! Without you, we are bankrupt!'

The Boy had scuttled back behind the counter. The stranger was still to say anything, and I hadn't seen their face, but I sensed poise. Their silhouette suggested strength and power, their glossy long hair shouted elegance and poise, down to the small of their back.

'We have something for you, make you feel right at home, yes? For our very own foreign correspondent,' said the Boy, eagerly.

He reached under the counter and pulled out a cardboard cone, into which he began layering sweating lamb mince from the hot plate, alternating it with chilli flakes and fried onions. It looked good, even if I suspected it would kill me.

'How's the story?' he asked.

The stranger grunted, a universal sign it wasn't going as well as they wanted it to.

The Boy called across to me, almost bouncing with enthusiasm:

'Clar is top, top journalist! Going to save Trinity with words!'

I pulled an impressed face and bobbed my head. I wasn't sure what to say, but I never am in these situations. Clar turned towards me, grinding their firm jaw awkwardly.

'I don't know about that.' They smiled modestly. Their voice was deep, with a rasp that suggested a late night. 'I'm just going to write it. Somebody else might have to save Trinity, but if I can show them the way…'

And then they winked. A shiver went through me. I had no reason to think they meant me. They obviously didn't mean me. But I couldn't escape the feeling that they did.

I left my tea, made my jumbled excuses and rushed out onto the street.

The street was quieter now. The last straggling workers were easy to weave between.

I reassessed my readiness for my meeting. I now had a working tablet, although I had questions to review, my Com was out of action, and there was still some bird crap on my shoe.

The entire strip between where I was and where I was going seemed to be cafés in the vein of the one I'd just run out of, but there was another concrete bunker that might sell something I could freshen my breath with alongside the newspapers, and looked to have the distinct advantage of being open.

I picked up a tube of lemon gel and flashed my Com to pay. I needed to check my credit balance. Not knowing what the exchange rate was, exactly, I could spend a fortune without realising it. I needed to exchange the battery on my Com, but I probably needed to make sure I could afford it first.

The entrance to the Administration building was not, in fact, entirely made of black stone but was glass fronted, albeit with that glass being heavily tinted, hence the effect from a distance. There were two giant, slow moving, revolving doors, next to a traffic loop.

I watched several TransPods pull in, slide their doors up and people in business dress disembark to the tuneless beeping of credits being extracted from Com wallets.

I made for the nearest entrance, before pulling myself up short with a start, much to the annoyance of the short woman behind me, who was straggling from her party because of the difficulty she'd had getting her giant bag through her TransPod's door. She dug me firmly in the middle of my back with a sharp elbow before she pushed past and on through the door. I was uncertain that it was accidental.

I sidestepped into a quieter spot immediately in front of the main window to avoid more muttering, tutting, elbow wielding staff members whose way I was definitely in. Putting my tablet into camera mode and reviewing my appearance, I smoothed down some hair and adjusted my tie.

I didn't look too unpresentable, other than the grease stain that I seemed to have picked up on the right cuff of my shirt. I dropped my arm. The jacket sleeve was long enough to cover it.

My breath was now lemon fresh so, other than the nervous sweat that had broken out on my forehead I was good to go. Only just over an hour early. My meeting, which I could now see from the alerts on my tablet screen was with a Mr Toun, started at nine.

I hated the rush and the panic and the sheer embarrassment that I usually felt when I was late, for anything, so I had a tendency to arrive stupidly early for most things unless I was actually running late, in which case I was bang on time.

Today I hadn't had a lot of choice in the matter. There weren't many trains from Ashuana City to Trinity so I had to arrive nearly two hours early, but this was familiar territory for me. I was good at killing time.

Maybe a circuit or two of the building would eat up enough of the hour that I wouldn't look insane if I checked in at reception. I wandered to the corner of the building and glanced down the narrow alley that ran down its side.

It stopped at a wall about ten metres down. It was mostly filled with bins. So that was out.

I could sit outside. The day was fine, and this area seemed safe enough. I looked around for one of those convenient benches that seemed to be such a feature of Trinity's urban landscape, but, predictably, there were none just where I needed them.

I could just walk, I thought, I knew where to find somewhere to sit, up on the PedWay or outside the terminal building, but I'd not felt very comfortable there before.

Maybe I had to bite the bullet and turn up too early for my appointment. I could absorb the judgement of a receptionist for an hour. And they'd probably have a bathroom I could clean my shoe up in.

My mind made up, I pushed the door and it scooped me inside.

The foyer was spacious, cool, and filled with light from the one-way glass at the front. The reception desk was central, a large oval shape, with two receptionists manning it.

I joined the shorter line for the woman on the left, but she tapped her ear to take a call on her Com, so I switched to the right-hand queue instead.

The knot of people at the front all turned out to be part of the same group and, once they'd followed a stern-looking woman with her hand in the air towards the security gates, as if they were a school party, it was the turn of the man in front of me.

His shiny bald head shone the fluorescent lights uncomfortably back in my eyes, so I searched for a more comfortable direction in which to look.

Giant screens hanging overhead cycled through pictures of trams and trains crossing high over the city, complex road junctions with boxy TransPods whizzing across, narrowly avoiding multiple collisions, and what looked like glass bubbles filled with commuters travelling through underground tunnels. They were obviously proud of their transport network in Trinity.

The generic businessman moved away towards the security gate, temporary badge in hand, so it was my turn. I stepped forward.

According to his badge, the receptionist's name was Ahji. He still had his head bowed as he tapped at the screen in front of him, completing something arising from his previous interaction, I presumed. I felt a rising panic about how to explain how early I was.

'Hello again, Sir.' Ahji was now looking up and directly at me.

I paused, hopefully looking as confused as I felt.

'I'm sorry, sir, I thought you were someone else.' Ahji looked momentarily flustered. 'How can I help?'

'Good morning,' I began. 'Ahji,' I added with a forced smile.

Ahji smiled back, but it wasn't any more convincing.

'Who are you here to see?' asked Ahji.

'I have an appointment,' I said. 'But I'm very early so I'm happy to wait. It's with Mr Toun. My name is Estrel Beck.'

I tapped my Com against the desk terminal to confirm my identity.

Ahji tapped at the touchscreen. His eyebrows shot up, before the unconvincing smile returned.

'Mr Beck.' Ahji scrutinised the screen. 'Standing in for Mr Burton. I trust he is well?'

I didn't realise that Crispy Burton had been here before. Trinity Administration wasn't, yet, a client of TrakcD Solutions. I nodded to confirm his continued health. That seemed to satisfy Ahji.

'I see here that Ernold Toun is running a little late. He is sorry to keep you waiting…'

'Oh, I don't mind waiting,' I said.

'Mr Toun is not yet in the building,' explained Ahji, 'but I'll make sure he knows you are here the moment he arrives…'

'I don't think that's necessary.' I leaned back. 'Just, you know, let me know when he's ready. I'm in no rush.'

That seemed liked a good thing to say, didn't it? Relaxed, accommodating, just like the sort of person someone like Ernold Toun would want to do business with.

'As you wish.' Ahji's smile never faltered but was losing some of its authenticity.

He tapped at his screen and printed out a temporary access pass. He handed me the card.

'That won't activate until nine. In the meantime, we have refreshments over here…' Ahji gestured towards a small collection of tables and uncomfortable looking metal chairs clustered around a coffee machine to the left of the reception desk. '… and our rest rooms are through the doors on the far side. Can I help you with anything else today, sir?'

I thought of the dead battery in my Com, versus the bird excrement on my shoe, and said 'No, thank you, you've been very helpful.'

I moved away, toward the tables.

'Have a doughnut, sir.' Ahji pointed at a tray on the side of the reception desk. 'They're fresh!'

I picked up a paper napkin from the pile and, with it, picked up a doughnut.

I took a seat with my back to Ahji, facing a large screen scrolling news headlines over pictures with the sound down.

Putting the doughnut on the table next to my tablet, I inspected my shoe. I needed to clean it off, but I didn't want to leave my doughnut unattended.

I didn't need a doughnut. I still wasn't hungry. At the same time, it would be a waste to abandon it and I didn't like waste. I shouldn't have taken it, but I was inevitably going to end up eating it.

I looked across at Ahji. There was no one waiting at reception anymore, and he was looking around the foyer at the people moving through. Smart people, people with purpose, serious people, with faces that spoke of busy agendas and places to be, in contrast to the dead-eyed masses trudging to the factories earlier. This place was making me feel uneasy.

The screen now seemed to be playing some kind of campaign ad, with slogans flashing up on every other beat. They spoke of "cleaning up Trinity" and "standing up to the elites" and "opportunity for everyone". I didn't recognise the youthful, vigorous looking man on the screen, but I assumed he was the candidate standing against the Mayor, who I think

I read was married to the Mayor's daughter. Estranged daughter, I think it was safe to assume.

I took a bite of my doughnut. Bright red sticky jam squirted out onto my tie. I knew it was already hopeless, but I dropped the doughnut on the table and went to wipe it, a vain hope that it wouldn't leave an obvious stain just before the meeting that was potentially going to kick start my career.

This would not make the "right impression, Estrel. Why can't you pull your socks up and act like someone who is serious..?". My dad's voice echoed through my mind.

I got up and ran to the bathroom, leaving a new story about wide condemnation for Resistance attacks on factory facilities to scroll unread across the screen.

The stall provided a safe haven to assess the damage. There was a sink and mirror in it, and a hand towel dispenser for me to wedge my tablet behind.

The mark wasn't too bad. My tie was a dark blue, and the jam had landed close enough to the knot that, if you didn't look too closely, you might have thought it was a shadow in a crease.

I grabbed some hand towels and wet them. If I sponged it a bit, it might take the worst of the stickiness out, and I had enough time to dry off before I was actually likely to see Toun. I dabbed at the tie until the towel stopped coming away red. That would have to do.

I contemplated sitting on the pan, lid down, to review my meeting prep away from the judgemental stare of Ahji, but decided that was unnecessarily paranoid, even for me. I should just get cleaned up and go back.

I grabbed another towel and ran that under the tap before dropping to one knee to clean my dirty shoe. As I knelt, my elbow brushed the jammy napkin that I'd brought in with me off the sink where I'd left it, scrunched up, and it fell to the floor too.

The bird poo had formed a white crust on the back of the heel and, as long as I kept folding the paper towel to keep it away from my fingers, it wasn't too bad a job. In some ways, it was a good thing that I'd left it. At least when dried it was less obvious what it was, and it didn't smell as bad.

That said, I was kneeling on the floor of a toilet stall, so awful smells were all around me. I tossed the dirty towel into the wastebasket and went to pick up the napkin, intending to do the same. It was unfolding, and something caught my eye.

There was writing on the napkin. That wasn't particularly strange, but this wasn't a brand name or a slogan. There were words scrawled in black marker, and blue ballpoint, and something that looked to be red crayon. Different handwriting, scribbled at different times, with different implements, with different levels of care.

But there was one word that held my attention. The first word, in bold capitals, in black marker, as if written expressly so that I would see it. It was my name. ESTREL.

CHAPTER 3

Standing up, I narrowly avoided banging my head on the sink. I looked around for a flat, dry surface to smooth the napkin out on, but everywhere was curves and a lot of it was wet, particularly after I'd been throwing paper towels around for the last five minutes.

I pulled my tablet out from behind the towel dispenser and sat on the toilet pan, lid down, smoothing the napkin out on the screen. There was only jam in one corner, so it was still fairly legible. As legible as it was ever going to be, at least.

ESTREL, it said, in black marker before switching to blue ballpoint. KEEP THIS NAPKIN ON YOU AT ALL TIMES. THIS IS IMPORTANT. YOU ARE IN A TIME LOOP.

I... *What?* It was undeniably my handwriting. A bit torn and splotchy in places, but my handwriting. I had even corrected the "n"s in "napkin" where I'd scrawled them a little too much, like I tended to. Also, most of my "E"s look like "F"s. Despite this powerful evidence, I was also certain that I hadn't written it.

ANYTHING YOU HAVE ON YOUR PERSON WHEN YOU RESET WILL ECHO INTO THE NEXT ITERATION. This had a question mark after it, which was crossed out. The next words looked like someone had added them later. The writing sloped off at a different angle. THIS NAPKIN IS AN ECHO. ADD TO IT. DON'T LOSE IT.

After this it switched back to marker. It said 8.03AM, crossed out. I checked my watch, just in time to see it change from 8.02 to 8.03. I shivered. That was unnerving. After that was 10AM, followed by 12PM and 2PM, all also crossed out, before the writing switched to the red crayon.

The times seemed to be more erratic after that: 5.56PM, 9.32PM, 11.43PM, 12.13AM. There was a line striking through all of them, apart from the last one. I presumed that was tomorrow morning.

So assuming that this message was, in fact, from a… what..? A previous iteration of me looping around the same period of time repeatedly? These times were… what? An attempt to narrow down the window?

It looked like I'd started out with a system, checking in every two hours. But then what had happened between two and six that first stopped me writing the time down, and then caused me to panic and write down the time whenever I thought of it?

That made sense, but it seemed that whatever happened I'd be OK. At least until thirteen minutes past twelve tomorrow morning, and *why am I even entertaining this notion? This is madness…*

I was too old for games. I was twenty-six years old.

Or am I? I thought *How much of that have I lived on repeat? How would I know?*

This was a ridiculous train of thought. I threw my head back and stared up at the ceiling. I thought about the flash of déjà vu I'd had encountering the Cleric on the train that morning. Was that a clue?

Echoes

What was the earliest déjà vu moment I could remember? Suddenly I couldn't remember anything.

Things had been strange since I got here, though. And this message I'd apparently left myself, in a place I'd never been to before. That was a risk. Was it only today that I'd figured it out?

Unless it was only today that it was happening. I thought about how odd I'd felt when I woke up from the nap I'd had on the train after I'd finished my breakfast. Was that it? It was just before I'd seen the Cleric, just before I'd arrived in Trinity. Just before seven o'clock.

So was that my hypothesis? I had somewhere in the region of seventeen and a half hours, of which I had already wasted just over one, to…

To do what? That was the question. The last thing written on the napkin, in large capital letters, appeared to be the answer. An answer.

It was at least an instruction. An instruction from my past about my personal future, a goal, a target, a *quest*?

I stood up.

'This is ridiculous,' I muttered under my breath.

It was a coincidence. A prank someone had left.

Left for me.

In my handwriting.

In a place I'd never been to before.

How did they know I'd take that doughnut? How did they know I'd take that napkin? It required such careful planning, such subtle manipulation to make me play along without even realising. Unless…

Unless I'd done it before.

Unless I'd done it many, many times before.

I took a doughnut, and I wasn't even hungry. No, that wasn't a sign of anything. If someone offered me food, I rarely rejected it.

I was feeling claustrophobic in the toilet cubicle. I needed some air. Air that didn't smell of synthesised flowers masking stale urine.

Back in the foyer, I sat back down at the table with my back to Ahji. On the screen in front of me, the young guy from earlier was standing in front of purple and yellow hoardings proclaiming "Jack White - There is another way".

He had his hands in the air, while a young woman stood slightly apart from him, smiling and leading the applause.

I looked at the napkin again. I couldn't deny that it was my handwriting, much as I wanted to deny that I'd written it. This felt like a situation where the one person I could trust was myself.

So, what? I accepted I was in a time loop? It seemed that way. So I had to find out how to get out.

I looked around. Ahji was busy with someone new at the reception desk. I could leave. I had an instruction, there at the bottom of the napkin. Should I follow it? I kind of felt like I should.

The only problem was that I didn't know what it meant.

The only other problem was that this handwriting was different, it wasn't mine.

It said one thing: FIND MOUSE.

I sat back. This was, at least, an instruction, a plan. It was, surely, better to follow clues like this than to flail around in the dark, relying on instinct and blind luck.

The words at the top of the napkin suggested someone who knew what was going on, had figured some things out and was passing on their knowledge to the next generation so that they could take the baton and run with it. Even though that person was me, I didn't feel like him.

The other person, the one expected to pick this thing up and solve the next part of the puzzle, that was also me and, well, see above. I was some overgrown kid playing at being a salesman, badly. What was about to happen that would change me so substantially? And would it hurt?

Unless it wasn't true. Perhaps it wasn't what it seemed. It was an idea, scribbled down for later. A ticket out of sales, an idea for a film, or a Com game, or… but why hadn't I made it more obvious? And why didn't I remember doing it? When had I had the time?

Even if I took it seriously, there were two things that gave me pause. The first was that I hadn't written this last instruction, and I didn't know who had.

It was most likely, I thought, that this past version of me had trusted whoever had written it and hadn't disagreed with the wisdom of this plan, as I'd presumably carried it around for some time after that, until the loop reset so that the words… what was it..?

Echoed back to me.

But it didn't have to have gone down like that. It is possible that I did not know someone had added to the napkin. Maybe they had slipped it back into my pocket while I wasn't looking. Maybe I knew, but I hadn't been able to do anything about it, because I'd been drugged, or lost the use of my hands.

That thought caused me to wince as the full range of painful methods that could render my hands useless flashed by my mind's eye in lurid detail. I shivered as I doubted the trustworthiness of the instructor. And this was only the first problem.

The second problem was that I didn't really understand what the instruction meant. FIND MOUSE. Not FIND A MOUSE. So was Mouse someone's name?

If so, it was unlikely that it was their given name, which

was going to make them hard to find. I couldn't look up someone called Mouse in a directory, if their real name was Christopher, for example.

Maybe that wasn't even what it said. The writing wasn't the clearest.

Maybe I'd misread. I looked again at the scrawled message, but I couldn't make it say anything else.

FIND MOUSE.

That was all it was telling me to do.

FIND MOUSE.

I sighed, lost.

'Mr Beck?' Ahji was calling me. I got the impression that this wasn't the first time, that he'd been doing it for a while and I hadn't responded. He sounded impatient.

'Mr Beck! Mr Toun has arrived in the building and will see you before his next appointment, if you want to go up? I've activated your card to give you access to the fourth floor for the rest of the day. Mr Toun's office is opposite the lifts. I'm sure you won't be able to miss it.'

Damn it, I wasn't ready for this. I had a head full of sci-fi nonsense and wet jam on my tie, not to mention a list of unrevised questions on my tablet.

'Just a sec,' I said, tapping the power button.

The tablet didn't respond. I checked the battery pack I'd bought at Café Konoroz and discovered that it was dead already. They had sold me a dud.

My head spun. I took a deep breath. With any luck, there was a screen I could plug into that would power up the tablet. I could make small talk while I set up. That was what people did on sales calls, right, made small talk?

I just had to put all thoughts of time loops out of the way for a bit. What if I broke out of the loop this time? What if I carried on with my life in a normal, linear way from now on?

I'd be glad to have made the sale. I would need that for when I got out of this bizarre, bizarre place.

I stood up; the world lurching a bit as I did so, like I was drunk. I nodded my insincere thanks to Ahji and stuffed the napkin in my trouser pocket.

Was I really going to do this? Meet a man I knew nothing about to talk about something I hadn't prepared? I found my equilibrium and put my right foot in front of my left. It really seemed like I was, I was moving towards the security gate.

Was this the right call? Should I be starting the hunt for Mouse, whatever or whoever that turned out to be?

I was halfway across the foyer now, still moving, one step at a time. Ahji was watching me, a strange expression on his face.

Every time I lifted a foot, it felt like it was made of lead and yet I kept going. Hurtling towards the abyss at a snail's pace. Ahji turned his attention back to his Com. I was certain that he shook his head as he did so. This annoyed me, but I wasn't sure how I could blame him.

Maybe the hunt for Mouse started with Toun. I didn't know that wasn't true. Maybe this was exactly what I was meant to do.

I had to make the best decisions I could based on the information I had available to me and what else was I going to do right now?

The gates were a bank of turnstiles with contact pads next to them. I tapped my pass on the pad and the barriers slid away.

One foot in front of the other.

One foot... Ahead of me the lift doors slid open, a red flashing number four displayed above them.

One foot in front of the other.

One foot... It looked like this was happening, then. This

was what I was doing. I was going up to the fourth floor to meet Ernold Toun.

I took a deep breath and entered the lift.

I stood inside the metal box, facing the open doors, waiting for them to close. In front of me stretched the wide expanses of the lobby, people drifting across it with coffees in hand, tablets tucked under their arms.

Of course, I could borrow a battery. I should have asked at the reception. I thought about going back now, but I couldn't face Ahji and his stare again. Toun probably had a secretary, I was good with secretaries. I just needed to be super apologetic and seem endearingly chaotic.

Excuse me, I'm really sorry, and this is a terrible thing to ask right before I'm due to meet your boss, but would you, by any chance…? Something like that. I had four floors to practise.

I ran down what I could remember about the question prep I hadn't reviewed. *Contract length… payment structures… service level agreements…*

Out of the corner of my eye, I saw something move, scamper out of the corner of the lift and out into the lobby. *Hey, was that a…?*

I saw the flash of light a split second before the doors closed in front of me. The heavy metal muffled the actual sound of the explosion, so that I wondered for a moment if I'd been right about what I'd seen. But the afterimage was still flashing in front of my eyes. I knew I had.

The déjà vu was so strong it was like I was stuck in a dream. I was sure I'd been here before. If this was what today was going to be like, I thought, it would be helpful to get these feelings earlier so that I could, for example, avoid doing things like getting into lifts in buildings that get their fronts blown off.

But I had little time to think about that as the wave of heat flashed through the cab and the entire building shook. I stabbed at the button to open the doors, but nothing happened. There was a sudden, lurching movement, making me fall to my hands and knees as the lift left the ground floor.

Panicked, I looked up. The numbers on the keypad were flashing, and above that, the small digital screen was scrolling letters. A-L-L. Pause. R-E-C. Recall?

Red light seeped through the gaps in the doors, a siren sounded from outside. None of this was reassuring.

I told myself it was some kind of emergency procedure. If the lift was moving, then that must mean that the shaft was still intact, so I was probably safest here for now.

For now. I imagined a second blast, rocking the lift as it took off the other side of the building. That didn't seem familiar, no déjà vu triggered.

Does that mean that it won't happen? Is that a rational thought?

What if I die? I wondered. Did I have to get to the end of the day to reset, or would my premature death result in my waking up at the start of this morning again, full of breakfast coffee and confused why the whole thing seemed so familiar? Or was I insulated from death?

If today wasn't my day, then was that true for every iteration? I didn't have a belief system that gave me a framework for fate that allowed me to believe that, but I was ready to reassess if it worked to my advantage.

The lift jerked to a halt.

'You have been returned to the Recall floor. Please evacuate the building...'

The doors slid open.

'You have been returned to the Recall floor. Please evacuate the building...'

I looked up from my crouch. All I could see was smoke.

Phil Oddy

'You have been returned to the Recall floor. Please evacuate the building...'

I wanted that electronic voice to shut up for a start. Also, if it wanted me to evacuate the building, why had it taken me to the first floor?

Choking smoke and dust filled the corridor. I went to stand up but thought better of it. Coughing and spluttering, I fell back to my knees, gasping for some actual air to breathe.

I scrabbled about for a moment, found some carpet, then thought better of that, too, and tried to crawl back to the relative safety of the lift.

I turned around, at least I thought I turned around, but I couldn't see anything anymore because of the smoke, least of all the lift. To be fair, the building appeared to be on fire and it probably wasn't the best idea to retreat into a metal box in a narrow shaft that ran through the middle of it.

But was it any wiser to carry on crawling into the smoky darkness, towards the tattered remains of the destroyed front of the building?

I was so disorientated I barely knew which way was up, and so all I could do was pick a direction at random and hope.

The air was full of smoke but it moved, and the motion suggested open doorways and large spaces coming off this one. I felt the heat all around me and imagined offices and meeting rooms, smelled the walls and the carpets melting.

The building creaked and groaned as it twisted and warped. There was the distant thud of falling masonry. Beyond all of it, I caught sirens and shouts, screams in the street.

But I felt no vibrations from running feet, heard no muffled whimpers from sheltered hiding places, nothing that led me to think that there was anyone in the vicinity. There was nobody here.

Echoes

There was nobody here. I was on my own. The lift had brought me to a place where there was no one who could help me. All power leached from my muscles and I collapsed onto my face.

I guessed I was about to find out what happened if I died. I thought about the Com games I'd played, the worlds I'd explored, the ease with which I'd stumbled into terminal trouble only to regen and get another go.

Was that what was about to happen? How did I score on this go? I didn't think I'd be gaining much XP for tapping out so early.

I turned my head to the side, gasped for some air that wasn't there. My lungs burned. The air was scorching, acrid, stifling me as I tried to find the strength to get out. Why was it so hard to stay alive?

This is it, then? I imagined the other Estrels, the ones who had made it further than this, who had scribbled all over the napkin, who had discovered the big boss,. Even if they hadn't completed the quest, they had survived.

I had failed. That was a given. I hadn't even made it to ten. Ten o'clock was the first time-check written on the napkin. How had I not even made it to the first checkpoint?

Where had I gone wrong? Was it getting in the lift? What had I done that I shouldn't have done? Or not done that I should have, that the others did?

FIND MOUSE flashed brightly in my oxygen-starved brain. The mouse. I should have followed the mouse. Like the white rabbit, I should have followed the rabbit. Not the rabbit, there wasn't a rabbit. I should have followed the…

'You can't stay here,' said a hoarse voice in my ear.

'What?' I could hear the sounds they were making, but I struggled to parse them into actual words.

'You can't stay here.'

Phil Oddy

Two firm hands scooped me up under my armpits. They hauled me to my feet. I had nothing to offer. I must have been a dead weight and if I'd been able to be impressed, then I would have been. Deeply.

As it was, I wasn't even grateful. This was just a thing that was happening to my failing body.

The unseen stranger wrapped powerful arms around my chest and held me tight to their body. I tried to help, but my feet weren't responding to any of the signals I was sending them, so I had no alternative but to let them drag me.

My heels caught on the carpet, sending painful vibrations through my feet to my hips. I was in no position to complain.

The stranger backed out of the corridor and into another room. My wobbling leg bounced off a desk. It seemed to be some kind of office.

The smoke was thicker in here. I couldn't see anything, but now my stinging eyes, feeling like daggers were being stabbed into them, were streaming with tears. The fog in front of me blurred.

I tried to say something but my throat was thick with smoke and, to be honest, I didn't know what I wanted to say, anyway.

The supportive arms let go and I fell, my heart staying where it was and ending up in my throat as I collapsed. I couldn't feel my body land on the chair, but my momentum halted with a jerk, forcing what air there was in my lungs out.

As it left me, I tried to gasp for more, but all I inhaled was more smoke. I choked out, 'Don't go,' but all I could see were the clouds that surrounded me. I was on my own again.

'Don't leave me,' I murmured.

Somewhere beyond the blanket I heard a grunt of exertion and the thud of something heavy hitting shattering glass. There was a rush of escaping smog being replaced with marginally cleaner city air. The smoke was thinning and I could make out a shape in front of me, leaning out of what was taking the shape of a window and pushing at something that made a metallic clank as it extended downward.

'Come on,' said the voice, again. 'You need to get out of here. And I could do with some help…'

As the powerful arms propelled me up from the chair, I pushed with my legs and found myself launched over a broad shoulder. My rescuer's collar bone dug painfully into my ribs as, together, we climbed out of the window and onto the fire escape.

My brain couldn't cope with the flood of oxygen, or the relief that hit me like a tidal wave. I passed out before we finished the descent.

CHAPTER 4

I came to as I was being bundled into a TransPod that seemed to have been waiting for us at the bottom of the ladder. I found myself gently laid on one of the bench seats in the back, my eyes half open and my vision foggy.

The stranger climbed in after me and, now that their frame no longer blocked the light from the street outside, I could see their face. Bolt awake, I went to sit up. Everything twisted on its axis and I fell back down.

'Easy,' said the stranger, who I recognised as Clar, the striking journalist from the café an hour earlier.

They turned and banged on the opaque partition that divided the passenger seating from the pilot. Someone on the other side engaged the gears and took off at speed down the alley.

'You were expecting to need to make a quick getaway?' I croaked, bracing myself against the side of the carriage to stop myself from sliding off the bench as the pilot took the corner onto the main road much too fast.

'I called someone when I realised things were going awry,' shrugged Clar, pulling long dark hair off their face and tying it up.

They had delicate features, high cheekbones, piercing blue eyes, and an air of vulnerability that I had not expected to see in someone who had picked me up off the floor with barely a grunt.

I sat up, my eyes clearing a bit more. The TransPod burst onto the TransWay and we swept past the front of Administration, weaving through stationary traffic under the PedWay.

The front of Administration was mostly missing now, people and emergency vehicles swarming around the gaping structure. Plumes of dust and smoke burst from the interior.

I was lucky to be out of there. We nudged past the last carriage of rubberneckers and picked up some speed, leaving the scene of devastation framed in the rear window.

This was an unexpected turn of events. I was feeling good to still be in the game, glad that I hadn't, yet, tapped out as what I presumed would have been the most ineffective Estrel to date…

And yet I couldn't exactly relax. I wasn't sure who I had just ended up in a speeding TransPod with, or whether it was pure coincidence that I'd met them earlier that morning, or whether any of this was an entirely good thing.

My rescuer was looking through the window, apparently trying to catch sight of something in the street that we were racing down. We'd turned off the TransWay and were barrelling along a narrowing street.

The buildings were as towering as anywhere else in Trinity but thin and pushed tight together. The traffic was quieter and the pedestrians more sparse. There appeared to be the occasional shop. I caught Clar's eye.

'I'm Estrel, by the way,' I said. 'Thank you for rescuing me.'

'I'm Clar.' Clar had either found what they were looking for or decided that it wasn't there. They turned to me, smoothing down the front of their blouse.

'It's fine. You were there, you looked like you needed rescuing.'

'I did. Thank you. Again. Did you..? Were you..?'

I didn't know what I wanted to ask. Or rather, I knew exactly what I wanted to ask, but I didn't know how safe it was to ask it. I needed to figure out if it was OK that I was in this Pod, and wanted to know where we were going.

I wanted to ask who Clar was, and if they'd been following me that morning. Vaguely, I remembered something they'd said in Konoroz's, something about showing someone the way. I wanted to understand that too. In the end, I settled for:

'Are we safe now?'

Clar laughed by way of a "no" and glanced back out of the window.

'No?' I asked.

'No,' they confirmed. 'I doubt it. We should keep moving.'

They didn't seem about to say anything else, but I was still reluctant to ask any more, so I waited, stretching the pause out to see if it helped. It didn't.

Just to check, I shoved my hand in my trouser pocket. The napkin was still there. The Echo.

Clar rolled up their sleeves, revealing tattoos covering their forearms. I recognised the symbol on their right arm. A black lion.

'You're Rosaanan?' I asked.

To be fair, it was pretty obvious, but it surprised me. Rosaan was a long way from Trinity. I hadn't met many Rosaanans, probably none in person. I always had an idea of them being rather traditional. Clar was shattering my expectations.

Clar nodded, sighed.

'I'm a writer,' they said. 'A journalist, I guess. I write things about this hellhole and sometimes people back home are interested and then I get paid. Today was one of those days. I was there to interview your Mayor.'

'Chaguartay?' I asked. I was impressed, but also felt the need to make one thing clear. 'Although not my Mayor.'

I loosened my tie and pulled out the small, gold elephant I wore on a thin leather thong around my neck. It had a fiery halo and a trident tail, the proud symbol of Ashuana.

Clar smiled.

'OK,' they nodded. 'How long have you been in Trinity?'

'You saw me fresh off the train, this morning, in the café.'

'I thought it was you, sat down in Konoroz's, right? So it's been an eventful trip so far, then?'

'You don't even know the half of it,' I chuckled. 'I do not know what's going on.'

I would not tell them the half they didn't know. Not right now.

'So you never got to meet the Mayor?'

'Oh, I met him,' replied Clar, as they banged on the pilot's partition. The Pod slowed to an abrupt halt in front of a terrace of battered houses. 'Met him on the executive floor, as arranged, but I didn't get through my first question before the building blew up and he disappeared through some kind of emergency evacuation tunnel.'

A thought dawned on me.

'You think he was the target?'

Maybe there was something bigger going on today. Maybe it wasn't all about me and my time loop after all. Or maybe it was about me and my time loop, but my time loop was about something bigger than I'd expected.

Icy dread grabbed me by the back of my neck. That would

significantly change things. I'd had a lucky escape, it seemed. Perhaps I needed to be careful.

'I don't... I don't know. He didn't seem surprised, Chaguartay, I mean...' They looked thoughtful. '... or his entourage. I think I smelled a rat, to be completely honest. But then...'

Clar stopped.

'Then?' I prompted.

'Then I found you,' finished Clar, 'and you looked like you needed help. This is me. I'm home now. Do you have somewhere you need to be?'

I considered this for a moment. If I did, I didn't know.

What was my next move? Had someone just tried to blow me up? Was my being trapped here - if indeed I was trapped, it astonished me at how quickly I'd accepted that this time loop was real - was it to do with this apparent attempt to assassinate the Mayor?

Or, if I thought I was understanding Clar correctly, this apparent attempt *to appear to attempt* to assassinate the Mayor.

'I don't think so,' I said, in the end. 'I'm thinking that I might lie low for a bit...'

'Then do you want to hide out somewhere safe?'

There was a stain on the table, left by the mould that Clar had wiped off. A lake of something that had partly dried after leaking from underneath the fridge had left the floor a nasty kind of sticky. The fridge itself buzzed with a determination that suggested it could explode at any moment.

The mug of tea that I was nursing, perched at the unholy table on a three-legged stool I was pretty certain hadn't been designed that way, was simultaneously perfectly brewed and covered in a layer of suspiciously persistent foam. This particular somewhere was only safe in certain senses of the word, it seemed.

It was unremarkable from the outside, and only remarkable inside in the sense that I didn't quite understand how anyone lived like this. To get to the kitchen, we'd had to pass a living room that suggested only one person did.

There was a collection of empty food cartons and discarded drinks cans at one end of the sofa, the one without the worn down cushion and the best view of the screen. The contents of the cupboards and of the buzzing fridge were basic and few.

It was shambolic, scummy, and it didn't smell great. It was a light year away from the carefully polished style of my companion. I had a feeling that Clar didn't live here.

I hadn't asked, however, because Clar didn't seem to stop moving. They were constantly checking something - their Com, the window, the door, the other rooms in the house.

Making tea had taken ages because they kept disappearing in between filling the kettle and pouring the water and removing the bags and adding the milk. It was a miracle it was still hot when it made it to my hand.

Something distracted me, too. On the counter opposite, buried in dust balls and cobwebs, I could see a black marker pen. I'd been staring at it for ten minutes. I wanted to check it out, but I really didn't want my suspicions confirmed.

A black marker pen. I pulled out the Echo, stared at the writing. It couldn't be, could it?

Everything that was running through my head, that this was about something bigger than me, didn't sit well. It wasn't in my nature to worry about the wider world. This wasn't even my world.

If that marker was what I thought it was, then it would be another push in a direction that I was reluctant to go.

Eventually, with Clar out of the room again, I cracked. I

put my tea down, stood up, and walked across to the counter. The stool fell over.

I wiped the fluff off the pen on my jacket. Smoothing out the napkin on a cleaner part of the counter, I stared at the row of numbers. It was just before ten o'clock.

I pulled the top off the pen and, because there was nowhere else to write it and because it didn't seem that it would matter, I wrote the number ten on the worktop. It looked identical, barring a small amount of leaching of ink on the napkin.

I realised that I wasn't breathing. Was this it? Was this where I'd written it the first time?

In about ten minutes, was some parallel version of me looking at this pen and an emptier napkin and thinking about recording the time to show how far he'd come?

Somewhere else was another version of me looking at a blank sheet of three ply tissue paper and thinking about trying to communicate to the rest of us?

Where did he get the idea? How did he even suspect that he was in a loop? Was that all to come? Regardless, we must have all passed through here at some point. This was definitely the pen. What about the explosion? Had we all been through that?

I wanted to write something, but I didn't know what to write that would add any value. I was still clueless, if I was honest.

There was a sound behind me, and Clar was back in the room.

'Sorry about that,' they said, pulling up another stool and sitting down.

I stayed stood where I was, shoving the hand clutching the marker pen into my trouser pocket to hide it. I hadn't got the measure of the mysterious Clar yet.

Phil Oddy

It felt like they had been following me around, although that could be coincidence. Was any of the explosion I'd just survived their fault?

They hadn't seemed too devastated about their big scoop interview with the Mayor being curtailed.

But much as I tried to distrust their motivations, they had stepped in to help when they could have easily left me to asphyxiate in a corridor. And not only had they got me to safety, but they'd got me to exactly where I needed to be.

I fingered the pen in my pocket. I thought I probably did trust them.

'Who are you?' I asked, as a general way into the wider topic.

To be honest, it felt like a stupid place to start, but it was what my brain had farted out in the moment. It didn't seem to matter.

Clar ran a hand down their face, looking exhausted.

'No, fair enough,' they agreed. 'I'd be concerned if I were you. Especially if you're from out of time…'

My breath caught in my throat. Had I said something? How could they possibly know? Suspicion levels shot back up to maximum.

'… I mean town,' they clarified, allowing me to breathe again. 'My name is Clar Triebel. I'm a journalist, I think we did that. I've worked in Trinity for five or six years, not affiliated with any of the Trinity channels, but I get plenty of work. There isn't a lot of interest in Rosaan, but I send the odd piece home. Trinity isn't as important as it likes to think it is. Not as important as it feels when you're in the middle of it all. Locally, I've developed a reputation as an independent voice. It doesn't pay well, but I get by. It helps that I'm from outside Trinity. It's hard to spend very long here without developing a political affiliation.'

Echoes

'Do you like living here?' I asked.

I almost asked if it was a good place to live, but I knew enough from the research I'd done, and the streams at home, and what I'd seen so far, to know the answer to that.

'It's a soulless place,' shrugged Clar. 'There's no culture, no joy. Chaguartay has built a machine.'

Clar sighed.

'But something kept me here. There's a division between the haves and the have nots, that I... I didn't think I could fix, but I thought I could shine a light on. The Factories run off the back of drones, propped up by tweak. The only escape is to work for the government, which is a massive, sprawling bureaucracy that largely exists to create work for itself and is so dysfunctional that no one has noticed that the Mayor is manipulating everything for the benefit and profit of him and his family. There's not enough anger here. Plenty of frustration, but no one's about to rise up and do anything about it.'

'Isn't there a Resistance movement? And the Opposition, they're led by Chaguartay's daughter. Surely she could make a difference. She must have the inside track?'

Clar shrugged again. They picked up my cup of tea and took a swig before pulling a face of disgust. It was surely cold by this point.

'Resistance play war games in the hills, there's no appetite to fight in the city. And Evie White - Chaguartay as was - is an impressive woman, but she seems happy to play second fiddle to her husband who is, frankly, nothing.'

'And Chaguartay? Now you've met him?'

Clar visibly shivered.

'I didn't have long, but I had long enough. Chaguartay is a virus. That man is chilling. I could feel the bile rising in my throat as he walked towards me, just an animal reaction to pure evil. When he sat down and shook my hand, I felt unclean. I knew I'd just touched something I couldn't wait to wipe off.'

'And then the building exploded?'

'And then the building exploded. Two pairs of hands grabbed his shoulders, hauled him up and suddenly he wasn't there anymore. I got up and ran and almost fell over you, gasping for air in the corridor. Now we're here. I think you can fill in the gaps.'

'You had a getaway car lined up.' That still confused me. Was that normal behaviour for an interview?

'Always do,' replied Clar, tucking their hair behind their ears. 'This is a dangerous place, and I'm in a dangerous profession. At least it is the way I do it.'

They reached into their trouser pocket and took out a Com device, which they placed in the middle of the stained table.

I stared at Clar's face, their blue eyes twinkling and a small, satisfied smile twitching at the corner of their mouth.

I was in a strange city, on my own, in a situation that made little sense. Either something that, hours ago, I would have insisted was impossible was happening to me, or it wasn't, but someone was trying to convince me it was.

I needed help; I needed an ally, someone to trust. My gut told me to trust Clar, and I needed to stop worrying.

They were holding something back, and I knew that. I knew I didn't know the full story, but there was something straightforward about them. I needed to trust them. Besides, I didn't have anyone else to trust.

'What is it?' I asked, breaking eye contact, which I'd held for slightly too long for it to be comfortable anymore.

I reached for the object they'd placed on the table. Clar grinned, pulling it towards them, out of my reach.

'That,' they said, 'is Stam Chaguartay's Com.'

I stared, the breath knocked out of me. My heart was racing, sweat breaking out across my back. Panic rose. Just when I'd got comfortable, I was frightened. This showed, at a minimum, a lack of journalistic integrity.

'You're not just a journalist, are you?' I stammered.

I had the urge to run, but my legs were weak and I felt glued to the spot. It was everything I could do not to slip down the counter into a puddle on the floor.

'Until this point, yes I was,' they insisted. 'But I'd gone to ask Chaguartay questions about a murder. They found one of his aides in an alley, shot in the back, a while back. A friend of mine was investigating, but he's now… indisposed…'

They dropped their head and exhaled. When they looked back up, a steely look had taken hold of their features.

'I think Chaguartay's involved, somehow, in all of it. So you're right, I have shifted my position a bit, but this might help me prove it. And it just fell into my lap, metaphorically and almost literally as well. In that it hit me in the groin when he dropped it.'

'Didn't he notice?'

'I guess the exploding building, and the bodyguards manhandling him out of the way, distracted him.'

'What are you going to do with it? I assume now you have a target on your back?' I was trying to control the panic, and I was failing. 'Are we safe here? Can he trace it?'

'Possibly,' admitted Clar. I wasn't sure which question that was in response to - I'd asked four. 'I assume he has access to the ComGrid. I'm trying to get rid of it. It's not like I can access it, it's got, like, layers of security on it. I just need to get in contact with someone who wants…'

'… to buy it?'

I thought I got it.

'It's a ticket out. And I've got to get out. This place is hell, and now I've met the man in charge, the man responsible, I can see that it's only going to get more hellish. You do not know how hard it is to get out of here.'

That felt ironic, given what I thought I now knew about my situation. I wondered whether to say something.

'I might,' was all I said.

Clar shook their head.

'I'm sorry if you feel like I got you mixed up in something. It wasn't my intention.'

'How are you going to sell it? Do you know people like that? Who'd be able to use it?'

'I know people who know people like that. More importantly, I know someone who works for them. You need a go-between for this kind of transaction. Someone they trust.'

'I can imagine,' I said. I couldn't imagine.

'This is their place,' Clar explained.

I narrowly avoided exclaiming "I knew it" out loud. This had all the hallmarks of being the place of residence of someone with a necessarily chaotic lifestyle.

Clar sighed and put their head in their hands.

'I don't know. Maybe this was all a huge mistake. I don't know what I'm doing. I'm in way over my head.'

This wasn't reassuring. *I* didn't know what I was doing. *I* was in over my head. So far Clar had seemed to be on top of things, it wasn't helpful to watch them unravel.

I went back to the table, righted and sat down on the wobbly stool. I found myself, almost without controlling it, reaching across the mould-stained table, taking Clar's hands from their face and holding them in mine.

Clar lifted their head up, there were tears in their eyes. I didn't quite know how to react.

'I... I'm sorry,' I said, although I wasn't sure what for. 'This is probably delayed shock. If it wasn't still ten in the morning, I'd say we needed something stronger than tea.'

Clar smiled, sucked air through their lips and blew upwards, lifting a loose strand of hair.

'It's OK,' they smiled. 'You didn't ask to be here.'

I looked across the kitchen to where I'd left the napkin. The *Echo*. I didn't. And yet maybe…

Clar pulled their hands back and stood up, wiping their eyes and straightening their blouse.

'This won't do,' they fussed, sniffing and trying to get their emotions, if not back in check then at least, away from their face.. 'But you're right, we shouldn't stay too long here. I'm going to make another call, see if I can speed things up a bit. We don't want to end up as sitting ducks…'

A door banged in another room. Clar snapped to attention.

'… or,' they continued, 'maybe there's no need.'

They started towards the kitchen door, and I made to get up and follow, but Clar motioned me back down with a hand gesture.

'I should prepare the ground,' they said. 'She's not expecting anyone else to be here. It'll be fine, it's just…'

Clar slipped through the kitchen door, pulling it closed behind them. I sat back, holding my breath to hear the voices from the hallway, Clar and a woman. Their tones were urgent, lowered, possibly strained. I caught a gasp, an expletive. But not in the woman's voice, from Clar.

The voices gained in volume, until I could hear them clearly, just outside the kitchen. I realised that they were on their way in and I scrambled from the stool, grabbed the napkin and stuffed it into the inside pocket of my jacket. The door swung open.

The figure standing in the doorway was not what I had been expecting. She was short and leaned slightly to the right, unsteady and unkempt. She wore a grey striped waistcoat over a stained white shirt, with a black bowtie unravelled around her neck.

Her hair was untidily gathered into a ponytail, but the band securing it was halfway down and at least a third of her hair had come loose. Her eyeliner was smudged. I had been expecting an underground fixer, but I seemed to be faced with a scruffy bartender.

The most surprising thing, though, was the look on the woman's face. Shock, confusion, but also recognition flashed across her as she took me in, stood at the far side of the kitchen.

Before I could speak, she exclaimed one thing, which took me by surprise.

'No!' she said. 'Not you!'

CHAPTER 5

The bartender, white with apparent fear, left the room and marched back down the hallway. Looking bewildered, Clar spun, shrugged in my general direction and followed her.

I remained rooted to the spot, not sure what to do. I'd apparently been recognised, but by someone I was certain I'd never laid eyes on myself. That had to be a mistake, surely?

It wasn't the first time that day that someone had thought they'd met me before, though. Ahji in Administration had made a similar mistake. *I must have a doppelgänger in Trinity.*

I heard Clar shouting from the hallway.

'Mouse? Mouse!' they called.

"*Mouse*"? With a start, I ran out of the kitchen and into the hallway.

This was Mouse? There couldn't be many Mouses around, and for this to be their house, where I'd only just uncovered the very pen that I - a different iteration of I - had used to write the Echo that pointed right back to them... This had to be important.

The hallway was dark and empty. Mouse and Clar appeared to be in the living room off the corridor towards the front of the house. I heard raised voices and an erratic thump of a fist on a wall.

'No!' shouted Mouse. 'What are you trying to do? I don't need this, Clar. I know what…'

I walked to the open doorway and then hesitated, uncertain what to do. I'd obviously caused a great deal of angst. This made little sense to me. If this was Mouse, who I'd had direct instructions to seek, didn't that make them an ally? Shouldn't they be more pleased to see me?

Although, of course, for this Mouse, this would be the first time they'd met me, so perhaps they needed to be won around, and only then they'd be prepared to help. Yet they seemed to recognise me, seemed to know who I was. So, did they think I was someone else?

Mouse was standing in front of the large screen on the wall. She turned to face me. Her eyes were wide, but I was relieved to see that she didn't seem angry. She still seemed scared, though.

'You!' she said again. 'I dreamed you! You're not real. You can't be real or…'

She screwed up her fists, pushed them into her eyes. Clar went to put an arm around her. I felt like I was intruding. Except that this all seemed to be about me.

'You can't be fucking real,' she muttered. 'You're not fucking real.'

'I…' I knew I wanted to counter that, however hyperbolic a statement it was. I still thought that they thought I was someone else. 'Who do you think I am..?'

'You're Estrel Beck, aren't you?' screamed Mouse, dispelling that illusion. 'Estrel fucking Beck!'

She drew out each syllable, punching them back at me, challenging me to prove her wrong, to be anybody else.

I was stunned.

'How?' I spluttered. 'How do you know who I am? How do you know me?'

'I don't!' groaned Mouse, which made no sense at this point. 'I don't fucking know you. You were a dream, a hallucination. You have got to be, or everything's fucked up like... Have you got the napkin?'

I really was stunned this time. As if in a trance, I pulled the Echo from my jacket pocket and unscrunched it before holding it out, hand quivering, to Mouse.

Mouse took it and stared at it, shaking her head and scoffing.

'I... It's exactly how I remember it,' she whispered. 'Except... what's this bit? FIND MOUSE? Ha!'

She held out her hand, half a smile breaking through the thunder on her face, giving the crumpled piece of paper back to me.

'I guess you've managed that already.' She shook her head. 'Here I am. Here I fucking am. Tell me what you need, Estrel, because it seems that your wish is my fucking command.'

I was lost for words. Thoughts were colliding head-on and the twisted wreckage was making it hard to articulate any of them.

'I... I don't know. I don't understand this.'

If the time loop was real, if the Echo was true, then Mouse was my biggest ally. But Mouse knew who I was, and what the Echo was. If the time loop was real, then how was that possible? I had understood that everything reset, except the Echo. Did that make the whole thing a hoax? What did that make Mouse?

'You seem to know who I am,' I said. 'Can you tell me what's happening to me?'

'No, no, no.' She took a step forward and slapped me on

the shoulder sympathetically. 'It doesn't work like that, my friend. You told me that.'

The warmth of the gesture confused but reassured me. An idea occurred.

'But you remember me. Does that mean you're an Echo too?'

Mouse chuckled.

'Am I an Echo? Yes, that's what you kept calling it. I remember that. But I don't know, everything else is kind of hazy. Like, ephemeral, you know?'

'What?' I didn't. Was that "yes" she was an Echo or "yes" I kept calling things Echoes?

'It's all a bit...' Mouse took a step back and waved her hands around her head to illustrate. 'Jumbled up, I guess. But I know that what you wanted was to create another Echo, a person who could help you, tell you what happened to, if you don't mind the expression, all the other yous.'

'Yes,' I was excited. 'Yes, that would be perfect. Like the napkin. So, what, I needed you with me when I looped? So that you'd remember.'

'Yeah, that's the idea,' Mouse said, rubbing her chin. 'But... It's not like remembering something you've done, or even something you've heard. It's like remembering something you dreamed. And that evaporates the moment you wake up. There are all these little bubbles of memories, but if I reach out to grab them, they float away, or pop. So I don't know what to tell you, Estrel, but I don't think I can help you.'

I shivered at the phrase "bubble of memory". I'd thought something like that, myself, only a few hours ago. There were too many coincidences here. I didn't like it. It was feeling like the whole thing was true, something I actually had to deal with.

I glanced at Clar. They looked completely baffled, which

was understandable. I was feeling pretty baffled, and I had most of the information I needed. They glanced back, and then shrugged.

'Time loop, right?' they said, as if it was a perfectly normal predicament to find oneself in. 'Don't worry about me. You two seem to have things you need to sort out. I'll follow along. Probably.'

Mouse sat down on a wooden chair.

'You can try me if you like. Ask me questions. See if you can spark any more recollections. But I can't give you anything. You'll have to get it out of me.'

I raised an eyebrow. This wasn't a complete loss. I looked behind me at the one sided sofa and chose a seat at the clean end. I knew what I wanted to ask first.

'How long have I got? When do I loop?'

Mouse nodded.

'Solid first question, that.' She thought for a moment. 'It's after midnight, I definitely saw my Com say "12". But then, I swear I checked it again, and it was, like, ten thirty. So, I don't know. Maybe that was a dream. Maybe they both were.'

'Helpful,' I sneered.

'I'm doing my best,' shrugged Mouse. 'I didn't ask to be your Echo. I have a distinct memory of dreaming of telling you it wouldn't work. You should have just written "go get another napkin" on the bottom of the first one and started writing on that one too.'

I looked at her, saying nothing. That would have been quite a good idea. But I had to trust that past-me had rejected that with good reason. An image of myself with all of my pockets stuffed with paper napkins, looking like I'd eaten all the pies, flashed through my mind. *A better reason than that,* I hoped.

'OK,' I agreed. 'Then how? How do I loop? Do I... Do I

die?'

This was, of course, what I'd been worried about all along. What was the event that sent me back through time to live the same day over again, and was it my death?

If Toun hadn't been early, and I hadn't been in the lift, would the explosion have killed me? What if Clar hadn't carried me from the building? How careful did I need to be for the rest of the day?

Mouse shook her head.

'Just happened. We were... in the generator room, underneath Eamer's. You came over odd and grabbed my hand and said "it's time" and then you disappeared. And then I woke up. Or I carried on. I can't really wrap my head around how this is working, to be honest.'

'The Echo bounced back to you and you woke up with it,' I said. It seemed I'd been thinking about this more than I realised. 'Whilst a future version of you carried on.'

'Look, I don't know what you're looking for, but I don't think I can help you much more than this. It's properly vague, and getting vaguer by the second.'

'No, wait, I'm...' I was thinking. Something was bothering me and I couldn't quite put it into words. 'When you got here, you were surprised to see me?'

'Yes, someone I thought I'd conjured up in a dream was standing in my kitchen,' laughed Mouse. 'Of course I was fucking surprised.'

'No, but it wasn't just that, was it?' I realised what the problem was. 'This isn't how we met last time. How we met in the dream. Was it?'

Mouse shook her head, her eyes flicking around, searching for the memory.

'No, it wasn't. I was at work, behind the bar in Eamer's. You came in looking a state. You ordered a drink. I served it.

Echoes

You couldn't pay. That wasn't a good idea. High jinks ensued and, believe me, that bit's fuzzy. You had a load of strange theories. I went along with them, for some reason. Dream logic. Except it wasn't a dream. You jumped back in time and… Let's not get into that again, shall we not? That's it though, that's everything. I have literally nothing more for you.'

I was silent for a moment, then made a decision. I placed my hands on my knees and pushed myself up.

'We should go then.'

'Go where?' Both Mouse and Clar remained seated.

'Eamer's,' I replied, more confidently than I should have done given I didn't know where, or really what, Eamer's was. It seemed to be important in my repeating timeline though, and I wanted to see the place I'd reset before. 'You've mentioned it twice already.'

'Woah, steady on,' Mouse stood up now, her hands gesturing that I should take things a little more slowly. 'I don't think that's a great idea. Do you even know what Eamer's is?'

I grimaced because, of course, I didn't.

'A bar?' I guessed. There had been enough context for me to feel that I was in the ballpark.

It was Mouse's turn to grimace.

'Lucky guess. But it's not a place you want to just stroll into.'

'Sounds like I did before,' I objected.

'And didn't you hear me say that high jinks ensued?' Mouse threw up her hands emphatically.

'High jinks sounds like something I can deal with.' I shrugged.

High jinks didn't sound too scary. I'd survived a bombing already, and made several strides towards solving the mystery of the time loop. I could cope with high jinks.

'I was glossing over the gory details,' confessed Mouse. 'Besides...'

She turned to Clar, who was still sitting down, jiggling their leg nervously.

'Clar needs to get this Com out of my house, and taking it to Eamer's is a terrible idea.'

'How so?' I demanded.

Mouse shook her head as Clar took their turn to stand.

'Thieves, Eamer, Black Knights,' they offered. I only had a vague idea of what the last of those were, as well.

'Some might say they're the same thing,' observed Mouse.

'Some might say we're wasting time here,' said Clar, 'and the more time we waste here, the more chance there is that someone's got a lock on this Com. Whatever we're doing, can we go somewhere?'

Mouse nodded.

'Yes, we need to get out of here. Somewhere where there's no one with a line back to Chaguartay. Which is why,' she turned back to me, 'Eamer's is a bad idea. That's before we get to all the other reasons. Most of the city is out of the question, on that basis.'

'I thought you were meant to be helping? I thought you were some kind of well-connected fixer who could fence a stolen Com unit without breaking a sweat.'

Mouse smiled and looked at Clar.

'I see you've been talking me up again,' she said. 'Naughty Clar. But now you come to mention it...'

Now she was talking to me again.

'You won't find anyone else in Trinity who can get you an audience with both the Black Knights and Opposition. Sometimes even in the same room...' They paused, thoughtfully.

'So why aren't we doing that?'

'Because we need to be careful!' she snapped. 'I thought we'd already done this bit. We need to avoid the Black Knights. They're Chaguartay's secret police, as good as.'

'So Opposition then,' I said. 'Can't you…'

'Can't move in this city without the Black Knights,' objected Mouse. 'We may need to get to Opposition in a more creative way.'

Her face brightened, a lightbulb moment occurring for her.

'Estrel!' she exclaimed. 'Maybe your insane theories aren't as random as they might appear.'

I was confused.

'What insane theories?' I asked. 'Are we going to Eamer's?'

'Not you,' scoffed Mouse. 'The other you. Last-time Estrel. I wasn't the only Echo he tried to create. Grab your bag! We're going for a hike.'

'Will you just shut up about it?' asked Mouse, in the back of the TransPod.

I stared at her. Clar had called back their emergency backup Pod, with its enigmatic, unseen pilot, and we were once again speeding through the streets of Trinity, passing through districts at a rate of knots.

I barely registered the change in colour, or architecture, or smells, as they flashed by, but the perimeter walls that always loomed in the background looked to be closer every time I glanced out of the window, so I assumed that was where we were heading.

Despite me making the case for going via Tunnel Terminus to collect my luggage, Mouse and Clar seemed to be of the opinion that it wasn't important and I could hike wherever we needed to hike in my suit and dress shoes. After all, Clar was wearing heels.

I took a good look at Clar's boots which, whilst they did

boast an impressive heel, looked pretty substantial. I thought they'd be fine.

Besides, I was less bothered about the hiking and more distressed by the potential loss of another Echo.

'Look,' I insisted, waving the receipt I'd retrieved from my back pocket in Mouse's face. 'This receipt has today's date on it. It's time-stamped for two twenty-three this afternoon. That hasn't even happened yet, but I found this in my bag this morning.'

Mouse took the piece of paper from my hands and peered at it.

'Oh yes,' she agreed. 'You couldn't fit the boots in your bag. You said that if you could prove you'd just bought them, you could pick them up again. I don't think that's how shops work, but you were adamant.'

'I don't care about that,' I said. 'But the contents of the bag were another Echo. I didn't pay much attention to them this morning, but what if there was something else important in there?'

'Like your sandwiches?' asked Clar. 'We can stop for food if you're hungry.'

'No, we can't,' retorted Mouse. 'We're escaping the city. We don't have time for elevenses. Look, Estrel, an Echo that doesn't immediately scream "I'm important!" to you isn't an awful lot of use, is it? You said yourself you were just confused by the contents of your bag. Unlike the napkin, which has your name in massive letters at the top of it.'

'Or you,' observed Clar, 'who immediately said, "Not you!" and tried to run away.'

'Not ideal, but still better,' said Mouse.

'But what if it makes more sense as the day goes on? It was my bag. I would have expected to have it with me all day.'

'Except you knew about the bag check.' Mouse was getting

exasperated.

'But I didn't use the bag check yesterday,' I persisted.

'Not yesterday!' cried Mouse. 'It was today. The same today you're living now! How come you're the one stuck in the time loop and you're the one who seems to understand it least?'

'Shut up,' I replied, petulantly.

That was abnormally rude for me, with someone I'd only just met. But I hadn't only just met her, had I? I'd known Mouse for at least a day, maybe many, many more. It's just that I didn't remember it.

I felt like she remembered more than she was letting on, though.

'Look, like I said, you seemed pleased about buying the stuff. You said, if I recall, that it was the only thing that had gone right for you today. That day. Whatever.'

'But why would I do that? I wasn't preparing for a hike, this wasn't something we were going to do on that day. We didn't meet until later, you said.'

I'd taken Mouse's point about the bag check, about the risks of me not carrying around a heavy bag all day.

'Sure.'

Mouse was looking out the window now. We were getting very close to the wall.

'So maybe that wasn't why, maybe I wanted to make myself do something different from the start, like go hiking and miss the meeting with Toun. But then…'

'Then we wouldn't have met,' said Clar.

'But we didn't that day either,' I said.

But if we didn't meet and go to Mouse's then I didn't get the pen, which meant that I hadn't added to the napkin Echo that day. So maybe it wasn't the best template for comparing today to. Unless…

'Unless we did, and I didn't mention it.'

'I'd be surprised if you did something and didn't mention it,' sighed Mouse. 'You talk a lot.'

'Shut up,' I snapped, again.

'We're nearly there,' said Mouse, ignoring me, and looking out the window as the Pod slowed. 'There'll be perimeter checks. Let me handle the admin.'

I wasn't really listening, cogs were whirring.

'But what if we did?' I said.

'What if we did what?' asked Mouse, clearly irritated now.

'Not you,' I dismissed her with a hand. 'Although… maybe you too.'

I turned to Clar.

'What if we did? Meet. Just like we did today, what if we did all of this… but we did it the today before last? And then I echoed myself to make sure I had hiking gear. Then I echoed that but failed to tell myself why.'

I sat back, hands wide, an expectant look on my face.

'Oh, Dear Creator, that's dumb,' moaned Mouse, shaking her head.

This left me hurt and offended, and I did my best to communicate that in my facial expression.

'I think it's plausible,' I maintained.

'Oh no,' Mouse corrected herself, 'I think it's entirely plausible. I just think it's dumb. If you really think that's a possibility, then I think you're doing this terribly. And I already thought that.'

'I…' I began, ready to defend myself, but it turned out that I had nothing.

Mouse cut me off.

'If you can't even manage, once you've figured out how this works, to build on what's gone before, to make sure your Echoes communicate everything you need to know to make sense of them, all the thinking behind your actions, then who knows how long you've been at this? How many times have you been around that loop, Estrel? How many Estrels have there been?'

'I…' I began again, '… don't know.'

I trailed off. Was this right? My head spun with sudden doubt. I felt like I was figuring this thing out, but I wondered if I was any further forward than any of the previous attempts I'd made. And Mouse was right. I had no way of knowing how many of those there had been.

'What's this even for?' continued Mouse. 'Chances are you're just here to fall in love or avenge a relative or something equally nonsense and inconsequential. But what if this really means something? What if this is important? What if the world, *my* world, depends on you completing whatever mission it is that the universe has sent you on and you keep fucking it up?'

'I…' I began, for the third time.

I didn't have an answer to that. It was entirely possible that what I was doing was important. In fact, I was taking it seriously because I thought it was important.

I hadn't actually considered that I was here to fall in love, or to avenge anyone. The thought that it might be nothing more than that had knocked the wind out of my sails somewhat.

'Shh, we're here,' said Clar to me, slumping back into the Pod seat as it slowed to a halt. 'Keep your head down.'

Wounded, I did as I was told. The window of the Pod slid down and a helmeted Uniform with an Authority badge stooped to look inside the vehicle.

He immediately saw Clar and me with our heads bowed, which made me wonder how necessary it had been to duck out of sight. I kept my head low and eyes averted, just in case.

'State your business?' the Uniform barked into the Pod.

I jumped in my seat. Next to me, I could hear Clar grinding their teeth.

From the corner of my eye, I watched Mouse turn to the window and flash something that they held in their hand at the Uniform.

'I have business on the Outside,' she said, simply.

The Uniform's face flashed death grey.

'I'm s-so sorry,' he stammered. 'I won't hold you up any longer.'

He took a step back. I lifted my head and caught sight of another man, dressed in a black jacket over a black shirt, leaning in to whisper something to the Uniform.

The Uniform reconsidered and drew his weapon, levelling it at us through the window. Mouse looked as if she were going to shout something, made a move as if to bang on the partition between us and the TransPod pilot, but she then seemed to think better of it and closed her mouth, dropped her fist.

'I'm going to need you to get out of the Pod,' said the Uniform.

'I know,' sighed Mouse, triggering the door and stepping out into the murky shadows in front of the wall.

Mouse had been gone for several minutes before either Clar or I spoke.

The Uniform had ushered Mouse through a door in the wall fairly quickly, not aggressively, almost apologetically in fact, leaving us behind, sat in the TransPod. The Pod pilot had powered down, and we'd been waiting ever since.

Lurking in the shadows the whole time was the man in black, pacing backwards and forwards as he watched us with a permanent scowl on his features.

'What do you think is causing the holdup?' I asked, keeping my voice low.

Clar paused for a moment, a moment for which I thought I'd kept my voice so low that they hadn't heard.

'Not sure,' they said eventually. 'I assumed it was something to do with your Knight there...'

I had wondered. I'd heard of the Black Knights, they'd been referred to a few times already today. This guy was evidently one of their number. The hairs stood up on the back of my neck as he turned and glanced in our direction again.

'The Authority guy seemed to change his tune pretty quickly after they spoke,' I pointed out.

'I know, and that's what worried me,' replied Clar. 'He was all ready to let Mouse pass and then... something happened. I couldn't work out if it was us he had a problem with, but other than making sure we weren't about to make a run for it, he's not seemed bothered about us.'

'Do you think Mouse is OK?' I asked.

She'd been annoying me on the ride over, but she'd thrown herself into some drama that really had nothing to do with her with relatively little complaint.

'Depends on who's in there,' said Clar, 'and why they took her in. Trinity isn't a place that it's easy to leave. It's part of the reason I'm still here. As far as I know, though, Mouse can move through the border at will. That's what I mean. If it had been you or me that got pulled in, it would have made more sense. I don't know what Mouse has done for the Knights to put her on watch.'

'You said she was well connected,' I reminded them.

'She is,' confirmed Clar, 'very well connected. That could be part of the problem. She needs to keep her connections carefully compartmentalised. If one set of connections found out that she has connections to one of the others, then that could spell trouble.'

'What kind of trouble?'

'This kind of trouble.' Clar scratched their head, then banged on the screen to the pilot's compartment and shouted. 'Jo Jo!'

The partition slowly rolled down, revealing the mysterious pilot for the first time. I wasn't sure what I'd been expecting, but it wasn't a teenage boy in full chauffeur uniform. His cap had slid down to a jaunty angle, largely because it didn't fit his head.

'Jo Jo, we might need to make a quick getaway here,' said Clar. 'You ready for that?'

'Just give me the signal,' grinned Jo Jo, showing only half the normal number of teeth. He flicked a couple of switches on the dash. 'We're primed and ready to go.'

He punched a few more buttons and a red light flashed rapidly. He saluted before the screen rolled back up between him and us.

'Nice kid,' I said.

This place was weird. It wouldn't be long before nothing surprised me.

'He knows how to drive,' shrugged Clar, 'and he's not as green or as young as he looks. You'd be surprised. I've been trying to get him to tell me his secret for ages. Anyway, he's got me out of a few situations in the past.'

'You think this is a situation?'

'It's quickly looking like one. If Mouse doesn't appear soon, we need to make a swift getaway. If Mouse does appear soon, we may need to make an even quicker one.'

'Is there any scenario where…' I wondered about putting this delicately, but decided against it. '… where it's Mouse we're having to make a swift getaway from?'

'No, Mouse likes to juggle several balls, has her finger in

many pies, but she's straight enough. I trust her. She wouldn't turn me in. She's had plenty of opportunities by now.'

'She doesn't know me, though,' I pointed out.

'You say that, but I wouldn't be so sure,' mused Clar. 'She knows she's met you before, even if that was in, I don't know, a timeline that never existed from our point of view or whatever.'

'OK, but she doesn't seem to like me then,' I refined my earlier position. I was far from certain that Mouse wasn't about to throw me under the bus.

'You don't know that,' Clar shook their head. 'She's like that with most people. She has a very low bullshit tolerance, so she asks a lot of questions. Then she sighs a lot when she's bored with the answers. I think she likes you. She definitely believes you.'

'Maybe,' I conceded. I hadn't seen a lot of evidence that she liked me, or thought that I was anything more than an inconvenience and an irritation.

'That she believes you is important, though,' continued Clar. 'More important than whether she likes you. You're in a situation and so she'll help you out. That is what she does. It's only you that needs her to like you.'

That was a strange thing to say. I didn't care if Mouse liked me.

There was a commotion in the shadow. It was hard to see what was going on until a figure strode out and started heading for the TransPod. I jumped in panic - I think I hadn't realised how tense I was - before I noticed it was Mouse.

She had a serious look on her face and ignored the attempt of the background Black Knight to get her attention. Clar operated the door, and it slid open to allow her to climb in.

'Get ready Jo Jo,' Clar muttered under their breath.

I wasn't sure that Jo Jo could hear them, but suddenly the

Pod's motor whirred.

'Out of here?' Clar asked Mouse.

'Out of here,' confirmed Mouse through gritted teeth. 'The way we were going, not so quickly that it looks like we're running, but quick enough that we're no longer here when they realise that everything I've just told them is a giant pile of horse shit…'

Clar nodded, like this was a well-known unit of haste. They banged firmly on the partition.

'Now, Jo Jo,' they said, and before they'd finished, we were on the move.

CHAPTER 6

We sat in silence as the TransPod weaved through the last few streets towards the tunnel that would lead us out of the city. Jo Jo wasn't holding back, but we still weren't moving fast enough for my liking.

I got the impression that this wasn't a well-used route. As another pedestrian dived into a doorway, and the back of the Pod clipped another bin, I considered that this might be a good thing, that it was less likely that someone could follow us. Not, at least, without us realising it.

As we entered the tunnel itself, and its mouth swallowed the dim street level light, the Pod clicked onto some kind of guided rail and, with a jerk, we started moving forward with more purpose. Mouse seemed to relax at this point.

'What did you say?' I asked.

'Hmm?' asked Mouse, looking straight ahead and apparently pretending not to know what I was talking about.

'To get us out?' I persisted. 'What did you tell them? And how much trouble are you in when they realise you made it up?'

And, by corollary, how much trouble am I in when they realise you made it up?

'I dropped some names,' Mouse shrugged, 'some influential names. And if, when, those names get picked up, there is every chance that the people who own those names will deny all knowledge of what we're up to here. Largely because they don't have any knowledge of what we're up to here. They may, even, deny all knowledge of me, largely because they don't actually know me, at least not by name. At least not by the name I just gave them.'

'That sounds like a house of cards just ready to tumble,' I observed. 'I'm surprised it held up long enough for you to make it out of the room.'

'I don't know.' Mouse continued to stare straight ahead. 'Everyone in this city is playing a game.'

She turned and looked at me. It was hard not to read something into it.

'I'm not!' I exclaimed indignantly.

'Clar isn't,' replied Mouse.

I didn't like her tone, but her statement felt definitive, that she would tolerate no more discussion on the subject. I thought about what Clar had said: "I think she likes you. She definitely believes you". I was far from convinced.

The TransPod stopped again, waiting for a metal grille to withdraw fully into the wall of the tunnel. Beyond it was the world outside Trinity, where the light was noticeably different, brighter, crisper, more vivid and real.

The immediate landscape was grey, rocky, steep slopes building up to the base of the city walls, but beyond that, the green carpet of the tree-filled valley lifted me. My arrival in Trinity seemed an age ago, and the relief of escape flooded my heart.

The rail continued down the rocky embankment and we lurched and tipped onto it, the Pod now travelling at an acute angle downwards. I could see, now we were up close, that the bank was littered with metal and glass. Broken shards and barbs glinted from between the dark rock, itself a jagged deterrent to anyone who might contemplate exploring it. Or climbing it?

I hadn't seen this from the viaduct this morning. I'd been too high up, only seeing the majesty of the landscape. Down here, up close, it was threatening.

'They're not keen on encouraging walkers,' I said, with a tone that was probably inappropriately light, but I still felt the weight of Mouse's vague insinuations in the silence between us.

I saw a shadow pass over Clar's face.

'They've had what Authority deems "problems" with people trying to enter Trinity,' they said, seriously. 'It's kept very quiet, even outside Trinity, but there are camps beyond the Northern Exposure, filled with people displaced from their homes by war or famine. Many of them have come thousands of miles, drifting through places that don't want them until they arrive at the edge of Trinity. This border is hard. There's nowhere left for them to go.'

'But that's inside Ashuana?' I had never heard of anything like this.

Ashuana was a vast country, of course, with a range of cultures and languages that morphed from one to another as you moved from East to West, but a migrant population building up on the border was news to me.

Clar laughed in response.

'The Ashuanan government is nothing like its neighbours,' they replied. 'You are lucky to live as you live, to enjoy the freedoms you have, but at the end of the day, they're still a government. They still govern you. They would probably tell you that your ignorance is your protection.'

We fell quiet. The awkward, oppressive silence returned to the Pod cabin.

We reached the bottom of the slope and the TransPod lurched back onto the level. Here the rail ended, bouncing us off onto the road again, although I could see that this quickly deteriorated into a track as it passed the tree line.

The chassis of the TransPod was low, and I didn't see how it was going to take us much further. Unless the forest was our destination, we were going to have to get out and walk, just as Mouse had promised. Or threatened.

'Where are we going?' I asked as the light in the cabin dimmed under the canopy of trees.

'Up,' said Mouse. 'Well, across first, but then up. There.'

She pointed at the brown-grey slopes that rose from the other side of the valley. Another geographical feature that had been hidden from me on my inward journey, the Northern Exposure rose high above Trinity, steeply contrasting with the gentle slopes of the opposite side of the asymmetrical valley. Even if they hadn't been at the mercy of the fierce winds coming up from icy plains to the south of Trinity, their severe gradient would have made it very difficult for anything to grow without sliding down into the Triton.

Suddenly that very river was below us and we trundled out from the trees onto some kind of bridge. It was narrow, just a single rail that the TransPod clung to like its life depended on it.

I glanced down and almost vomited at the sheer drop from the side of the TransPod. Our lives did depend on it. I closed my eyes and hoped the Pod's grip was firm.

I'd been much higher, I told myself, only a few hours ago when I'd been heading in the opposite direction. We were close to the valley floor here, although not close enough. But then I'd been travelling in relative comfort in a substantial vehicle rather than being piloted by a kid over a ravine in a city taxi.

I was still none the wiser why any of this was happening. I had to remind myself that I'd come on a sales visit for a meeting that hadn't happened. If everything had gone according to plan, I would be having lunch soon. Probably sandwiches and pastries wheeled into the conference room.

We'd be agreeing to terms, maybe even toasting our future relationship. Had any of that happened the first time? Any of the times? Was it always chaos and danger? Was I always this terrified?

I realised that the fear had made me hide. I'd not faced the big decisions, not faced any decisions, really, other than to go along with everything that had been put to me, pretty much since I'd arrived this morning.

Drifting to a meeting, being rescued by Clar, driven out of the city by Mouse. I wasn't exactly directing events myself.

But this was happening to me. This was my mission, my quest, my problem to solve. I needed to do something, exert some control, however small. With precious little information to hand, I seemed to only have one option.

'I want to go back to Eamer's,' I said.

I didn't, not really. Mouse had put me off the idea earlier, but I couldn't break away from the feeling that the place was important, at least to my previous iteration. And my previous iteration had been trying to leave me clues.

I had rejected one Echo when I left it with The Face at Bridge. I couldn't ignore this one.

'No, no, you don't,' said Mouse, distractedly.

She was staring out of the Pod window, looking for something.

'I told you, that's not a place for you. It went badly before. That's definitely not how you solve this thing.'

'You don't know that,' I replied. The vagueness of Mouse's

description of what had gone badly didn't fill me with confidence that it was the truth. 'I don't think you know much, to be frank.'

'Who's fault is that?' scoffed Mouse. 'Leave a better Echo next time.'

'I'm going back,' I said, as the TransPod slowed further.

I went to bang on Jo Jo's screen.

'We're getting out,' shrugged Mouse. 'We're here. You can go back if you want. I don't fancy your chances of getting back into Trinity. You let me burn that bridge, somewhat...'

She slapped her hand against the pilot's partition and Jo Jo brought the Pod to a complete stop, next to a small patch of gravel and a grassy bank.

The door slid open and Mouse climbed out, closely followed by Clar. I paused and shoved my hand into my jacket pocket.

The napkin and the marker pen were still squashed at the bottom. I gritted my teeth.

OK, my problem to solve... I'd found Mouse. Maybe I did need to stay, so that I could discover why that had been important in the first place.

And ignore the fact that she'd effectively closed off all other options.

The path through the thin line of trees at the bottom of the slope was well worn, but the incline was already steep and tree roots made it tricky to place a foot without twisting an ankle.

Clar had discarded their boots within a couple of steps. My dress shoes were still on my feet but were cutting my heels to shreds and scraping the skin from my smaller toes. Mouse strode on ahead, oblivious to how much her companions were struggling.

I gritted my teeth and attempted to trot my way up to the

front.

'So where are we going?' I panted. 'Specifically, I mean. This place appears to be the middle of nowhere.'

Mouse kept up her determined pace.

'Up the hill,' she said, not a trace of breathlessness evident.

'You have a gift,' I observed, 'of finding exactly the thing to say that will piss me off the most.'

Mouse paused, turned, and grinned.

'Not a gift,' she said. 'It's too easy.'

Compared to the sullen stand-off we'd had in the car, this felt like good-natured teasing, which made it altogether easier to ignore.

'What's up the hill?' I asked.

'That,' agreed Mouse, 'is a better question.'

She shortened her stride slightly, as if in acknowledgement that we were getting along better now and she didn't need to punish me with every action. I downgraded from a trot to a walk.

'Up this hill, there are people. People we need to see.' Mouse cast a glance over her shoulder at Clar. 'Or rather people that they need to see.'

She stopped walking.

'People who can hack Chaguartay's Com.' I filled in. 'Find out what's on it.'

'Let's hope so,' said Mouse, as Clar came spluttering up. 'You OK?'

'Are we nearly there?'

I looked at Clar, breathless, sweating and red in the face. They could pick me up like I was a rag in the middle of a burning building, but they had no aerobic capacity to speak of. At all, it appeared.

'Where are we going anyway?' asked Clar.

I turned expectantly to Mouse, wondering if she was going

to make Clar work as hard for answers as I'd had to.

'Is it much further?'

'It is,' nodded Mouse, confirming my suspicions.

Clar's shoulders dropped.

'You need to get rid of that Com,' Mouse said. It wasn't a question, it was a statement of fact. 'So we're going to give it to some people who want it.'

'I thought we'd just be handing it over to Opposition,' said Clar.

'That will not work. Opposition can't be seen to be so closely connected to a criminal element.'

'A criminal element?' protested Clar.

I realised that Mouse had meant them.

'You stole the Mayor's Com,' reasoned Mouse. 'You're a criminal element. We need a middle man if we want to get it to the people who can use it to do some damage. And by damage I mean effect much needed radical reform.'

'So we're going to see the middle man?' I clarified.

'We are,' nodded Mouse. 'But I don't like standing around in the woods like this. It's not safe. You ready to move?'

Clar pulled an obvious face of reluctance.

'I could just go,' they said, looking back down the hill. 'You don't need me for this. All I wanted was to get out of Trinity. You helped me do that. I could just run.'

Mouse laughed out loud, looking down at Clar's grubby, scratched feet.

'Well, one: you can't and two: you haven't. If you were going to run, you wouldn't have got out of the TransPod at the bottom. Jo Jo could have taken you anywhere you needed, but you let him go back into the city.'

'Believe me, I wish I'd thought of that ten minutes ago...'

'What about the murder?' I asked. 'What about your friend?'

Echoes

'If I learned one thing during that very brief encounter with the esteemed Mayor,' Clar mused, more loudly than seemed strictly necessary, 'it's that he's very well protected. Pretty much untouchable. At least by the likes of me. I got lucky with the Com. If someone else wants to push that luck, then that's for them to take on. I'm out…'

They took a step to the side, right up next to Mouse, and dropped their voice. I had to lean in to catch their words.

'Don't react,' they said, 'but we're being followed. I felt there was something wrong, but I've just seen them hide behind that tree.'

Mouse turned her head to stare up the hill.

'You need to hurry up,' she exclaimed. 'These are not people who like to be kept waiting.'

I felt a bit lost. It was as if Mouse was deliberately ignoring what Clar had just told her. Which I then realised was exactly what was happening, and that this was something I should play along with.

I looked in the same direction as Mouse, trying not to show the fresh jolt of adrenaline that had just flooded me, making me want, surprising as it was, to rush the hill.

I'd seen them too, a glint of something between the leaves, a single branch moving at shoulder height.

If anything, the slope appeared to get steeper ahead, but the top of the tree line was in sight. That felt like somewhere we needed to get to, although I guessed we'd be more exposed.

But if we were exposed, our tail would have to decide to expose themselves as well or to stop following us.

'If we're going, should we just go?' I volunteered, trying to sound impatient.

Mouse and Clar said nothing, but started walking, catching me out and leaving me several strides behind. This time Clar matched Mouse's pace, despite their lack of footwear, and I realised that they hadn't been struggling, they'd been surveilling.

I ran to catch up.

I was breathless by the time we broke past the last line of trees. In front of us spread the bleak expanse of the Northern Exposure, sparsely dotted with the few clumps of grass and bush that had found a foothold in the grey, chalky soil. It was hard to tell where the hill ended and the clouded grey sky began, but it was still a very long way to the top, if that was where we were headed.

'How many did you think?' Mouse now asked in a hushed voice.

'Just the one that I saw,' replied Clar. 'But they moved fast. I don't think they were on foot.'

I couldn't believe that any vehicle could have made it up the steep, root tangled path we'd just climbed. Surely the only way up was on foot? I tried to say something but my breath and therefore my voice failed me.

'Terrain Boots?' asked Mouse, surprise in her voice. 'Not Authority then?'

Clar shook their head.

'They don't have that kind of equipment. There's no call for it inside the City walls.'

'Fuck,' spat Mouse. 'Then they're Military, in which case we're fucked, or the Black Knights, in which case we're super fucked.'

'I thought you had clout with the Knights?' Clar pointed out. 'That's why they swallowed your bullshit at the checkpoint. I thought that's how you got us out of the city.'

'Yeah,' Mouse's pace slowed, and she rubbed her chin.

She chanced a glance over her shoulder, which I copied. I saw no one.

'I've been wondering if that might have been too easy. It's

possible that I wasn't as clever as I thought I'd been and that they always intended to let us leave.'

'Great!' Clar threw their hands up in the air. 'So you've brought us out here to be killed?'

Mouse pulled a face.

'Now I think about it, it's what I'd do,' she admitted, stopping in her tracks. 'I'm sorry. I might have really fucked up this time.'

Clar and I stopped walking, too. I wanted to say something, but I couldn't quite articulate what was speeding through my head.

I was scared, that much I knew. Mouse had a look of uncertainty on her face, which I hadn't seen up to now. I saw Clar seemed to process similar thoughts as the three of us stood, trapped in indecision.

But despite what I felt, my brain was tickling me with a "what if…".

What if I reset when I died?

What if I, actually, couldn't die and would just wake up again this morning, on a train headed back to Trinity?

Then, all I had to worry about was whether my death would be quick, or drawn out and painful. But even the most agonising of deaths would be instantly forgotten, surely?

Instantly forgotten… I needed to make sure I kept my Echo and didn't have to start again from square one. What if they went through my pockets, removed the napkin?

I barely had a clue what was going on as it was. I couldn't afford to lose what meagre knowledge I'd amassed. Sticking my hand in my pocket, I pulled out the marker pen.

I needed something more reliable, less ephemeral. Something that couldn't easily be taken off of me.

I popped the lid off with my mouth, rolled up my sleeve, and bared my arm. I started with the letter Y for YOU - I didn't think there was any need to start with my name if I'd written the message on my own skin.

I felt the barrel of a gun in the small of my back.

CHAPTER 7

There were two of them, it turned out.

The one Clar had spotted darting between the trees was not the same one who had the barrel of his rifle rammed into the small of my back, but he soon caught up and was now awkwardly trying to pat Mouse down.

Whilst we outnumbered our captors, the guns made a big difference, and they were only being wielded by the other side, which was enough for me to conclude that the best thing to do was cooperate, especially as I was the one with the gun poking me in the back. Mouse seemed more interested in trying to get a good look at the insignias on her frisker's fatigues.

I saw the penny drop and her face light up.

'You're Resistance?' she asked. 'Oi, watch where you put your hands.'

'Sorry,' muttered the youth, slightly more sheepishly than was necessary given the balance of power.

After the dire warnings of Military personnel, or Black Knights, being on our tail, that they were Resistance was a relief to me. They were, after all, who we were on our way to meet.

'That's fine,' replied Mouse, primly, with a note of sarcasm. 'It's nice to see you're a respectful terrorist. But it's very convenient because we're on our way to see you guys.'

The other, apparently more senior Agent, who I hadn't seen yet as he was still standing behind me, put his hand on my shoulder and exerted some pressure.

'Shut up. On your knees,' he barked.

I fell to my knees, and in doing so, I dropped the pen in my hand. I felt the gun again. This time it was against the back of my head. I was sweating and, for the second time in half an hour, swallowed down the urge to vomit.

'I suggest you take a leaf out of your friend's book and cooperate,' he snarled, sweeping his gun from Mouse to Clar and back again.

A quicker, braver man than me might have chosen that moment to make a move, propel themselves backward to knock him off balance, or try to take him out at the knees with their shoulder. But by the time any of this had occurred to me, the second Resistance Agent had their gun trained on my head and the moment was lost.

'Just trying to save you some time,' shrugged Mouse, proffering her wrists for cuffing, 'but I get it. There's a process to follow, protocols, standard operating procedures, what have you…'

'I don't need to cuff you,' came the stern reply. 'I've got a gun. Just turn around and walk.'

He accompanied this instruction with a toe planted between my shoulder blades. I stopped myself from falling with my hands, scrambled to my feet and stumbled forward. To my relief, Mouse dropped her hands and turned to do the same.

'Lead the way, Agent Carlsen,' barked the senior man.

Agent Carlsen turned and picked his way through a small

patch of gorse.

'You can go first,' the first Agent said to Clar, shooing them with the barrel of his rifle, 'and I've got my eye on you…'

'Agent, is this really the time?' Mouse all but fluttered her eyes.

The game she was playing was making me nervous.

'One foot wrong, one word out of place, and I shoot him,' said the Resistance Agent, without a hint of humour.

I saw Mouse swallow and, to my relief, adjust her expression. Quietly, she fell in behind Clar. I felt another rough shove in my back and I stumbled forward, following behind.

I felt the increasingly familiar jolt of déjà vu, but this time attached to actual memories, rather than the dim echo of something I might have done in another reality.

The sullen line of silent walkers, trudging together, but with only their thoughts for company, this was every childhood holiday I'd ever experienced, with my elder brother Thurstan leading the way and my dad at the back, better placed to fire off admonishments to anyone who stumbled or wandered out of line.

I realised that, much as it had on every childhood route march, my head had dropped and I was staring at my own feet, counting the footsteps.

> *One, two. Inappropriate footwear.*
> *Three, four. Feet cut to ribbons.*
> *Five, six. Now we really were hiking.*
> *Seven, eight. "Are we nearly there yet?"*

I lifted my gaze. We seemed not to be headed for the brow of the hill, but for a small pile of rocks about a hundred metres away. Agent Carlsen dropped from view.

'Should have known, secret lair,' whispered Mouse. 'See

what I meant? Boys with toys, playing at being soldiers…'

I was very grateful that the man behind me didn't appear to hear her.

The entrance to the bunker nestled in an indent in the hill, a concrete pillbox with a heavy iron door. Agent Carlsen strained to prise it open and, once it was free, it swung outwards with a heavy violence that almost knocked him off his feet.

Inside, it was too dark to see, but he descended into the void down a flight of steps. Clar followed, with Mouse close behind, leaving me no option but to proceed the same way, especially not with the other Agent on gun waving duties at the rear.

Once inside, it was impossible to even see my feet anymore, and I descended carefully, my toes exploring the dark in front of me, convinced I was about to step out into nothing and plummet to my death right up to the point that my heel made contact with the next step.

Occasionally Mouse's head would loom into view, or I'd hear the noisy clatter of my captor stepping down behind me, but otherwise I could have been alone in the dark. Again, the shot of déjà vu, but I squashed this one. That wasn't a helpful memory right now.

There was the clang and the creak of another door opening and a milky white light washed into the stairwell. I could see, ahead of me, Carlsen and Clar stood in the entrance to a narrow tunnel, which sloped downwards into the hill.

Behind them, Mouse stood on the bottom step, her hands braced against the walls for balance. That would have been a good idea, if I'd thought of it.

'Come on,' said Carlsen, and he moved into the tunnel.

Silently, we all followed. The tunnel smelled of damp earth

and standing water and, whilst there was some light here, it wasn't powerful enough to illuminate much below the knee.

My foot occasionally splashed in something unseen as I tramped along. My socks were now waterlogged inside my insubstantial business footwear, although I only knew because my feet were slightly heavier to lift. I couldn't really feel them anymore.

As my eyes adjusted to the murk, I saw another door up ahead. The Resistance Agent in the lead banged on it with the barrel of his gun. The loud clanging echoed around us in the confined space, causing my brain to rattle in my skull. We waited for an answer.

'No one home?' muttered Mouse in front of me, under her breath.

'What was that?' came a stern voice from behind me. 'I could just shoot you.'

'But then you won't find out what I've brought you,' said Mouse out loud.

I wanted to shout out, wanted to kick her from behind to stop antagonising the gunman. In this cramped tunnel, in the half-light, anyone behind me shooting at Mouse was likely to put a hole in me at the same time. I held my breath instead.

There was a pause. The tone of voice in which he said "… one of the others can point out where, on your corpse, I could find it…" did little to calm my nerves.

The door, apparently less heavy and higher tech than the others, slid smoothly open, flooding the end of the tunnel in bright light. Blinking furiously to adjust to it, we emerged into a high-ceilinged, circular bunker.

Curved screens lined the walls running around the perimeter, from the floor up to well above head height, with regular breaks for doors. We were deep underground now, and the earth above our heads was clearly visible through the glass at the top of the dome.

In the middle of the room was an array of screens and Com equipment, some of it looking like it was decades old, arranged around a figure in a wheelchair, who wore similar fatigues to our captors.

I heard the crackle of an incoming transmission. That kind of static suggested analogue Com tech. I didn't think I'd ever seen a working one.

'I don't know, Kap, the door just blew off...' came the voice over the Com. 'It's... inside... it's weird. Hold on.'

The Agent in the wheelchair, who I presumed to be Kap, stabbed at a button, cutting the voice off, and raised his head to survey the new arrivals.

'What's this, Wright?' he asked the Agent behind me.

'Found them coming up the hill,' replied Agent Wright. I could still sense the Agent's gun waving around behind my head. 'Heard them talking. I think they're Authority.'

Mouse swung around at that point, looking exasperated and apparently determined to have her say, waving gun or no waving gun. To be fair to Mouse, I was still in the way of a clean shot. To be fair to me, that made pretty much anything she did or said at that moment feel terrifying.

'Seriously?' She almost screamed it, the sounds echoing off the closed-in walls and shiny metallic surfaces. I noticed even Clar winced.

'I don't think they're Authority, Agent Wright. That one looks like he's a bank manager who's been forced to do survival training.'

Clearly, he meant me.

'Why are you wasting my time?' Kap stabbed at the button again. 'Report?'

'I don't know, Kap,' continued the crackling voice, 'it's like something covered the whole place in... in webs.'

Echoes

'Webs? What do you mean webs? Give me visual.' Kap stabbed the button again, to talk to the room. 'Was there something else?'

'What do you want me to do with them?' asked Wright, sounding less sure of himself.

'Let them go? Give them some shoes?' Kap stabbed the button again. 'You're right, Jones, that looks like an army of spiders has shat all over it. It's weird but I don't know it's anything to do with… Hang on a moment, there's something I need to deal with.'

He cut Jones off again and turned back to us.

'You're still here,' he observed.

We were still there. I wasn't happy about this, either. As far as I knew, there was still a gun pointed at me, but I wasn't so certain that was the reason.

The expression on Mouse's face troubled me. That wasn't a new feeling, but I had a sense that she would not allow herself to be dismissed so easily. I, on the other hand, was ready to accept some dry shoes and retreat.

'We're here to see Toshock,' Mouse said, stepping out from the line and towards the centre of the room.

Silence hung between her and Kap.

'We're here to see Toshock,' she repeated.

'I heard you,' said Kap. 'You can't.'

'I think she's going to want to see us. I think we've got something she'd be very interested in.'

'If she was here, I'd ask her,' shrugged Kap, 'but she's not here.'

'I don't believe you,' said Mouse. I had to admire her gall. 'General Toshock hasn't left this bunker in years.'

'Until today, apparently,' snapped Kap, now clearly annoyed, wheeling his chair from behind his monitors, and positioning himself toe to toe with Mouse.

His stare was piercing. I was glad it wasn't focused on me. Mouse seemed to take it in her stride, however.

'Where did she go?' she demanded.

'Is not a thing I'm going to tell you,' laughed Kap.

Mouse walked around Kap's wheelchair and made a big show of looking at the screens on the walls of the bunker. Most of them showed maps of Trinity. A lot of red dots flashed at various points around the city.

I scanned for the Bridge, traced the line along to the rail terminal, then followed my route this morning over the PedWay and up to the Administration building. It was one of the red dots.

'Since she left, things haven't been going well?' hazarded Mouse, who appeared to have drawn the same conclusion as me.

'Since she left, Trinity has been blowing up,' confirmed Kap. 'Would you know anything about that?'

'Not just that, though..?'

Mouse was fishing in a way that made it appear that she already knew the answers. I suspected she was just busking, though.

Kap sighed, resigned. He would not get us to leave, at least not without giving Mouse something.

'Not just that. There's... weird shit going on.'

'I heard. But when you say "Trinity has been blowing up", you mean multiple explosions, right? All over the place. That's what these...' she waved her hand at the screen '... dots are?'

'All over the *fucking* place,' Kap sighed, wheeling himself back to take another look at the Com monitor.

'Not just Administration and... whatever that spider shit was?' Mouse was tracing routes over the map with her finger now.

'Not just Administration,' confirmed Kap. 'Not just the

Dome. Not just the Citadel. Not just fifteen other spots all over…'

'The Citadel?' asked Mouse.

'Who exactly are you?' asked Kap, raising his eyebrows. 'Why am I telling you this?'

'I don't know why you're telling me anything,' grinned Mouse, 'but I'll keep asking questions if you're amenable. My name is Mouse, though. This is Clar Triebel.'

She didn't seem to think I was worth identifying.

Kap paused.

'You're Mouse?' he said, eventually. He phrased it as a question but he didn't deliver it as one. 'Makes sense.'

He chuckled to himself.

'And you,' he looked to Clar, 'I've heard of you. Channel Rosaan12, right?'

'We were in Administration,' said Clar. 'I was. Me and Estrel here.'

I was grateful to Clar for bringing me into the fold. Kap looked up, stroked his bristled chin.

'Hi!' I said, weakly raising a hand.

'I wondered when you were going to say something,' he said.

I looked nervously at Carlsen and Wright, who was still holding his weapon out in front of him. He wasn't exactly training it on anyone, but I wasn't exactly out of the firing line either.

They seemed unmoved by the conversation unfolding around them, but also not about to engage in it.

Kap turned to Wright.

'I think you're dismissed, Agent,' he said. 'You're not serving any purpose here anymore. I don't think these people are from Authority. I don't think they're going to give me any trouble.'

He glanced at Mouse.

'Other than an incessant torrent of questions,' he continued. 'Get inside the walls. We have people we need to get out.'

Wright nodded and gestured to his companion to join him. They disappeared back out of the tunnel and I finally felt able to breathe again.

Kap turned his attention back to Clar.

'You were in the first explosion?' he asked.

'I didn't realise it was the first,' said Clar.

They took a step forward. Mouse grabbed the back of a swivel chair and pushed it towards them. She pulled another towards herself and sat down, a lead which Clar followed.

So we're sitting down, I thought, looking around for a chair for myself. There weren't any more.

'Well done on getting out,' nodded Kap. 'They made a real mess of the place.'

'Who did?' asked Mouse. 'I take it this wasn't your doing?'

'No, it wasn't us,' Kap shook his head. 'But you've hit on the critical question there. Your guess is as good as mine. It wasn't us, but after that? Take your pick. Knights, Devoted, Authority, Administration… There isn't an organisation in this city that doesn't have a paramilitary wing.'

'But Administration wouldn't blow themselves up, that doesn't make sense,' objected Clar. 'And you just said that the Citadel was a target. So…'

'So nothing,' shrugged Kap. 'It's election season. All bets are off. I wouldn't rule out a false flag operation. Or multiple factions involved. Or someone trying to pit them all against each other?'

'Are you suggesting what I think you're suggesting?' asked Mouse.

Kap shrugged.

'I don't know. But you've got to look for who benefits from all of this. And by all of this, I mean Trinity slowly tipping into civil war.'

Clar laughed hollowly.

'Who could benefit from that amount of chaos and destruction of accepted norms?'

I looked at each of the people ranged before me. This conversation was making me feel like even more of an outsider than I already was.

It seemed to be a given that everyone knew who could benefit from that amount of chaos and destruction of accepted norms. That seemed like the aims of an avowed terrorist organisation, but if it wasn't them…

I could only guess, but by reputation I supposed they meant Mayor Chaguartay.

I had a horribly sneaking suspicion that my purpose here, today, was connected in some way to the bombings. It seemed like too much of a coincidence, but I didn't want to say anything as I wasn't sure I understood how far we were trusting Kap. He appeared to notice my discomfort.

'Are you going to sit down?' he asked, gesturing towards a small stool tucked underneath a trolley stacked high with partially dismantled Coms.

I pulled it out and sat down, feeling stupid as well as lost.

'Anyway,' Kap turned his attention back to Mouse, rubbing his hands. 'If I heard you right over the decidedly antiquated mics in the tunnel, you have something for us? I assume you wanted to give it to Toshock, but as we've established, she's not here. So is this something that would also interest me?'

Clar pulled the Com from their pocket. They smiled.

'I think, given the accusation you just made, that you'd be very interested in the Mayor's personal Com unit.'

Kap's jaw dropped open.

'Suggestion, rather than accusation, I would have said to anyone who asked me,' he said. 'But yes. I don't know where you came from, but you may just be the people I didn't know I needed to meet.'

The first perk of being people that Kap wanted to meet was, apparently, access to the kit cupboard, something that both Clar and I badly needed.

It wasn't a cupboard, in fact it turned out to be a side room: "If it's locked, then it's Toshock's quarters and you're a door too early, if you end up in the kitchen you've gone too far," were Kap's instructions.

The room had rows of clothing neatly hung, banks of drawers and, behind a glass wall, weaponry and ammunition I couldn't even begin to give a name to.

'Med kits are on the shelf over the door,' called Kap from the other room. 'Something tells me you'll want to start there?'

Clar had, in fact, already found them and pulled out a bottle of antiseptic and several rolls of bandage.

'Sit down,' they said. 'I'll sort you out and then you can bandage me.'

I was about to protest, but as I went to do so, something dug into my heel with a pain so violent that I found myself unable to move any further, causing me to tumble into the chair in front of me with a clatter. I thought better of arguing and worked off my shoe instead.

It was at this point that I realised that my socks, which I'd thought were waterlogged, were in fact soaked in my blood. I steadied myself before I fainted and pathetically held my foot out to Clar.

'This is just embarrassing,' I said. 'You weren't even wearing shoes...'

Echoes

'I suspect,' they said, 'that this happens to me more often than you think. Whereas I don't suppose you're a big walker?'

I had to concede that, although I did so without actually saying anything. I was in awe of Clar's ability to appear so hardened and capable whilst also remaining humble and empathetic. And their ability to maintain a presence while saying nothing.

Throughout the journey here Mouse and I had been bickering, but Clar had been nothing but thoughtful, even when they didn't speak. Taking a lead from their book, I resisted my urge to fill the silence between us with words as Clar bathed my feet in the bright pink liquid.

Involuntary yelps as the antiseptic seared my wounds, on the other hand? Those couldn't be helped.

Wrapped tightly in clean bandages, however, the haze cleared and I could stand. Clar's feet were filthy dirty but only mildly scuffed. They didn't react to their antiseptic bathing and shrugged off any more than the most cursory of bandage. We found socks, thick, woollen and reinforced, in a drawer and boots hung on racks behind the clothing rails.

'Not the Terrain Boots,' shouted Kap, 'but if you need a weapon…'

It seemed he activated something because the glass screen slid back, giving us access. Clar jumped straight in, taking down handguns, weighing them in their hand, checking their action as they slid the safety back and forth, loading, reloading.

I picked up something that looked manageable, went to aim at something imaginary, and failed to bring the gun above waist height.

'I wouldn't start with that.' Mouse stood in the doorway. 'It's deceptively hard to wield. As I think you just found out. Here…'

She stepped into the cupboard and took the gun from me.

She picked up something much smaller and more delicate - I think I could have fitted it in the inside pocket of my jacket - and placed it into my grip. It was certainly more manageable.

But it still didn't feel right. Watching Clar skilfully manipulate another firearm, I realised I didn't know what I was doing. I put the gun down.

'I think I'll pass.' There was a note of regret in my voice.

'Suit yourself,' said Mouse. 'Come on, Kap's trying to track down someone who can crack this Com for us.'

She moved back towards the doorway.

'Aren't you going to take anything?'.

Mouse stuck her hand in the back of her waistband and pulled out a solid-looking handgun.

'I've been carrying the whole time,' she grinned. 'Wouldn't be without her. I thought young Carlsen was going to take her off me, but he was too shy to touch my bum.'

She disappeared back into the bunker.

'You got what you're looking for?' I asked Clar.

'Hmm,' Clar looked up from their weaponry. Their eyes sparkled. 'Getting out, you mean?'

'No, the gun I mean,' I said, but then I realised what Clar had been saying. 'But yes, earlier on you said you needed to get out of the city. We're out now. Why are you sticking around? Why are you tooling up?'

'You never know. When Mouse is around, the possibilities are endless. It's best to be prepared.'

'No, but if you're not going back, if you're going home, why do you..?'

Happy with their choice, Clar hooked a holster off a peg and pushed past me, clapping me on the shoulder as they passed.

'I can't leave you on your own, Estrel,' they said. 'She would eat you alive...'

CHAPTER 8

Back in the bunker, Kap recalibrated his screen and threw the image up onto the walls. New icons covered the map of Trinity, flashing and beeping. All three of us moved closer to peer at the icons, although I certainly wasn't sure what I was looking at.

'Each one of those is one of my Agents,' explained Kap.

He tapped at his screen. One icon flashed red, near an Accommodation block.

'That's Jones, hot on the trail of her giant spiders.'

Another in the Citadel.

'There's Begrandt, trying to mop up what he can from the Clerics.'

Two more outside the city walls.

'That's Wright and Carlsen, your new best friends, skulking somewhere outside. This...' he tapped again, 'should be Batt...'

Nothing changed on the screen.

'What does that mean?' asked Clar.

Kap shrugged.

'Agent Batt is out of range? He could be underground, but

he'd have to be a long way down, deeper than Research. Way up in the sky, maybe. He could have left the city, but he'd have to have gone a very long way in a very short period of time. I can't find his device on the ComGrid, either. He's missing, put it that way, and it's almost impossible for me to lose an Agent.'

'Could the link have got damaged?' Mouse was scanning the walls, trying to spot something that no one else could.

'Unlikely. It's pretty much everything proof, and bonded to his spine, so if it's damaged, then Batt's probably dead, and I'd still be able to see where his corpse was. Theoretically, if he got vaporised, I guess that might take the link with it, but I'd have picked up a surge of energy that strong and, again, nothing.'

'Could he turn it off?' I asked, trying to be helpful.

'You heard the bit about it being bonded to his spine, right?' scoffed Kap. 'No, he couldn't have turned it off.'

'I don't know,' I said, sheepishly. 'Maybe he could have done it with magnets or something.'

If anyone heard, they didn't show it, and I decided not to say anything else. I wasn't even sure why I was here now. I kept getting buffeted along by events and convincing myself that I'd chosen for this to happen.

My priority was trying to stay close to Mouse. I still had this nagging feeling that being with Mouse was important, would get me answers, but so far it hadn't helped at all.

If anything, it had taken me even further away from my primary goal of figuring out what was going on with me.

'And Batt is your hacker?' asked Mouse.

'Batt is my hacker,' confirmed Kap. 'Without him, I can't help you. Unless you know how to operate the kit yourself?'

Mouse swivelled her chair to face Clar.

'It would be easier if we'd brought Jo Jo with us, but I've seen it done,' they said. 'We're wasting time if we don't.'

'I'll take that as a yes, then.' Kap gestured at a cluster of consoles on the opposite side of the bunker. 'Be my guest. I've got some Agents to locate.'

Mouse and Clar stood up and busied themselves attaching cables and entering commands, filling the wall screens with scrolling code. I looked around, lost. Kap paused his chair as he wheeled away, turning to face me.

'You won't help?' he asked. Maybe demanded. I felt interrogated.

'I don't know I can help,' I admitted. 'This isn't my thing. I don't know what I can do.'

'What's your thing?' asked Kap.

'Well, software,' I admitted. 'But sales. And in logistics. I seem to have wandered out of my comfort zone.'

'I don't know,' mused Kap, with a faint smile. 'I think you could still be useful around here. You want to join the fight? For the soil and the soul?'

I raised my eyebrows. This was promising. It felt good to be taken seriously for a moment, rather than argued with or ignored, which was mostly how the last few hours had gone.

'If you've got something…' I said.

Kap raised his eyebrows, as well, in response.

'Kitchen's behind you. You'll find the tea in the tin.'

I did, indeed, find the tea in the tin, and some mugs in the cupboard that didn't seem to have anything growing on them. I wasn't willing to touch anything else in the cramped corridor of a kitchen.

There was a fridge door, but it didn't seem to respond to me pulling at it, and I didn't want to know what was sticking it shut. I filled four mugs from the boiler tap and dropped bags into each one.

I was wasting time. I needed to get out, get back to Trinity, try to find out if I'd left myself any more Echoes to guide me. Otherwise I was going to reset out here, in the middle of nowhere, having learned nothing.

I hooked the tea bags out with my fingers and flung them into the sink. *I should have taken a gun.*

I carried two of the mugs out and placed one in front of Kap, who was deep in conversation over his Com array. He lifted his head and nodded his thanks without completely taking his eyes off the screen in front of him.

A face loomed out of smoky darkness, eerily lit by out-of-shot flames.

'That's just the thing,' the face said. 'No one's seen the Superious since Devotion this morning.'

Kap scratched at his head agitatedly.

'Fuck. He's disappeared too? Abducted as well?'

I wondered who else had disappeared. *Chaguartay?*

'Could be.' I assumed the Agent on the line was Begrandt. Kap had said he was dealing with the Clerics. 'More likely, he's buried in The Catacombs. He likes to go walking, apparently.'

'Walking?' asked Kap. 'That's very fucking inconvenient of him. Is there anyone looking for him?'

'Armies of Clerics, from what I can tell,' said Begrandt. 'They're pretty worried. He's not a young man. Or a well one.'

'Right,' Kap slurped his scalding tea without reaction, 'well, let's hope they find him then. You need to be back here. I'm holding the fort on my own at the moment.'

'What about Wright? You've got Carlsen up there too, right?'

'Like I said, I'm holding the fort on my own up here. Kap out.'

'Begrandt out.'

The screen went blank.

Mouse and Clar huddled over a couple of terminals by the

far wall. Strings of apparently random letters, numbers, and symbols scrolled across the wall behind them. I moved over to hand Mouse her mug just as she let out a shout of delight as Clar did something at their terminal that caused the nonsense on-screen to resolve into words.

'Nice!' cried Mouse, punching the air.

'Don't get too excited,' cautioned Clar, visibly less so. 'I don't know I've decrypted that much. "Sender", which unsurprisingly is always Chaguartay. And maybe half the subject?'

'So we can't see who they're to?' Mouse took her cup of tea without acknowledging me. 'That's less exciting.'

'There's an auto-wipe set up as well,' Clar sighed. 'I've got a bot running that will stop it kicking in, but I don't know how long that will work for. We need to move relatively quickly.'

'How long have we got?' asked Mouse.

'Your guess is as good as mine,' Clar shook their head, leaned back in their chair and exhaled slowly with their hands behind their head. 'But we should get what we can while we can.'

They glanced at me.

'I'll grab your tea,' I explained. 'There isn't any milk.'

I scuttled back to the tiny kitchen.

This was good, that they were making progress. But what was next?

First, they just had to get the Com to Resistance, then we could focus on me. Now they had to decrypt the Com's data.

That made sense, given Kap's obvious lack of present personnel. And yet, they weren't Resistance themselves. The plan had been to hand over the Com. Not to stick around helping.

Why did they care? Why did Clar care? They'd said their aim was to get out of Trinity. And yet when I'd asked they'd said they were staying around to protect me.

So, what *was* next? What if they found something on the Com that they just had to follow up? What if we spent all day on Resistance missions and never got to focusing on me?

I didn't have all day. Or rather, I did, but that was all I had. I needed to make something happen. To call their bluff. I couldn't afford to keep getting strung along.

I picked up the two remaining mugs and strode back into the bunker. Mouse was reading off the screen on the wall, what appeared to be a series of Com subject lines.

'"Chaguartay - Re: call..."' she read. '"Chaguartay - Re: call..." This is gripping stuff. "Chaguartay - transfer..."; "Chaguartay - Re: Minutes of..."; "Chaguartay - TrakcD meeting..."'

She had my attention. My head jerked up, the force of my involuntary movement causing me to spill hot tea on my hand. I let out a yelp and put both mugs quickly down, balanced precariously on the edge of the nearest terminal.

'You OK?' asked Mouse.

I moved closer, peering at the screen, looking for the name Mouse had just said out loud.

'TrakcD?' I asked.

'Yes,' said Mouse. 'I don't know what that means. Looks like a typo.'

'I know what it means,' I said, because I did. I worked for TrakcD Solutions. 'That's the name of the company I work for. The TrakcD meeting, that's why I'm here.'

There was silence in the bunker for a moment, while everyone turned their heads to stare at me, openmouthed.

'Interesting,' said Kap, reversing out from behind his Com array and wheeling himself closer. 'I wondered when we'd find out what the point of you was.'

I sneered at that, but only inwardly. I continued staring at the screen. The rest of the text was still unreadable.

'What's this gibberish after it?' I asked.

'It's still encrypted.' Clar pointed at some of the less interpretable text. 'But I think that some of those strings are the hashes to unlock the rest.'

'Damn it,' spat Mouse. ' So close. How are we going to figure out what's code and what's encoding?'

'*We're* not.' Clar tapped something on the keyboard.

'Sorry. How are *you* going to figure out what's code and what's encoding?'

'I'm not either.' Clar hit a key and sat back. 'I'm going to use the routine I've just written to brute force it. Let the machine hack itself.'

They looked very pleased with themselves. They swigged their tea.

'That's disgusting,' they said, swallowing awkwardly. 'Can you just get me some water?'

I didn't really want to leave the scene, but I obediently went back to the kitchen, carrying Clar's mug as well as mine.

Everything looked very different now. There I had been, trying to figure out how to get away from Com cracking and on to figuring out what was going on with me. I hadn't stopped to think that they could be the same thing.

I needed to have more faith. FIND MOUSE. Mouse might not know what that meant, but whoever wrote it wrote it for a reason.

I took a sip of my tea and realised it was pretty much cold by now. I tipped the contents of both mugs out into the sink. Then I paused.

One mug had Carlsen's name scrawled on the bottom. For a moment I'd thought it was a message, another Echo. What would it have said? "Keep going Estrel, you're on the right track…"?

And what if it had, once, but I'd not been here on the next loop and it had wiped the Echo? How could that work? My brain started ticking.

What if I did it? Took something now and kept it until tomorrow, just before I looped. When did Mouse say it happened, just after midnight?

Or ten thirty. Maybe judge it just before that. Find something, take something, write something down. Good path, bad path, "you're on the right track", "you're wasting your time".

I opened up the cupboard above the sink. A cardboard box, half filled with salt crystals, sat right at the front. I pulled it out and ripped off the side.

I could use this, it was perfect. A brand new Echo. If I wrote on it later, and didn't let it go, then next loop I'd open this cupboard and there it would be. My next instruction. I just had to do this wherever I went and I'd create loads of new Echoes...

Maybe some of them wouldn't work out, but I'd leave those places. If this mug said "Estrel! Leave now!" I'd get out of there, taking it with me. That would give me more time to go somewhere else, find another Echo, make another Echo.

Surely, *surely*, over time, I'd end up with more and more until... Until I'd mapped out the route I needed to take. I'd start out bouncing around like a pinball, but over several loops, over many, many loops... over *infinite* loops...

I didn't need to think about that, but how many times over had I wasted already?

I pushed the thought away. That was a sunk cost. This was a plan.

I put the ripped cardboard into my inside jacket pocket and refilled the mugs from the tap. I needed to update the napkin, Echo number one, with the new plan. Now I'd thought of this, I couldn't afford to forget it.

By the time I got back to the huddle of cryptographers, the nonsense strings of characters on the screen were churning rapidly.

I needed a pen.

'Do we need a drumroll?' asked Mouse, banging the table with her palms.

The churning stopped. All four of us peered at the resulting text. Mouse stopped her drumroll.

'It's still gibberish,' she said, staring.

We were all staring. I scanned the screen, trying to make sense of it. There was no sense to be made.

'Hold on,' said Kap. 'That bit there. 5#4qw++pD. That's not gibberish. It's a call sign. That's our call sign.'

'Your call sign?' asked Clar.

'Here, the bunker,' he clarified. 'That message isn't meant to be decoded by anyone but us. That sign tells us we own the hash. It needs to be fed through one of our Coms.'

'But the message comes from Chaguartay,' objected Mouse. 'Why would he be communicating with you?'

Kap held his hands up defensively.

'Not me,' he insisted.

His eyes were flicking all over the place. He did not look comfortable at that moment.

'Who? Your comms guy?' asked Mouse.

'Could be,' agreed Kap, glancing over his shoulder. 'But… I review the logs. I think I'd notice. And I trust Batt.'

'But you don't trust Toshock?' asked Clar, following Kap's line-of-sight back to the door of Toshock's quarters.

Kap's hands stayed up.

'I didn't say that.'

'But you don't, do you?' asked Mouse, standing up, a thoughtful look on her face.

Kap sighed.

'She's got the only Com that doesn't route through the log. She needs to communicate securely in her position. And you never know who's watching. It wasn't about me, it was about everyone else...'

'... except it seems like it might have been about you after all,' murmured Mouse, walking across the bunker towards Toshock's door.

Kap dropped his head.

'Fuck's sake Tosh, what are you doing?'

'Can you get into her quarters?' asked Mouse, approaching the door. 'You said it was locked.'

'Of course,' Kap shook his head, swivelling his chair to face the door. 'She wouldn't let me monitor her Com use, wouldn't accept a spinal link, but she was perfectly happy to hand me the keycard to her personal quarters.'

'I think you're being sarcastic,' said Mouse, placing her hands on the door panel. 'But I'll let it slide. Which... aha...'

The door clicked as Mouse pushed it backwards. With one motion, she slid it to the side.

'I'll leave you to make your own jokes,' she smiled, and stepped through the open doorway.

Toshock's quarters were narrow and spartan, a single bed against the far wall, neatly made; a small metal closet with the doors closed and a similar metal desk next to the doorway with a brand new desktop Com on top.

Clar followed Mouse inside, after which there wasn't much room for anyone else, and I had to stand behind Kap's chair in the doorway.

'It wasn't actually locked,' explained Mouse. 'I just pushed.'

'Why would she leave it unlocked?' I asked.

'She didn't leave of her own volition,' said Kap.

'Bingo,' said Mouse, bending down. 'What time did you arrive in the bunker, Kap?'

'I slept here,' he replied. 'My quarters are across the other side of the bunker. I heard nothing. I don't think she would have gone without a fight…'

'I didn't say she was forced out,' shouted Mouse, her head under the bed. 'Just that it wasn't her choice. Someone could have been holding some information over her. I think we might guess what that information was.'

'That makes more sense,' agreed Kap. 'It's hard to imagine her coming off worse in a fight.'

'Or,' said Mouse, standing up, 'there were a lot of them. Either way, she didn't choose to leave. She wouldn't have left the clue we're looking for if she had. Look inside the desk, Clar. There's nothing under the bed. I'll take the closet.'

'You seem very certain you're going to find something,' I said.

I looked at Kap.

'Are you OK with this?' I asked him. 'You've only just met these people and now they're ransacking your superior officer's room?'

'Hardly ransacking,' pointed out Mouse, carefully removing a pile of folded sweaters and placing them behind her on the bed. 'And I think we made a reasonable case for why she'd be perfectly fine with it. If she's got nothing to hide.'

Kap shrugged.

'It's dog eat dog, isn't it?' he asked. 'Loyalty is a luxury in this city. Leaves you vulnerable to being double crossed. I'm happy to shift my allegiances in light of new information. And they brought me Chaguartay's Com. Those are compelling credentials, to be fair.'

'I can't get in here.'

Clar grunted through gritted teeth, pulling at the drawer under the desktop.

'Look for a key,' they said to Mouse, who was searching the pockets of the garments she was removing from the closet.

'I know but, really, you really believe that the leader of the Resistance to the Mayor is conspiring *with* the Mayor?' I asked Kap.

'Beliefs are hypotheses to be tested, my friend,' called Mouse. 'And at the moment that one is holding up well to scrutiny.'

I had to admit that seemed fair enough.

'We're not finding much here,' observed Mouse, pulling out a rack of camouflage jumpsuits. 'Except that her ironing is immaculate.'

'We get Carlsen to do the laundry,' said Kap.

'Can you try to get the desk Com on?' Mouse said to Kap. 'Estrel, go and pick up the mayor's Com.'

I left the doorway and went back to the workstation that Clar had just vacated. Chaguartay's Com was plugged into the equipment with several wires, all of which I pulled out.

The Com started to beep. I panicked, tried to plug a connector back into a socket that it obviously wasn't made to fit.

I hadn't been paying any attention. How many wires had been coming out of it when I started? I didn't even know that. There were five on the console, but it hadn't been that many, surely? *Think, Estrel, was it two? Three?*

'Everything all right out there, Estrel?' called Kap. 'What's that noise?'

'It's, uh,' I started. 'I, uh... It's beeping. The Com. I don't know what I did...'

That was a lie. I knew what I did.

'I can't make it stop.'

'The auto-wipe! It's shutting down!' shouted Clar, the banging sound of them trying to force the drawer stopping.

They appeared in the doorway, looking urgent.

'Get it here. If it shuts down, it'll wipe and we won't be able to get anything off it. We need to grab what we can while we've still got time.'

I was already crossing the room by this point, holding the beeping machine out in front of me, desperate to get rid of it, to pass it on to someone who could absolve me by fixing what they could of my mistake.

Clar ripped it out of my hand, spinning and grabbing a cable from the Com on the desk, which Kap hunched over, a green light from its screen bathing his face. Clar stuck the cable in a socket rather more successfully than I had managed, and the beeping stopped.

'Too late?' asked Clar.

'No, I'm copying… ah, rats.'

Kap sat back. I glanced down. The small Com screen was dead.

'I'm sorry, I-I didn't realise…' I stammered.

'No, I should have thought,' sighed Clar, 'when Mouse told you to get it. You needed to leave it attached to the mod pack. But you weren't to know that. Did you get anything at all?'

'One or two,' said Kap, scrolling through. 'I'll see what I can decrypt. Let's hope it's not just his shopping list…'

Clar went back to banging around at the locked drawer and I remained, hovering, behind Kap's chair. He opened a file. My face appeared on the screen.

'Woah, Estrel,' breathed Kap. 'It looks like they were expecting you.'

I stared. There was something strange about the image on the screen. It was a grainy still from some kind of security footage, captured mid-turn, with the figure in it unaware they were being watched.

And it was me, unarguably, indisputably me. But I couldn't place where it had been taken. It looked like some kind of laboratory. There were benches with flasks and tubes in front of me, and behind my shoulder, in the shot's corner, what looked like a cage.

I also didn't look right. My hair was shorter, I didn't recognise my clothes; I had never worn a lab coat, not since high school. And I looked older. Not by much, but my face looked more worn, my eyes deeper set, an extra hint of a jowl evident.

'Looks like you were having a tough day,' joked Kap.

I laughed it off. It was eerie though, staring at me, so recognisably myself and yet so alien. It reminded me of the reflection I'd seen in the train's window. I squashed that thought. It creeped me out.

Mouse was behind me now, and Kap scrolled. It was the message about the meeting, the one with TrakcD in the subject line. The agenda, my name, several attached documents I recognised from the message Crispy Burton had forwarded me.

But no mention of Crispy Burton. I pointed at the date at the bottom.

'What's this?' I asked.

'Sent date?' Kap looked up at me, quizzically. 'That's why it says "Date Sent" next to it…'

'That can't be right, though,' I said. 'That's a week ago.'

'More or less, yes,' agreed Kap.

'But that can't be right,' I insisted. 'My name's on this, my picture, although I don't even know where that's from. But it was sent a week ago. I didn't even know I was coming here until yesterday. That's got to be wrong…'

'Curiouser and curiouser...' muttered Mouse from behind me.

'Mother...' swore Clar, uncharacteristically, raising their leg and kicking at the stubborn drawer with their heel.

To everyone's surprise, it popped open.

'It's filled with notebooks,' they said, grabbing a handful and passing them to Mouse. They tossed a few at Kap, who caught them and passed one over his shoulder to me.

The notebook was leather bound, well used and bent in every direction. I flicked open the front cover. It was filled, as everything seemed to be at that moment, with apparently meaningless letters, numbers and symbols handwritten in careful script across the page.

'More code,' I said.

'Same here,' replied Kap, running a hand over his face. 'I feel like we're trapped in some kind of game.'

'Or a nightmare,' I said, 'on the night before an exam.'

This was probably truer for me than for everyone else. Right now, I didn't know that I had the energy to keep looking, to keep questioning, to make sense of everything being thrown at me.

I flicked through most of the pages. They meant nothing. I allowed my eyes to relax and defocus. Nothing meant anything. That felt like the helpfully unhelpful kind of remark that Mouse would have made.

I looked up at her, leafing through the pages of a large desk diary. It was strange that someone would keep so many handwritten notes, especially when they owned so much Com equipment.

Half a thought formed in my mind, but there was something else. I couldn't quite put my finger on what was bothering me, but... There was something about those characters, something oddly familiar.

I knew what it was, or what I thought it was. I stuck my hand in the pocket of my jacket and dug around until it closed around the scrunched up paper of the Echo. I smoothed it out against the page in front of me. It was staring me in the face. I was right.

'It's the same writing,' I said. 'Toshock wrote this.'

'Wrote what?' asked Mouse, putting down her own book and coming to look over my shoulder.

She gasped.

'No fucking way.'

I held up the napkin and pointed at the words written at the bottom. The letters were much bigger, but undeniably written by the same hand. Toshock's hand. They read: FIND MOUSE.

CHAPTER 9

I turned my back and walked away from the doorway. I dropped the notebook to the floor.

'Estrel?' Mouse came after me. She seemed concerned. 'Estrel, are you OK?'

I didn't know if I was OK. My mind was reeling. Sweat pin-pricked my skin as a wave of raw, panicked heat washed over me.

Behind me, in Toshock's quarters, I could hear Clar rapidly bringing Kap up to speed. "… time loop…" they said, and "… Echo…" and "… FIND MOUSE…". I didn't register Kap's reaction, I didn't have the capacity.

The same thought was thundering through my mind repeatedly. Toshock wanted me to find Mouse. Chaguartay was working with Toshock. Ergo…

'I'm OK,' I said, but I didn't mean it.

"Who are you?" was what I wanted to say, but I wasn't ready for the answer.

I shouldn't be here, I thought. I wanted to run, to take out the ripped off piece of a cardboard box from my pocket and scrawl "Run!" on it.

Not for a moment had I ever considered what I was considering now. I'd assumed I was stuck in this situation for good reasons, that I needed to put something right, do something good. I hadn't been in Trinity long, but I knew enough to see that the status quo was a dangerous situation and that I, naturally, aligned with the people fighting against that.

At no stage had I ever thought that I was here to help the bad guys.

'So what, you're working with Toshock?' asked Clar, following us out of Toshock's quarters and cutting between Mouse and me.

'No, I'm not fucking working with fucking Toshock,' snapped Mouse, taking a step back. 'Just because…'

'Just because,' I suggested, 'she wrote on a piece of paper, that I was told explicitly to keep on myself at all times so I'd never lose what was written on it, that I should find you?'

'Yes,' insisted Mouse. 'I don't know why she wrote that. I don't know how she knows who I am, or why she thought I'd be useful to you. Other than by reputation, I know nothing about her, or you, or why I'd be useful to you. I know nothing. I'm not working with her.'

'So you knew nothing about me coming here, didn't know that it was all planned, even before I did?'

'No!' Mouse shouted.

She was close to me now, in my face. I felt the speckle of her spit on my face, the heat of her denial in her breath.

'Is this even real?' I groaned. 'Is this whole time loop thing some elaborate hoax to confuse me, to disorientate me for…? For…'

'For what?' demanded Mouse, nose to nose. 'What is any of that meant to achieve?'

'I don't know,' I screamed. 'You tell me!'

'I would if I knew!'

Mouse stamped her foot.

Her eyes were pleading with me. I wanted to believe, but at that moment I also wanted to rip her head off. I felt muscular arms around me, a voice in my ear, Clar's voice: 'You need to calm down, you need space to think. Just listen to her…'

'It's an emphatic denial.' Kap wheeled himself into the room. 'If only it were convincing.'

Mouse turned on him.

'Not convincing?' Mouse's voice was high, loud, angry. 'Tell me this, Mr Faithful Lieutenant who, incidentally, seems to have turned on his superior officer on the flimsiest of circumstantial evidence… why, if I knew what Toshock was up to… appears to be up to… would I, on obtaining the one piece of communication equipment that would incriminate her, bring it immediately and without question, unprompted and unrequested, bring it here to the very place that not only could uncover that fact but where the knowledge of that fact would do the maximum damage? Why would I do that?'

'I don't know,' Kap shrugged. 'Why would you do that?'

'I wouldn't fucking do that!' Mouse threw her arms wide in exasperation. 'I wouldn't fucking do that and I didn't fucking do that. I didn't know! Estrel, think about it. That note could have been written at any point today. It probably hasn't even happened yet. Even if… *Even if* Toshock is working with Chaguartay, is working against the Resistance… *has been* working against the Resistance… maybe it's with a higher goal in mind! Maybe she sees the error of her ways? You might save her life. Maybe I do. Maybe… I don't fucking know! Who knows what's coming up for you, for us, for the rest of the day? But I'm not working against you, and so, as it stands, this does, if anything, exonerate Toshock rather than incriminate me!'

'I believe her,' said Clar, quietly releasing me.

Everyone turned to look at them.

'I believe her.' Clar sat down and took a deep breath. 'We've not known each other long, but I think we know each other well. Mouse isn't... isn't a guarded person, doesn't hold people apart from her. It's easy to get to know her and... I don't know what I'm trying to say. She genuinely didn't want to help you, Estrel, a few hours ago.'

That seemed like an odd way to persuade me.

'Maybe because she knew what we'd find out...' I muttered.

'No.' Clar spoke loudly, cutting me off. 'No, I don't believe so. You really spooked her, turning up in her kitchen like that. I know that was my fault but... I think I know her well enough to know that she was scared, but she could see what the right thing to do was. To help you. And so she did it, despite her reluctance. I think that's who she is. I think she does the right thing. So even if I'm wrong about this latest turn of events being as much of a surprise to her as it is to the rest of us, even if she has a connection to Toshock... I trust her. I think she's doing the right thing. And if she's not ready to tell us what that is, I think we should trust that too.'

'Thank you,' said Mouse. Then, more quietly, to Clar: 'Thank you.'

This was a stretch for me.

'I mean,' I started, 'that was well argued and everything but...'

Again, I wanted to ask, "but who are you?" but I couldn't bring myself to do it. They could have left me overwhelmed by smoke in a burning building. That had to be worth something.

'I don't know. I've only just met you, any of you, and whilst one of you saved my life and one of you is apparently so important that I must, whatever I do, find you and...'

I trailed off, waving a hand at Kap vaguely.

'It's OK,' said Kap, picking up on my lost thread. 'I'm as much in the dark as you are. I don't think I'm important to you. The Creator knows that would make my life simpler.'

'Right, sorry,' I said. 'Whether or not I should trust you, I don't. Not all of you, and not completely for any of you. But I think that's OK. I don't think I should trust any of you, no more than you should believe in me...'

I regathered my thoughts.

'One thing is clear to me though: I need to find Toshock. I think we have that in common. Where do we start?'

Considered nods broke out amongst the group, which was gratifying. There was sense in focusing on our common goal. We could figure out what came next when we'd found the errant General.

'I can't track General Toshock,' said Kap, 'but there's no point in her going anywhere but Trinity. We have to assume that's where she's gone, and that's where you previously met her and she wrote on your Echo thingy. I say you get back into the city. I certainly don't see her coming back here. Not now.'

'Great,' I agreed, 'let's go?'

'I don't know it's going to be that easy to get back in,' said Mouse. 'I kind of blew several cover stories getting us out of there earlier. And they'll have figured out that nothing I said to them was true by now. They're slow and wrapped up in red tape, but they're not stupid. Not even institutionally. Authority will be on the lookout for me, and the Knights will not be happy with me either. I suspect we'll get taken in the moment anyone lays eyes on us. So if our aim is to get back into the city, then having that anyone be the border guards would be a dangerous move.'

'You'll get arrested, surely. Clar and I should be fine. Neither of us has done anything wrong,' I objected.

I still wasn't altogether against the idea that ditching

Mouse would be safer.

'Well, you left the city without permission,' Mouse pointed out.

This seemed extreme to me.

'That's a crime?' I asked. 'I don't even live here. How can going home be illegal?'

'It's not a crime,' said Clar, 'particularly not now you're out here. No one is going to come looking for you, but it's definitely a reason to hold you if you try to get back in. Going in and out of Trinity is suspicious activity. You could be working with Resistance.'

'Which you kind of are,' laughed Kap, grimly.

'So that's it? There must be ways,' I protested. 'You actually are Resistance. You have Agents in the city…'

'Yes,' nodded Kap 'Yes we do. Do you want to know how we do it?'

'So, all of this is underground,' said Kap, pointing at the screen, which now displayed a large schematic diagram of a complex of rooms and tunnels. They extended out beyond the city walls.

'This shaft here,' he pointed, 'comes up into a tunnel that slopes upwards and hits the bunker just behind that door there.'

He gestured over his shoulder at another door, between the kitchen and the supply cupboard.

'If you go through there and follow it down, you'll find yourself right above the Research complex just outside the walls.'

'That's real?' Clar took a step forward, peering at the screen. 'I'd heard rumours, but I didn't think they could be true. It must be really deep.'

'You'd be surprised,' shrugged Kap. 'Massive laboratory

complex just under the surface of the street. People ignore what's right in front of them all the time. You can't expect them to pay attention to things they can't even see. But it's there, extending from under the city, so you can just drop in and pass under the city walls unseen. They've got tunnels running all over the place. You can pop up pretty much anywhere you like.'

'Security?' asked Mouse. 'It can't be that easy.'

'Don't need to worry about that.' Kap shook his head. 'We've infiltrated their security. We run the entire operation. I can give you passes. He slid open a drawer and pulled three fobs out. These will get you in and out of Research at will. So you've also got an escape route when things get sticky.'

'When things get sticky?' I asked.

'If,' Kap laughed. 'If things get sticky.'

'Right.'

'What? You're not expecting things to get sticky?'

I let that slide.

'What kind of laboratories?' I changed tack.

'Oh, they've got a bit of everything,' said Kap. 'R&D, robotics, medical, biological, genetics, temporal theory, there's a particle accelerator down there… You know. Science.'

'Who are we going to encounter down there?' asked Mouse, before repeating: 'It can't be that easy.'

'It should be,' Kap shrugged. 'On the whole, you're going to find disinterested scientists. You might catch up with one of our guys. If you're lucky, you'll track down Toshock without even having to surface. I can give you this…'

Kap pulled open a drawer and fished out a Com unit. This was boxier and looked heavier than the Com model I was used to.

'Field issue,' he explained. 'It's an entry level Com inside a pretty much indestructible casing, so it's low powered, but it'll plot our implants for you. See who you can find.'

'I thought you couldn't track Toshock?' Mouse queried, turning the ancient Com in her hand.

'No, I can't,' said Kap. 'But maybe she's not alone. I've still not found Batt. I don't know how he turned off his implant. Maybe she did it. If you pick him up again, I'd run at him. That's your best bet.'

'You think it could be as simple as that?' asked Mouse. 'She's hiding down in Research? Is that likely?'

'It's not unlikely. Unless she's being actively shielded by Chaguartay, she won't be able to stay above ground in Trinity for very long. She'll trip a camera within five minutes and Authority will be down on her in no time.'

'You seem to be turned around on whether she's working with Chaguartay,' said Mouse, flatly. 'You would imagine that would give her immunity.'

'I would,' said Kap. 'So yes, I guess I'm coming around. It sits easier with me she's playing some kind of high-level chess than she's betrayed everything that I believe in…'

'Assuming she's still alive,' said Clar.

No one really responded to that.

'And on that note,' said Mouse, brightly at odds with the mood in the bunker, 'shall we go?'

Kap led us down a long, gently inclining slope. The ramp itself was concrete, although the walls, wide enough for the three of us to walk abreast behind Kap as he rolled ahead, were the bare rock that they had bored the tunnel through.

We said nothing as we walked, keeping our own counsel with our own thoughts. My thoughts were careering wildly between contemplating the tangled mess of my situation and considering how hungry I was.

I hadn't eaten since the train that morning and that seemed

several lifetimes ago. In some senses it could have been, it was before the point I thought I'd jumped back to. I wondered if that had any bearing on how hungry I was, although to be fair it was now well past noon, so my stomach, used to regular mealtimes, was within its rights to protest.

The tunnel was ruler-straight, disappearing into the darkness ahead. There was no light other than that which seeped in from the bunker via the doorway behind us, but Kap tapped at a control on his chair and a pair of headlamps attached to the underside of the armrests lit up the way.

'Handy,' I said, striding out slightly so that I moved next to Kap.

'I have my uses,' grinned Kap. 'You're going to need these in a bit, though.'

He passed me three sturdy flashlights. I wasn't sure where he'd got them from. I hadn't seen him bring them.

'You're not coming all the way?'

'I've got a bunker to guard, and I'm not even sure who I'm guarding it from right at the moment. Plus, whilst this first bit is very smooth sailing, it's going to get tough going for someone of my limitations fairly soon. I don't really do shafts…'

'Thanks for your help, though,' I said. I meant it. 'It's only recently I was wondering what the point of Mouse dragging us all the way out there was, but…'

I hadn't looked at it this way yet, hadn't had time while clinging onto the rollercoaster of a day I was having.

'… I feel like I'm getting somewhere. Really getting somewhere, like some stuff is getting clearer.'

'I'm glad you think so,' scoffed Kap. 'I don't have a fucking clue what's going on.'

'Well,' I backtracked, 'I mean, I don't either. But I've got a next step. We've got a next step.'

Phil Oddy

I glanced over my shoulder at Clar and Mouse. Mouse had promised that when we'd dealt with the Com, we'd focus on me. Now we'd dealt with the Com, and she was following through on her promise. Maybe that was worth a modicum of trust.

The end of the tunnel loomed ahead, Kap's lights reflecting off it. There didn't appear to be anywhere to go when we arrived there, though, no obvious doors or corridors off to the side.

It was only once we got close that I spotted the metal hatch set into the concrete floor. Next to it, on the wall, was a small panel with a contact pad and some lights, which were glowing red.

I stepped to one side of it and together we waited for the others to catch up.

'When you're ready, tap your fob there.' Kap pointed to the contact pad on the wall. 'The hatch here will open and you can head down. Go one at a time, there's not a lot of room in there and if one of you falls, you'll take the others out. When you're in the shaft, close the door above you. At that point, this light here will turn red. You can't open it again until it goes green.'

He pointed at one bulb on the left-hand side of the panel.

'What turns it green?' asked Clar.

Kap glared.

'I'm getting to that,' he growled. 'Don't make me lose my train of thought. You do not want to be stuck in there. You'll need to tap the panel at the bottom of the shaft to get out. That opens the hatch at the other end but be careful, it's set into the ceiling so if you stand on it when you open it you'll fall, and the ceilings are pretty high down there. You could break something, which would make it hard to close it behind you, which is what will turn the light green again. Until you shut

Echoes

the hatch at the other end, anyone left up here is stranded. OK, so far?'

We nodded, keen not to interrupt again.

'Sure?' Kap checked.

I had a question.

'If the ceiling is high, how do we get down from the hatch? And shut it behind us?'

I thought it was a reasonable question. Kap didn't.

'There is a ladder,' he said, 'attached to the wall. Anyone else want to ask something stupid?'

We didn't. If there was anything else, then it was Mouse's turn to ask about it.

'As I said,' continued Kap, 'When the hatch at the bottom closes behind you, this light will turn green and whoever's at the top will know they're good to follow. If it turns red again before you tap it, that means that someone's coming up. Probably one of ours, but, you know, be on your guard. In case they're not. One of ours.'

I didn't find this particularly reassuring.

'I presume there's a similar light at the bottom?' asked Mouse.

Kap nodded. Apparently, this one wasn't a stupid question.

'So if there's anyone down there, they know that we're coming?'

'That is true,' admitted Kap. 'But again, they're probably either scientists who won't care, or Resistance. Or at least Resistance affiliated. And if they're not, you've got guns.'

'I haven't,' I pointed out.

'Then that flashlight is heavy,' said Kap, clearly improvising. 'You should be OK if you need to bop anyone on the head. Seriously though, it's only going to be a bemused scientist or a friendly Resistance Agent.'

'There aren't any unfriendly ones?' I asked.

'Get them to Com me,' said Kap, 'and I'll vouch for you. Seriously though, you've got nothing to worry about down there. Think of Research as your safe haven. No one can get you there. Just be careful when you resurface in Trinity. You're not supposed to be there, remember, and Authority has a way of spotting that. And then dealing with it. You really don't want to be dealt with.'

'Thanks for that,' I sighed.

I looked at Clar and Mouse.

'Who's first then?'

I didn't really want it to be me.

'Mouse should go first,' said Clar. 'I'll stay with you.'

I was more comfortable being alone with Clar than with Mouse, but I didn't feel fully confident that I trusted Mouse not to summon a battalion of Black Knights to wait for us at the bottom. I still didn't want to go first though, although I would not tell them why.

'I think you should go,' I said to Clar. 'Get down there and secure the area. Don't worry about leaving us. Besides…'

I glanced across to Mouse.

'I think we have some things we need to talk about.'

'If you're sure,' said Clar, stepping towards the panel. 'You should come after me. Just in case…'

'In case?' I asked.

'Just so I know you're safe,' they said, squeezing my hand.

It seemed that Clar, despite their speech back in the bunker, didn't entirely trust Mouse either right now.

'See you around,' said Kap, turning his chair and wheeling himself up the slope. 'If you find Toshock, tell her she's got a lot of explaining to do.'

The hatch slid shut as the darkness swallowed Clar. Mouse

cast her torch around the floor and picked a spot that looked slightly cleaner than the rest, which was spread with grease and dirt. She sat down with her back against the end wall.

'So now we wait,' she said.

I paced up and down a few steps, not sure what to do with myself. Things still felt prickly between us.

I thought I wanted to patch things up, hence "we have some things we need to talk about", but I still wasn't sure where I stood with her. I had decided to trust her, faced with limited alternatives, but I also wasn't sure whether I should. None of this was giving me a simple place to start.

'Sit down.'

I did, but she'd taken the cleanest spot, so I tried to squeeze in next to her, my right elbow brushing her arm as I lowered myself to the floor

'Cosy…' she said, sternly.

'Sorry.' I shuffled to my left as much as I could bear before my hand slid into something slimy.

'It's OK,' she laughed. 'I must say, given your entire mission for today, as far as it's written up to now, is to find me, you don't seem happy to have done so.'

'I, er… I thought you'd be more useful to me. Instead, you dragged me all over the countryside and now my feet hurt and I'm hungry.'

'I apologise for focusing on the task at hand,' grinned Mouse.

She reached into a pocket of her waistcoat and pulled out a bar of chocolate, which she unwrapped and broke in half. She offered one piece to me.

'But we're headed back now, and we've got you a new mission. Find Toshock. That was pretty useful of me, wasn't it?'

She seemed cheerful, even though it was barely twenty

minutes since we'd been screaming in each other's faces. I wasn't used to this.

I couldn't let go of anything. Minor disagreements in my childhood still caused me enough pain that I buried them in strata of memory. But she seemed to have shrugged the whole thing off, as if I hadn't accused her of working with Chaguartay. It was confusing, but refreshing. I decided to give it a go.

'To be honest, I hadn't completely decided that I wasn't looking for an actual mouse when you just kind of turned up,' I admitted. 'I don't know that I can actually claim to have found you.'

I took the offered chocolate.

'Thank you.'

'All ends up the same,' Mouse shrugged. 'But you've found a shortcut today. You should alter your instructions. Cross out FIND and replace it with ACCIDENTALLY HIDE OUT IN THE HOUSE OF.'

'The House of Mouse? I'm not sure…'

I shoved the chocolate in my mouth and pulled the napkin out of my pocket again.

I smoothed it out against my leg and mimed crossing it out with a finger. Of course, now I had a new Echo plan, but Mouse didn't need to know about that. I was going to struggle though, now that I'd lost the marker.

'Have you got a pen?'

I swallowed down the chocolate. I could instantly feel a boost that I knew was not chemically possible in such a brief space of time, but which calmed the gnawing pangs in my stomach.

'Nope,' Mouse shook her head. 'Besides, that sounds idiotic. Don't write that. It's a good job I don't have a pen.'

'I should write something though,' I said. 'You're right.

I've learned things along the way today. All that gets lost if I don't write it down.'

I waved my finger around, miming writing.

'I do remember that.' She sighed and put her head back against the wall. 'From the dream, from yesterday, from…'

I remembered her berating me, in the Pod, for getting the terminology wrong. She seemed to be letting her guard down now. I had a feeling that this was about as vulnerable as she would allow herself to get. I decided to be kind about it.

'The language is a minefield,' I agreed, 'but I know what you mean. When you mean. What do you remember?'

'You said you needed me,' she whispered, looking me straight in the eye.

She was very close to me again, but this time, there was no anger. Her breath stroked my cheek as she spoke. My heart leaped. This felt very intimate, in a way that I couldn't really process, given the way I thought I felt about this woman.

'I…'

I really didn't know what I was going to say next, but I stopped when I spotted the glint in her eye. She was playing with me. *More cat than mouse.*

'You were always talking about losing your way, about forgetting what you'd learned,' she said. 'We might have had this conversation before. You haven't got a lot of space. There's no way you could write everything down. You said that's why you needed me. You needed me to remember.'

I stuffed the napkin back into my pocket.

'That didn't really work out, did it?'

'Nope.'

She shook her head, rolling it against the wall behind her, causing a shower of dust to fall down her back. She sat forward, irritatedly trying to scoop it out.

'It did not. But you're right, you need to solve that. What's

Phil Oddy

your next big idea?'

I suddenly felt that scribbling on mementos from everywhere I went was maybe not the way to go. There was no big idea. I had to make this up as I went along.

If I still had my bag, I could put something in there. What had been in there this morning? The sandwiches, the waterproof gear, the… an icy shiver went down my spine. My tablet.

The battery had been dead. I'd used my Com and nothing had seemed out of the ordinary, but I hadn't been through my tablet properly before the explosion at Administration. Now it was somewhere in the rubble.

But what if? What if Mouse, and the bag, hadn't been my only attempt at a different type of Echo? What if I'd had the answer all along? I could easily have left myself copious notes on the tablet. I needed to know.

The light next to the security panel turned from red to green. I leaped up, gripped by a need to get down the shaft and back into Trinity. I wasn't sure how my companions would react when I told them where I wanted to go, but I would not tell them just yet, so I could deal with that later.

'I guess it's my turn, then,' I said, pulling out my pass fob.

'I was scared of you, you know,' said Mouse, staring at the ground.

'Scared?' It seemed ridiculous. 'Of me?'

'Not *of* you, maybe. But by you. Meeting you like that. It threw me. I wanted to run away.'

'You didn't run away…' I paused.

'No,' said Mouse, 'no I didn't. I'm glad I fought that instinct. I hope I did help.'

'I'm glad that you did,' I said. 'And yes, you helped.'

'See you at the bottom.'

I tapped my fob against the panel, and the hatch opened.

Echoes

Below was the reality of the darkness. I hadn't been thinking about that. I swallowed hard.

'See you at the bottom.'

CHAPTER 10

The hatch closed, and darkness enveloped me. Instantly I felt a shiver of cold.

Gripping tightly onto the rung of the metal ladder that ran down the vertical shaft, I took a deep, musty breath. Sweat pricked my brow as my heart thumped loudly in my ears.

Not a shiver of cold, then. It was fear. I was afraid of the dark, of the concrete coffin that surrounded me, squeezing in around me, driving the breath from my lungs.

I fought to take another breath, but something held me tightly, stopped my chest from expanding.

'Damn.'

The word was barely audible without the air to force the sound from my mouth.

I fumbled for the torch. I'd wedged it in the back of my trousers and I struggled to get my arm behind my back to pull it out. Eventually I had it in my hand and, on the third try, pushed the button to turn it on.

The contrast with the all-encompassing darkness of seconds before was blinding. I screwed my eyes shut until the flashing afterglow faded, pointed it downwards and then eased the pressure on my eyelids to allow the light in. I couldn't see the bottom of the shaft.

'Damn.'

I tried to take a breath again. This time it hurt, a wheezing, grating pain. I knew this. The panic was rising.

I closed my eyes again, more gently, and without thinking about what I was doing, dropped the torch. One second, two seconds...

With a clang and a crash, I heard it break at the bottom. Two seconds, that wasn't so far. I could deal with that. And the shaft went straight down. I couldn't get stuck.

I summoned up the determination to prise one foot off the ladder and, shaking through my entire leg, I jammed it one rung lower. I felt as if my heart had stopped. But I did it.

That was one less that I had to worry about. One at a time, that was how I was going to have to do it. And I was going to have to do it. I couldn't stay here. I forced another foot down a rung, shuffled my hands down a bit.

Perhaps I could do this.

Suddenly the thing I'd been ignoring ever since Kap had mentioned climbing down a shaft burst through the layers of denial I'd buried it under.

I was ten years old, clinging to roots attached to a sheer rock wall. We'd been walking, another endless route-march in bright winter sunshine, a day that was cold and blinding.

We'd stopped for lunch, greasy pasties wrapped in wax paper. I'd devoured mine and gone to explore, the ache in my legs and the blisters on my feet disappearing the moment that I was free to move as I wanted to.

I dug an arm down sandy rabbit holes, picked berries from the salty bushes, tiptoed as close as I dared to the cliff edge before stopping, taking in the view, then inching forward a fraction more.

While my father lectured Thurstan on his expectations for his eldest son's very great future, and my mother tended to my younger siblings, I tasted freedom, just for a moment. I couldn't remember when I'd been happier.

I'd been jumping between hillocks. I hadn't known enough to see that the ground was unsafe, although the line my father took later was that I did know and I should have seen and that was what I got for deviating from the pre-planned path.

Now I was lost in the dark, all alone. No one knew I was there. I could hear the waves rushing in, feel the cascade of sandy earth on my head. I felt my chest compress, felt my head spin.

Just like I had then. I had to hold on, had to hold on, had to hold on until someone found me. I was about to learn that it didn't matter what I did. No one was coming. I was on my own.

No one was going to help me.

'Help.'

It was barely more than a whisper. I looked up, tears pricking my eyes. I was lost.

I forced my eyes down, trying to find a chink of light, and a chink of hope, straining to hear a suggestion of someone coming to help me.

Nothing.

All was darkness, all was silence. Once again, no one was coming. I was on my own.

No one was going to help me.

The fear ripped through me. For the second time in my life, I felt the strength I needed to hold on seep away, for the second time I welcomed the prospect of release, the end of the agony.

This time, maybe it would come. At least this time I might have the chance to start again. Or it could be the end. I didn't think I minded that either.

I let go of the ladder.

Phil Oddy

Crumpled at the bottom, I felt the cold metal of the lower hatch on my back. The impact had initially left me numb, but I could now feel my fingers and toes as I flexed them. They hurt, but I could feel them all move.

I probed my mouth with my tongue. I could taste blood, but I couldn't find anywhere that it might be coming from, so I swallowed and the metallic taste faded.

It seemed I was in one piece.

I was going to be OK.

All I had to do was wait for the search party, wait for Thurstan to find the entrance to the cave and come and get me.

Only I wasn't in the right place.

I had to get where he could find me. He wouldn't find me if I didn't move.

I had to pull myself along on my elbows, dragging throbbing feet and legs behind me, scraping my way on the sand, splashing face down into pools slick with seaweed, salt water searing my wounds.

I imagined I could see the beams of his torch playing on the wall already, hear his voice echoing towards me.

I gripped the bottom rung on the wall, tried to stand.

No, this wasn't right, there shouldn't be a rung. There shouldn't be a ladder. If there had been a ladder, I wouldn't have had to fall. I narrowed my eyes and brought the light into focus.

It wasn't a torch beam; it was red and bright. I reached out a hand towards the light.

There was a bleep and the hatch beneath me swung outwards, dropping me out of the shaft and into the dependable arms waiting beneath.

'What happened?' Clar set me down on my shaky feet. 'I heard a thump on the other side of the hatch and then... nothing. The light was red and I couldn't get you out of there. I tried to call to you, but I didn't want to shout. I didn't want to attract attention.'

'It's OK. I'm OK. I fell, I'm a bit shook up but I'm fine. I'm...'

I put my hand on the wall to steady myself. It was like waking up from a dream.

'I had an awful experience once. My subconscious seemed determined to relive it.'

The green light next to the panel in front of me turned red.

'Guess Mouse is on her way.'

Clar glanced up and down the corridor. I followed their gaze and took in our surroundings for the first time.

In one direction, the corridor ran in a long straight line, and it bent into a corner about half as far away behind us in the other. The walls were a dirty white, the ceiling tiled with grey polystyrene. The floor was mostly dusty concrete but, at several points, broke into small black and white patterned tiles. At the far end of the long corridor, about two hundred metres away, a pair of white swing doors blocked any further view.

I wandered up to the bend and peered around. Another couple of hundred metres down that there was another set of doors. Nothing led off it in either direction, no doors, no side corridors. There was nowhere to hide.

'We're exposed here, huh?'

I realised why Clar was looking so twitchy.

'I'm not a fan,' said Clar. 'I've not seen anyone yet, but this corridor must go somewhere. Hopefully, it's not somewhere popular, but it's only a matter of time, and then we're sitting ducks. If you've any ideas for a cover story for when that happens, I'm ready for suggestions.'

'Maintenance?' I suggested. 'That might explain our

potentially unnatural interest in this hatch. We're just checking that the light controls work properly, by following each other up and down. We just need our colleague to come down and we'll be out of their hair…'

'Your lies are way too complicated,' said Clar. 'You won't be able to keep that up.'

They weren't wrong.

'Maybe it's fine,' I said. 'Kap didn't seem to think people would question us passing in and out of this place. He said that Resistance Agents do it all the time. How did he describe them? "Largely disinterested scientists"?'

'That's the kind of flippancy that worries me,' said Clar. 'It's all very well that Resistance Agents pass through here all the time. Can you pass as a Resistance Agent?'

'Fair question,' I admitted. 'I've only met three. I dunno…'

I looked up and down the corridor.

'How does it go?' I recalled what Kap had said. '"For the soil and the soul…"?'

Despite their generally serious demeanour, Clar did at least laugh at that.

'OK, stop. Maybe you're right, maybe it doesn't matter. If anyone comes, we just walk, pass them and then loop back for Mouse. If we look like we're supposed to be here, people will suppose that we are.'

'And hope that Mouse doesn't drop on their heads in the meantime?' I looked up at the hatch, which remained stubbornly shut. 'How long did it take you to get down?'

'A couple more minutes than this,' said Clar, reassuringly. 'I wouldn't expect her just yet. And you were much longer.'

'Actually, I was much quicker,' I explained, 'but then I lay there for a while until I figured out where I was.'

'Maybe you don't mention that to Mouse,' advised Clar. 'I don't think she'd understand. Me, I'm relaxed about the lingering echoes of childhood trauma. Mouse is a bit more "pull yourself together and deal with it".'

I stared at Clar. They were constantly surprising. I didn't think I'd mentioned childhood trauma. Maybe it hadn't been a comment about me.

'Are you OK?' I asked.

'Pitch darkness, confined space… I wasn't a fan of that shaft either, it's just that you weren't there to hear the screams of terror…'

We left the comment hanging for a while. There didn't seem to be a need to address the subject any further. But after a minute, the silence got awkward.

'OK, so Mouse incoming,' I said, to break it.

In my head, I started counting down. *Ten, nine, eight…* I wasn't sure what I was counting down to. I had no way of knowing that Mouse was actually about to appear.

I could always start again when I got down to zero. At least this way I was keeping my brain occupied. I didn't like standing here any more than Clar did.

The air in the corridor shifted, ever so slightly, with a hint of the brush of a door opening and closing and the squeak of heels on polished tiles. Our heads snapped around to the doors at the far end of the corridor, but there was no sign of anyone.

Clar flicked their eyes the other way, put their finger to their lips. I nodded in agreement and crept to the corner, where I crouched and peered around carefully.

Two figures headed in our direction, the set of doors in the distance swinging behind them. They wore civilian clothes, but with black jackets over black shirts, it was obvious who they were.

It was also obvious that they were more than capable of spotting someone peering around a corner, even if they were crouching. As I scrambled backwards, I saw their right hands going for their belts.

'They don't look like scientists,' I hissed at Clar, as I ran towards them, less worried about being quiet now that I'd been spotted. 'It looks like they've got guns. Black Knights, I think I've been here long enough to recognise that.'

My heart was thudding in my chest.

'I think we cancel the plan.'

'The walking past them plan? I think that plan now ends with us getting shot in the head by a pair of Black Knights. I suggest we...'

The light on the panel turned from red to green and the hatch swung down between the pair of us and the corner, which was now being rounded by the Knights, who had started running and were holding their guns in front of them. I looked up just in time to see Mouse jump down. She had her back to the approaching Knights.

'Are you...?' she began.

Clar grabbed her by the shoulders, firmly, and spun her on the spot.

'Fuck!' she yelped. 'Why aren't you running?'

We turned around and ran.

We ran hard, my already thudding heart trying to escape through my throat, my thighs burning, my shins stabbing. Without knowing the range of the guns the two Black Knights were waving, we seemed to stay far enough away that they weren't confident enough to shoot.

We crashed through the doors and braced our backs against them. Ahead of us, the corridor branched left and right.

'Which way?' I screamed as the first bullet ricocheted off the doors behind us. 'Do we split up?'

Mouse took in the situation quickly.

'We split up,' she panted. 'I'll go left, Clar, you go right.

Estrel, follow whoever you think is least likely to get caught. If you see another shaft, get up it. Hopefully, it will surface inside the city walls.'

'Right,' said Clar, already moving towards the right-hand fork. 'How do we find each other?'

Mouse paused for a moment. The glass behind her left ear shattered. She dived to her right.

'Eamer's,' she said. 'I can't think of anywhere else. We can't go back to my place. That might be my fault, but...'

'Your fault?' asked Clar.

'Me and my big mouth. I might have suggested that it was a Resistance safe house. To the border guards. Throwing them a bone. I was improvising.'

'OK...'

Clar took a step towards Mouse. Two more shots thumped into the door.

'But Eamer's? Is that really a good idea? Given who we're currently running from? It's not exactly neutral ground, is it?'

'Three blocks east, there's an alley,' Mouse said. 'It runs down the side of the Custom House. There's a door, won't be locked. The stairs will take you down to the generator room. It runs all the way under Eamer's. I've... left supplies. You'll be safe there. In the belly of the beast. It's not ideal, but I don't know that we've got any other common ground. And it gets Estrel close to where he needs to be. Where we think he needs to be.'

'I thought we'd moved on from that. What about Toshock?' asked Clar.

What about my tablet? I thought, but I hadn't had a chance to bring up the idea that it might be another Echo and there wasn't time now.

'I don't know,' protested Mouse, 'but we have to move! They're going to be banging at these doors any second. Come on!'

Mouse broke into a sprint, and disappeared around the left-hand corner, as Clar turned back towards the right. I stayed where I was, my back against the door, waiting for the bulge as two running bodies hit the other side.

'You're coming with me,' said Clar, turning their head.

'No.'

I surprised myself. I hadn't exactly made a decision, there hadn't been time to think that much, but I did know what the right thing to do was. I couldn't let these two strangers risk their lives for me.

'Go. You've done enough. This isn't your problem.'

Clar narrowed their eyes but barely broke stride and, crucially, didn't stop. I took a deep breath. Any second now.

I felt calmer than I thought I would. I didn't know what would happen next, but if I got captured I'd be free again in a matter of hours, reset back to the beginning of today. And if they shot me, then who knew?

It had been troubling me all day. Maybe I was about to find out. Maybe I'd still reset and resurrect, as if nothing had happened. Because nothing would have happened. And if I didn't reset?

I'd felt it in the shaft. It hadn't left me yet. The prospect of death didn't worry me. In a way, it would be a relief, albeit one I would never actually feel.

At least I'd be free of the loop. My conscious self had only experienced it the once but my spirit was tired, flagging. This could be a way out, at least.

'Nothing to lose then,' I muttered to myself, as I felt the first thump on the other side of the door.

I pushed back with all my weight. *Buy them some time. Hold back the river.*

There were grunts, another shove. The door opened

slightly before I could push it back. I forced my weight against it again and it swung the other way, but only as far as the foot wedged in it would allow.

Hands reached through, I edged away. It was enough to reduce the amount of force I could apply and I found myself flung forward by the opening door, two Black Knights pushing their way through and tackling me to the ground.

My face hit the floor, pain smashed through my head from my nose. I tasted blood again. My arm was gripped, twisted, and thrust awkwardly into the middle of my back.

I gritted my teeth as the other arm, trapped under my pinned body, was forced the same way. I felt several of them give way, spat out the pieces.

'This our guy?' said a voice.

'This is our guy,' replied the other.

My slowing brain took the words in, struggled to put them in order. They were looking for me? I thought it was strange that they hadn't fired more. I thought they were trying to kill us, though. They wanted me alive?

'Any sign of the other two?' said the first voice.

'I assume they ran,' said the other. 'It would be about right for Mouse.'

'That was Mouse?'

A knee on my back pressed my chest into the ground, squeezing the air out of me.

'That was Mouse. She's in trouble when Eamer finds her.'

There was a laugh, a harsh, humourless, cruel laugh.

'Come on, tie his hands.' I couldn't tell which was which anymore. 'Get off him. He'll be easier to move if he's still conscious.'

Unlucky, I thought, as the blackness enveloped me.

Part Two

CHAPTER 11

'One.'

I heard the voice, but struggled to open my eyes. My lids were heavy, the weight of sleep pushing down on me.

I wondered where I was. *Push back, wake up.* My body was coming back online, but only slowly.

As sensation returned, orientation reestablished, I realised I was sitting in a chair. My legs felt stiff, so did my arms. I couldn't raise up my lolling head. My tongue felt fat, too big for my mouth, pushed against the sharp edges of broken teeth. I tried to lift a hand to rub my eyes, and discovered that I was bound at the wrists, the plastic of my cuffs cutting into the skin.

'Two.'

I heard the voice again. I hadn't jumped back to this morning, then. Whatever had happened to me, it wasn't a reset.

I wasn't dead. I was somewhere new.

It was cold. I shivered as I thought about it. The last thing I remembered was giving up.

No! Capture...

I thought they were going to shoot me. It had seemed

inevitable, so I'd tossed the coin, thrown the dice.

Death or respawn. Either seemed to be a reasonable option.

Chalk that iteration up to experience.

Except I'd achieved nothing. Nothing that would last. No Echoes updated.

If anything, I'd lost several, one in my bag, another in Mouse, maybe the tablet... I couldn't chalk anything up to experience. I hadn't had any experience to speak of.

I fought to open my eyes. Had they drugged me? And if so, who were they?

'Three.'

My eyelids sprung apart, as if a force holding them shut had snapped. Interesting. This was not what I was expecting.

The chair I was sitting on was the only furniture in an otherwise bare room. It was white. The walls were white; the ceiling and floor were also white. I had to blink several times before my pupils constricted enough for the glare not to hurt.

I realised I wasn't wearing my own clothes anymore. I wasn't wearing shoes or socks, although my feet were still bandaged, and instead of the suit and shirt I'd been wearing earlier, I was now dressed in an all white overall made of a heavy canvas.

New clothes.

That meant that the napkin was probably gone. Another Echo lost. I wished I'd been able to go through with the writing on my arm idea.

I looked around. There was nothing to see.

'Hello?'

My voice cracked as I spoke. My throat was dry. I ran my tongue over my chapped lips.

'Hello?' There was no response. 'What are you counting?'

I moved my head, stretching my neck a little. It snapped

painfully as I moved to the right. I flexed my fingers underneath the cuffs and tried to stretch my legs out. They were pulled back almost immediately by the rope that I hadn't noticed tied around my ankles.

'Four.'

I stopped moving.

'What are you counting?' I demanded, again. 'Is it me? Is it something I'm doing?'

Silence.

Beat.

Silence.

'You've stopped,' I observed. I closed my eyes again, took a deep breath, and held it. What would happen if I did nothing?

'Five.'

My eyes snapped back open and I let out the breath. Behind me I heard a hiss, which sounded like every automatic spaceship door on every science fiction show I'd ever streamed.

I heard footsteps approaching my chair and then stopping behind me. I tried to turn my head, tried to see who had come into my prison, but again there was pain when I tried to turn and I couldn't look behind myself.

'What have you done to my neck?' I asked.

'Nothing,' said a voice from behind me.

It was a woman's voice, deep and calm. In any other situation, I might have found it reassuring. The restraints impeded that a bit.

'Nothing specific, anyway,' she continued. 'You were quite resistant to the Knights who took you into custody. You may have sustained some unintended injuries.'

Oh, well, as long as they were unintended. I didn't say that out loud.

'I don't know to what extent you appreciate the seriousness of the situation you have found yourself in, Mr Beck, but...'

'How do you know my name?' I asked.

My mind flashed back to the message on Chaguartay's Com. I was expected here. People knew who I was. Even if the pictures they'd taken of me were less than flattering.

'We know a lot about you, Mr Beck,' she replied. 'More, probably, than you know yourself.'

This annoyed me. It seemed like a line, and one from a terrible movie at that. But I couldn't discount the possibility.

I'd already seen enough to suspect that I was being manipulated. Certainly manipulated into coming here. Possibly manipulated since I arrived.

I had a choice to make. I needed to decide what would give me the best chance of finding something useful out.

She seemed in the mood to talk. Was the best approach to unsettle her into defensively revealing something she shouldn't by talking back? Or should I keep quiet and let her string her own noose?

Talking back wasn't very like me, though, and I wasn't entirely certain that I could pull it off. I stayed quiet.

'Hmm.' The woman behind me noticed. She seemed annoyed that I wouldn't react. *Good.* 'Do you even know why you're here, Mr Beck? Do you have any idea what you're destined to do if I let you?'

Destined to do... If I let you... The adrenaline hit me with a jolt. Who was this woman? Was she the instigator of the time loop?

I had assumed its purpose was to make sure I did something, to make sure that I didn't miss it. I hadn't considered the possibility that it was to stop me from doing something.

Did that mean that there wasn't a way back? Was I trapped, imprisoned forever? Who would do that to a person?

I was just... well, just me. What could I possibly be about to do that would require such an extreme imprisonment? *Why don't you just kill me..?*

'What I need to do, Mr Beck,' continued the woman behind me, 'is to take you out of the equation. I have some knowledge of who you are, and of what the purpose is of your being here. I don't know which iteration of yourself you are. In many ways, it doesn't matter. I will only meet you today, in my timeline, and I judge you are getting rather too close to what I'm trying to achieve today.'

She paused at this point. My mind reeled, but I continued to say nothing.

So, the time loop wasn't down to her, then. She wanted me out of the equation. Was what I was meant to do something to do with stopping her, and *what I'm trying to achieve here*? Who was this? *Toshock..?*

'I mean you no harm, Mr Beck,' she said, in response to my continued silence.

I had to contain the *Ha!* that threatened to burst from my mouth at that point, but, to be fair, I was unharmed so far. Despite being shot at, tackled to the ground and then tied to a chair.

I almost got blown up earlier, as well. And fell down a shaft, although that was mostly my fault. Being tied to a chair in an empty room was one of the safest places I'd been all day.

'You don't look comfortable, though,' she continued. 'You'll understand that I need to keep you here for the rest of the day until you reset. But I can make you more comfortable.'

As an offer, it seemed friendly enough. I braced myself, ready for my wrist bonds to be cut. It turned out that wasn't what she had in mind.

'Five.'

And, in that moment, I realised what the counting had been for.

'No,' I said. 'No, no, no…'

'It's OK, Estrel,' she said. 'You won't know anything until you wake up tomorrow morning.'

'My Echoes…' I began.

I could almost feel her grin, even though I couldn't see it.

'Oh, no,' she cooed. 'You're going back to square one. Four.'

I could resist. Hypnotism is just a trick of the mind. I didn't need to succumb. *Just ignore the countdown, try to drown out the noise.*

I started to hum, low in pitch and volume. The vibrations filled my skull. I could resist. I wouldn't succumb.

I lost my tablet.

I lost my bag.

I lost Mouse.

I lost my marker.

Now I'd lost my napkin.

If I was trapped here, and I seemed to be well and truly trapped here, then I'd reset with nothing. Echo-less.

No way of telling my next iteration what to do.

No way of telling him, me, what was happening.

How many times around the loop had it taken to have that realisation in the first place? How had I even figured it out?

I must have accidentally created an Echo at some point. Done something, held onto something impossible just long enough for it to be dragged into the next loop.

Maybe I'd bought something and kept the receipt in my pocket, like with the boots, bearing a time that hadn't happened yet.

Maybe I'd recorded something on one of my devices and

hadn't lost them before I'd had a chance to charge their batteries.

Maybe their batteries hadn't been flat yet. Did battery reserve echo as well?

A jolt of electricity shot up from my leg, tingling its way at first and then ramming a hot iron bolt up through my thigh. I shot up in the air, but was quickly pulled back, painfully, by my ankles. I crashed back down into the chair. My teeth clenched, my throat scorched, my concentration broken.

'Three.'

My eyelids drooped, the weight of them too much for me to keep open. I tried to say something, although I wasn't sure what I was trying to say. The words died in my dried, cracked throat.

'Two.'

The weight of sleep was pushing down on me. *Push back, wake up,* I told myself. My body was slowly taking itself offline again.

Sensation dimmed, the world tipped sideways.

My legs felt heavy, so did my arms. My head lolled, and I couldn't raise it up. I tried to raise a hand to rub my eyes.

'One.'

I don't remember what came next.

I dreamed.

I had a sense that you weren't meant to dream when you were hypnotised.

I had a sense that you weren't meant to realise that you were hypnotised when you were hypnotised.

So perhaps this wasn't hypnotism. I couldn't move, though. Or maybe I could, but I couldn't figure out how.

It was getting hotter in the room. My thighs were slick with sweat. I could feel the plastic of the chair through the linen of not-my trousers. The suit clung to my shoulder blades, and I couldn't move enough to peel them away. Salty sweat stung my wrists, where my restraints had dug into the flesh.

I could feel my pulse race, feel the panic setting in. I closed my eyes and breathed deeply to calm myself down. Then I realised my eyes were already closed. I closed them some more.

From the depths of my dream I could hear something, distant voices, phasing in and out. The sound was vague, an echo of muttering, just out of my hearing.

I couldn't make out words, only the shape of mumbled secrets, the suggestion of something I needed to know. I couldn't tell where they were coming from.

Maybe I was being watched.

Perhaps they were the reflected sound of something I didn't remember having said out loud. Possibly, they were a recording designed to disturb and disorient me.

I worried they were a figment of my imagination.

They came again, distorted, squeaking and buzzing as if from a speaker system that wasn't equipped to deal with these resonances. Maybe my brain wasn't equipped to deal with these resonances.

Slowly, the squeaks and buzzes settled, coalesced around a rhythm, found a common pitch, morphed into something more meaningful. A man was shouting, pleading. He sounded distraught, on the edge, his voice breaking, wailing.

If it was as simple as just hanging onto something in my pocket, why did I choose the napkin? The napkin was flimsy, easily ripped and torn, very hard to write on clearly, especially with a pen that gave out a lot of ink.

Surely it would have been easier just to write something down on a regular piece of paper and keep it in my pocket for the next loop. I could have taken all the space I needed, mapped out hypotheses to be rejected and crossed off.

Why not an entire notebook? Why the napkin, which there was every chance I would never see If I made different choices at the start of the day and never went to the Administration reception.

How much time did I spend every loop pondering this? How long before I figured it out and decided to stick with it? Oh, Dear Creator, did I never figure it out?

Was I so worried about making a mistake, about messing things up, about letting myself down, literally, that I just went along with what I'd done before?

I was too scared to come up with a better idea in case it wasn't? That sounded very much like me. Oh, Dear Creator, that's exactly what happened.

'No!' I think he shouted. 'No! You can't do this!'

He sounded like me. Not how I sound in my head, but how I'd sound recorded in a large, empty room, and then played back through tiny, tinny speakers.

I saw myself in the bunker, at Mouse's place, on the train.

I saw myself in a cellar, on a hilltop, running down a darkened street, falling.

I saw myself disappear a thousand times.

I saw myself, angry, fist hitting a table, in tears, wrapping my arms around Mouse… no, Clar, no… someone else I did not recognise.

I saw myself, tired and soaking wet, euphoric and triumphant, furious and out for revenge, shuffling, strutting, storming into an empty bar and taking a seat on a stool, dancing on the table, sweeping an arm across the bar sending glass flying in all directions.

I saw myself back in the bunker again, with Kap and Clar, with Kap and Mouse, with Mouse and Clar.

I saw the woman I didn't recognise grab me by the elbow

and a look of anguish flash across my face.

I saw her lips move, but her voice was nothing more than a whisper.

I strained to hear better.

'No!' I think I shouted. 'No! You can't do this!'

The pictures dissolved, the voices faded out, time passed. I couldn't tell how much.

I was colder. The fabric sticking to my thighs was icy now. My fingers were numbing, the lack of feeling creeping up my hands but not yet reaching my stinging wrists.

I flexed my toes, at least I thought I did. I couldn't feel them. There was a chill across my shoulders that I couldn't shiver out.

The voices chimed now from the corners of the room, louder, more melodic, the resonant frequencies of the room articulated in their speech and reinforced through repetition. Any relation the sounds bore to actual words was lost.

I lost focus again, let the time flow past me because I couldn't hold on to it anymore.

'Three.'

My eyes opened, blinking, fighting the waves of suggested sleep and the sharp brightness of the light.

Eyes closed: I felt myself slipping back into the vortex, the world spinning past me, too fast.

Eyes open: the white blinded me, a searing pain to the back of my skull, too bright.

But it was the light I grabbed, tolerating the glare, each blink getting gradually shorter until, squinting but eyes still just open, I was in the room.

Back in the room? Had I been there before? It seemed very familiar and yet starkly alien. My thoughts swam, memories floating just out of reach, every grasp in their direction causing a ripple that pushed them ever so slightly further away.

I realised I had missed the beginning of the count. I didn't know which way it was going.

'Four.'

Up. I was being brought back. What did that mean? How long had I been under? Did this mean it was time for me to reset?

The room was white. My groggy eyes eased open a little more. Floor to ceiling. Floor and ceiling. Everything was white.

I looked down. The chair I was sitting on was white. My clothes, which were not mine, were white. I didn't dwell on how I was wearing them.

The ropes binding my ankles were white and, presumably, the restraints I could now feel chafing my wrists raw, which were behind my back, behind the chair, and immovable… they were probably white too.

I thought I had been there before, earlier. I didn't know how long ago, how long I was out for. It seemed familiar, but I couldn't zero in on the memory, couldn't rule out that it wasn't déjà vu.

More déjà vu? Déjà vu about déjà vu? I may have done this, woken up here many times. Or this might have been the first. Another ripple. Another memory bobbed away.

Start again.

'Five.'

The voice cut through. I opened my eyes, properly now, and the murmurs fell away. It was silent now. The room was the same, still empty, still white, but it was dark. Not pitch black but a grey, murky light that washed everything out.

I tried to move my wrists and ankles. They were still restrained.

The voice spoke again. It was a woman's voice, but it was not in the room. I couldn't tell where it was coming from, echoing around, from no obvious speaker, no obvious source.

Phi Oddy

The sounds just seemed to appear in my head. Someone was saying my name.

'Estrel. Estrel.' My name, repeated.

This was a different voice. Different from the one I heard... When? Different from the one that was behind me.

I grunted.

'Estrel,' they said. 'Can you hear me, Estrel?'

I grunted again. My mouth felt full of my tongue. I couldn't open it to form the words. I raised my head and dropped it again. The effort was exhausting, but I hoped it was meaningful. It seemed to be.

'Estrel, I need you to respond,' the voice persisted. 'I need to know that you can hear me. We don't have much time.'

'I can hear you,' I whispered.

'That's good. Now I need you to listen. I need you to listen to what I say, but most of all, I need you to understand. I need you to understand because I can't tell you what to do.'

'I don't know what to do,' I mouthed.

'I remember,' the voice said, 'but Estrel, this is dangerous. I can't tell you what to do. You have to figure it out yourself.'

'Just tell me.'

I felt empty and broken. Nothing made sense anymore. I wanted to get out. I wanted this to be over.

'Stay with me, Estrel,' said the voice again.

I tried to pay attention.

'I need you to hear me. I need you to listen. I need you to understand, but I can't tell you what to do. It's too dangerous and it won't work. But I want to help.'

'Help,' I repeated.

I think there were more words that I wanted to say, but they escaped before I could get them out.

'You're going to have to figure this out for yourself, Estrel,' the voice sounded urgent, scolding. 'But I'm going to tell you a story. I just need you to listen. And to understand.'

'I was born beyond Ashuana, far from Trinity, in the eastern deserts,' the voice began. 'I was born a water bearer, in a tiny hut huddled around a deep, ancient step well. The well had been there long before we arrived, our people, but it gave us life and a purpose. I learned how to drop my water carrier below the surface, letting the water surge in. The air, forced out, would break for the surface, causing a spurt that would hit me in the face. Every time I squealed with delight; the water was fresh and tasted as blue as it looked, but this prompted tuts from around the platform. I grew up to the sound of tuts, but I didn't care about their disapproval.

'"That's your problem," my mother would say, scolding me, most mornings. "You are not better because you do not take your work seriously."'

'"I am no worse," I would insist, holding my chin up high and looking down my nose at her. And I was happier.

'Being happier helped. The work we did was hard. The women had calf muscles like horses, backs that cracked, dank smelling clothes that never had time to dry. These were the prices paid because we were born into our work. I was truly born to this life. Mother carried me down to the water every day whilst I grew inside her. I kicked as she bent and her belly dipped below the surface. The day after my birth, she wrapped me and carried me down the well for another day's work. That's taking your work seriously.

'Each level of the well was a square. The waters never got that low, but I assume that at level zero it disappeared to a point. It was the height of summer, and we were working on level five. Behind, a queue formed on the stairway while we filled our carriers and started the walk back up. At the end of each stairway, there was a choice of two more to the next level.

Phi Oddy

If someone was coming down one, then you had no choice but to take the other. I liked to race up, so that I always got to choose, forcing my sister to take the one that was left.

'When I was too young to know better, I imagined I could, given enough time and determination, take every feasible route from the water back to the top. I soon learned differently. Level five had thirty-two staircases. Level six had sixty-four. By level twenty-five, you could choose over sixteen million different routes. If I lived to be a grandmother, I wouldn't cover a thousandth of them. Our work was ridiculous. I couldn't take it seriously.

'The priests blessed the water that we brought up and they poured the blessed water, with grand ceremony, over the Great Wheel. The Great Wheel towered over our village, blocking out the midday sun. It sat between two giant statues of the Creators, who between them held the mighty axle on their shoulders and allowed the Wheel to turn in the wide groove that they had gouged out of the desert soil.

'Day and night, we descended into the well and brought up the water for the priests to make the Great Wheel turn. The Wheel turned with a grinding and a roar that echoed down the well, that we felt in our feet and saw in the ripples on the water. Water running off the Wheel soaked into the parched earth and, in time, found its way back into the water table, back into the well, and back into our water carriers. The Great Wheel drove the Great Machine.

'I asked what the Great Machine was for; I was told that the Machine stopped the sky from falling. I never saw the Machine, it was buried deep below the surface, in the Temple, where only the Priests could go. I asked how a Machine buried under the ground could hold up a sky, way up in the heavens; I was told that the Machine stopped the sky from falling. I asked what would happen if the well dried up and there was no more water for us to bring to the Priests; I was told that the blessed water powered the Great Wheel, which drove the Great Machine, which stopped the sky from falling. My mother sent me to my bed until I stopped asking questions. I didn't want to carry the water until I was old and broken, calves like horses, a back that cracked. My clothes already smelled. But I didn't want the sky to fall.

'On the day I decided I would let it fall anyway, I lifted my water carrier and took the empty stairway, two steps at a time to make sure I beat the girl coming down and got my pick of the next pair of stairs. In my mind, it was the last opportunity I would get to make this choice. Behind me, the women with empty carriers cursed as they shuffled down the steps to level four. When I go to the top, I poured the water directly onto the ground. The priests beat me. The next day I was back in the well.

'On the second day I decided to let the sky fall. I dashed my water carrier on the steps and came up from the well empty handed. The Priests beat me three times harder than the time before. They shut me in a hut on my own, with the door tied closed and the windows nailed shut. When I escaped, they caught me, brought me back and beat me two times harder again. When I told them I would carry the water again, they praised the sky, but I knew I did not mean it. I did stop splashing the water and squealing, and I did stop running up the stairs. I stopped asking questions and in time they stopped watching. But by that time I knew I didn't care if the sky fell, as long as it fell on the Priests.'

I felt the room slipping away, my trance beginning to envelop me again. I fought it. There had been no count. I didn't have to go.

The words I was hearing washed over me, washed through me. I had stopped understanding, but I hadn't stopped listening. I still heard.

'On the day I left, I just walked away, and no one saw me go. I was calm, but I didn't go where they expected me to go. I came west, walked until I reached Trinity, a city where the sky was already falling, but nobody wanted to acknowledge it. I decided to stay. What about you, Estrel?'

'What about me?' I croaked, the haze descending.

Nothing made sense.

'How many times have you been down the well?' the voice asked me, 'Have you poured your water on the ground yet? Or do you still see the sky when you look up?'

I shook my head. *How many times?*

'How would I know?' I moaned.

'Did you try to escape?' they asked. 'Are you ready to walk away?'

I understood.

But I didn't know. I'd been looking at this whole thing as a learning experience.

What if I wasn't learning?

What if I was tying myself down?

What if, slavishly following what I thought I'd done every time before, I wasn't building a picture of what was happening, but was retreading the same ground, repeating the same mistake?

Over and over and over. Or, and this struck me and it was so much worse, what if I was going backwards?

What if the napkin was a panicky response to something going wrong? Like a flat battery?

What if I'd lost information, lost clarity, lost the bigger picture?

What if, with every loop, my horizons got closer, my perspective narrowed?

What if I now knew less than I'd ever known before?

Echoes

I'd been assuming that this process was all about growth. But I could easily see how I, disorganised, scared, so damned stupid, could have made it all about inertia, or decay.

The mist rolled in.

CHAPTER 12

Now I was somewhere else, shrouded in a thin mist. I could see for about ten metres and beyond that, there was blackness.

What was I going to do with this information? Was it information? It was a theory. Several working theories.

Maybe I was wrong about all of this. Second guessing myself into abandoning everything as a bad job would have been just as typically, authentically me.

I'd lost all my Echoes, so I didn't have many alternatives here. Was that what I was doing? Was I trying to make it OK that everything had gone wrong, and I was going to have to start again with nothing?

Did I have to start again with nothing? Was there a way I could take a new Echo back with me, something that would lay out my options, allow me to consider everything on a new day, with a new start?

With my hands tied, I couldn't write anything. I couldn't keep anything on me. I didn't even think that this overall had pockets. What would I take back with me? My mind? Could I implant something, bury something deep in my subconscious? Like a self hypnosis, maybe some kind of suggestion.

Wait.

I sensed someone was standing beside me, and I turned. It was only then that I realised that I, too, was standing, and that I was no longer tied. I flexed my wrists, cut from their bonds, and my feet, cut from walking too far in unsuitable footwear. Both felt fine.

It seemed sudden, unbelievable. Was I dreaming? Still hypnotised? Hypnotised again?

'Where are we?' I asked the stranger.

They turned, and I recognised the Cleric from the train earlier that morning. He was still dressed in his azure robes. Up close, I could see that he wore a ring in his nose and several in each ear. His skin was rough and weather worn.

'You did this,' said the Cleric. 'You tell me.'

This was frustratingly cryptic, and I could only think of one answer.

'I'm dead, aren't I?'

The Cleric laughed and placed a hand on his own chest.

'No, you're not dead. I might be though.'

'How come you're dead and I'm not?' I asked. I wasn't usually one to see departed spirits.

'I can see through you, Estrel,' said the Cleric.

'What do you mean?' I spluttered. This was rich. I had done nothing. 'I don't... see what? I'm not... I've got nothing to hide!'

'No, Estrel,' he said, and I realised that this was the second time he'd used my name. 'I don't mean...'

'Who are you?' I demanded. 'How do you know my name?'

'Those aren't the right questions, but my name is Lek. I know your name because we've met before, although you probably don't remember it.'

'On the train?' I offered, to show that I did.

Echoes

'Not then,' said Lek. 'That was a way we met, a start for us, but that was in another life and all that's left is the trace of recognition you felt. That iteration of me was not destined to know you, nor you him. He will lead a simple life and die young.'

'So you're not him? You're...' I struggled to define what I meant. 'You're not from this timeline. You're from my past?'

'Your past, your future, none of it is important right *now*,' said Lek.

That's what I'd been waiting to hear. I wasn't that important; I wasn't that significant. Why did I think to assume that my purpose here was something meaningful? It could just as easily be the case that I was being forced to live the same day, repeatedly, for some more trivial, more petty end.

Money, power, influence. Those were big motivators to do something dastardly and screw the casualties - ie. me. *Or love*, I thought. I hadn't lost my sense of humour in all this, then.

'So,' I said, about to sum up something I could not fully comprehend, 'you're probably dead, from another timeline...'

'Not another timeline,' Lek corrected me. 'From a timeline, but not the one you have come from.'

'That's the same thing,' I protested.

'No disrespect, but it isn't. I can't be from another timeline, as we're not in a timeline right now. We are... the best way to think of it is that we're *outside time*.'

'Outside time? How did we..?'

'You tell me,' grinned Lek, his face wrinkling into a lifetime of folds. 'You brought us here.'

'How? And why? And why would I bring you here?'

'That's a lot of questions,' observed Lek. 'You need to ask fewer questions. It would help to calm your mind.'

'Would it?'

'It would,' Lek nodded. 'Especially since they all have the

same answer.'

Now he was just being deliberately obtuse, I was certain of it. A thought struck me. I wasn't particularly au fait with the religion that the Clerics adhered to, but I was not a man of faith myself. We were on our own. Death was the end. You made your bed…

This should feel weirder. Communing with a holy man at the end of time? That wasn't me. I didn't believe that this was a thing that could happen.

'Just because you don't believe it doesn't mean that it's not real,' Lek pointed out, apparently reading my thoughts.

I gaped at him, speechless.

'Also, it's not the *end* of time. We are merely outside it. Think about it like a kind of respite from everything you've been going through. Over and over…'

'How do we get back?' I asked. 'Do we get back?'

'You probably should,' said Lek. 'But there's no rush. The world will still be there when you're ready for it. Make it wait.'

I looked down to see what we were standing on. Despite the thickening mists, I wasn't cold, but I couldn't feel the ground with my bare feet.

To my shock, we appeared to be standing on a cloud, but that wasn't the most surprising thing. The cloud was visible through my feet, my translucent feet. I checked my legs, my torso, held up my hands in front of my face. I wasn't completely there.

'I know what you're going to ask,' said Lek gently. 'It took you a moment to realise, didn't it? You're wearing a bit thin.'

That sounded like a bad joke. I said as much.

'Every time you loop is like taking a copy of yourself,' explained Lek. 'You've done it so many times now that the clarity is degrading, the original image is wearing out.'

'But you don't look like this!' I protested.

Echoes

'I'm probably dead,' Lek reminded me, 'and if I am, then I don't count. Not anymore.'

'But I don't look like this normally,' I insisted.

'It's all relative. A faded copy in a splintered timeline doesn't stand out, necessarily. If anything, the world around you is fading faster than you are.'

'What do you mean?' I asked, losing the thread of the explanation again. 'Splintered? splintered how?'

'Every time you loop, you copy yourself,' said Lek, 'but every copy needs a new timeline to exist in. Only that's not possible, to create a new timeline. So instead you split the one that was there before. Make do with half of what you came from.'

'And I can't carry on doing that forever.'

The conclusion here was kind of obvious.

'You can't carry on doing either of them,' agreed Lek. 'The timeline is weak. Reality can't sustain. You must have noticed things seeping through. Hints from other times you've lived through today.'

I knew that I had. More times than I wanted to admit.

'You've done a good job of holding it all together so far, but you're not the man you were, either.'

'So what do I do? I assume that's what you're here to help me with.'

Lek grinned again, the wrinkles extending past his face and furrowing his shaven head.

'Finally, you're getting the hang of this. Yes, that is why you brought me here, even if you didn't know that you had.'

'So what do I do?' I asked, again.

'Weren't you listening to the story? You pour your water on the ground.'

'What does that mean? I make a fuss, protest?'

'You break the cycle,' said Lek, simply.

'Yes, but,' I didn't feel like I was getting a lot of help, 'break the cycle how?'

Lek held his hands up.

'That's up to you,' he said. 'But you don't have many chances left. The universe cannot cope with many more fractures. I'm sorry to tell you that reality is kind of depending on you.'

'That's not much pressure, then.' I couldn't help but make a joke. The whole thing seemed ridiculous. 'The whole of reality in my hands…'

'It's important.'

Lek was serious. I felt bad about my joke. But the whole thing *was* ridiculous.

'I've taken something of a risk coming here. I wouldn't do that if it wasn't critical.'

'You've… I thought you said I brought us here,' I objected.

'I did,' said Lek, 'and you did, but I may have had a hand, in a roundabout way. Someone needed to do something. We're not supposed to, but…'

'You're… who's not supposed to?'

I was feeling manipulated again. Possibly I was getting close to whoever had caused me to exist in this time bubble in the first place.

'The Devoted?'

Lek laughed.

'I won't say that we don't have an interest within the Citadel,' Lek paused, corrected himself, 'I mean we *had* an interest. This is all a bit fresh. But you're looking in the wrong place if you're trying to pin this on someone.'

'Yes!' Finally, somebody got it. 'That's exactly what I need to find out.'

'No,' said Lek, firmly. 'You don't need to find that out. Exactly the opposite.'

'How do you mean?'

'I mean,' said Lek, turning away, 'exactly that. You can't know. The would be the end of everything.'

'That's not helpful,' I said, to Lek's back.

'I can't be helpful,' sighed Lek. 'Not in the way that you want. You have to figure it out for yourself.'

'Quickly.'

'Quickly.'

'That's all you've got for me? How am I supposed to do that? Every time I loop, I lose it all.'

'Echoes, Estrel, you're all about the Echoes,' Lek stepped into the mist, shaking his head.

'You're going?'

Lek turned. I wasn't sure how he'd got so far away so quickly. He was on the edge of the darkness. It was wrapping around him, dissolving his body, leaving just his head floating in the mists.

'I have to go,' he said. 'But you've got this, Estrel. It lies within you.'

'I...'

This was frustrating. I wanted to scream in his face. My voice left me just as I needed it, though.

'I...'

Lek, now just a smiling face, faded from view.

'Within you, Estrel,' he said.

I was on my own. I was completely on my own.

I woke with a start.

This time was different. There was no counting, no slow slip from trance to consciousness. This time I was asleep and then, with a jolt, I was awake.

My vision cleared, a fog that wasn't really there burning off in the glare of the White Room. Thoughts and images darted away from me, disappearing over the horizon, leaving me with an impression of their impact.

I felt a wrench, but I wasn't sure why I felt it. Something had changed, but I didn't know what it was. I sensed a presence in the room. I couldn't tell if it was real or remembered. Something else was different.

The room was the same, my chair was the same, but I realised my wrists were no longer bound and my ankles were no longer attached to the chair legs. I was still wearing the white suit. My feet were still bare.

I stood up, out of the chair. My joints creaked, and it took several paces before I could properly straighten my spine, but I seem to be otherwise unharmed.

I turned around and braced myself, holding onto the back of the chair for support while the head rush I experienced subsided. There was no one else in the room, after all. I'd been freed and left to fend for myself.

The door, it turned out, was the only thing in the room that wasn't white. It was blue and directly behind where I had been tied. With caution, I approached and put my ear against it.

I could hear the thrumming of machinery vibrating through the wall, but nothing that would suggest that there was any danger in opening it. Looking around, there didn't seem to be an obvious handle, but neither was there any sort of panel or button.

I took a step back. Without warning, the door slid away into the wall with the same whooshing hiss I had heard before. I jumped to one side to avoid being in direct sight of whoever was going to come through but, after thirty seconds with nothing happening, I allowed myself to creep closer again and peer around, into the corridor.

Both directions were empty, either of people or of much in the way of features. It was familiar, in that it looked very similar to the one I'd run down some hours previously. The dirty white walls, grey polystyrene ceiling tiles and dusty concrete floor suggested that I hadn't left the Research facility.

I looked back into the White Room and wondered what sort of experimentation happened in there, then wondered if I'd experienced it, then wondered what I couldn't remember.

I breathed a sigh of relief, which did little to calm my now racing heart. Whether accidental or because of the actions of some guardian angel, I had an opportunity to escape. I was going to take it.

If only I knew which way I needed to go. I looked left and right along the corridor. There was negligible difference in the two options. It seemed to be a fifty-fifty thing.

A voice echoed in my head. *"Have you poured your water on the ground yet?"*

What did that mean? How would I know, even if I understood the question?

I looked at the chair I'd left. There was nothing on the floor. That was a relief. For a moment, I thought that my subconscious was trying to tell me I'd pissed myself.

There weren't any pools of water anywhere else in the room, either. I turned back to the corridor and stuck my head back out, looking from left to right again. *Show me something,* I begged. *I'm lost.*

I realised that the right door panel hadn't slid inside the wall completely. On the left side it had vanished, but on the right a small sliver of blue outlined the empty door frame.

I pushed it. Something whirred and ground; a gear slipped a little. I stopped pushing, and the noises stopped. It seemed to be stuck, jammed somehow.

I looked down at the floor. There was something wedged under it.

I dropped to my knees and examined it further. It looked

like a wad of tissue paper stuck under the door. It couldn't be, could it? I didn't believe that prayers could be answered, didn't believe that I'd prayed in the first place and yet...

I wiggled the wad of paper out, being as careful as I could not to tear it any more than was necessary. It was dirty, and even more tattered than when I'd last seen it, but here it was again, jam stain and all.

My napkin, my Echo. I unfolded it and smoothed it against the clean white floor in the room. There it was, the initial, mind-boggling message to myself. The list of times, corrected and updated. The words FIND MOUSE.

But now there was something new. It was small, squeezed into an empty corner, and carefully detailed in red. A series of lines leading from a large capital U, branching and winding outwards. Each branch ended with an X except one. At the end of that one was a crudely drawn picture. Of a mouse.

This was surprising. I thought I'd lost the Echo, had dim recollections of trying to figure out how to make a new one, whilst in the grip of a hallucinatory trance, or whatever that had been. And now it was back, not just intact, but with brand new information added for me.

This was either incredibly helpful or incredibly suspicious. It was in the room where I'd been held, sedated and categorically told... I thought... that they would keep me there until I reset without the benefit of an Echo.

So this had to have been left for me by whoever had set me free from here. An ally, one who couldn't show their hand but was working behind the scenes to fix things for me.

The voice who had told me the story? The first voice was a woman's. I was certain of that.

I thought the second voice was as well, but I wasn't so sure that it was the same person.

It was all so hazy. I was struggling to remember what

they'd said. Something about a well, I thought, but it was as vague as the dream I'd just awoken from.

Back to certainties, then. Whoever left this for me had also freed me. Ergo, they were trying to help me, ergo I should follow the map. And for whatever reason, I did feel like I wanted to find Mouse. Unless it was all a brilliant double-bluff.

I had no way of knowing. I just had to pick a course and commit. It was time I took responsibility for my actions. I had nothing much to go on, but I was going to keep the faith.

FIND MOUSE.

I refolded my Echo and put it in a new pocket before leaving the white room and turning to the right.

CHAPTER 13

I knew something bad was waiting for me around the first corner. It was the smell that gave it away. Hot, wet, sweet metal hung in the air.

I heard nothing, but proceeded with care anyway, pressing my back against the wall and inching to the corner until I could see enough to feel confident that there was no one there.

Except for the dead body. Around the first corner, there was a dead body.

They were greyer than I'd expected, their blood pooling in their lap from a shot to their abdomen, much darker and stickier than I would have imagined. *Like jam*, I thought, bile rising at both the sensual clash of that thought and the smell that was even more revolting now that I knew what it was.

The name stitched into their uniform, which I recognised as being Resistance issue, was Jones. I thought I should check if she was carrying anything that would serve as the weapon that I felt I was going to need, but I didn't want to. Her pockets were too blood-soaked, the stench of her recent death was too cloying.

Phil Oddy

I breathed out, backing away from Agent Jones until my heel struck something soft and I turned to see what it was.

It was an Agent Knope, who had little face left. I vomited on the floor next to his body.

There was a room with an open door further down the corridor. I approached cautiously, turning every few paces to check behind me.

I swept my gaze like the weapon that I didn't have. The shudder of my adrenaline-soaked body, the jolt with every heartbeat, made the entire process even slower.

Apart from the constant background electrical hum, everywhere was silent.

It did not surprise me to find a third body, labelled Begrandt, in the upended chair that lay on the floor just inside the doorway. I stepped over him, into the room which was dark but small enough that all but the tiniest far corner was visible with the light from the corridor behind me.

The room served as sleeping quarters, with a fourth body spreadeagled on the bed, thrown backwards by the force of whatever had made the significant hole in their chest.

I closed my eyes briefly, steeled myself and, avoiding slipping with my bare feet on the pool of Begrandt's blood, took another step inside. Already, I was getting used to the smell, and numb to the bloody horror of the scene.

All of this still scared me, though. It had obviously taken a struggle to get me free, and I wasn't sure which side of the firefight I was now looking at. Whoever had taken out the Resistance Agents strewn around the place was not someone I wanted to meet unarmed until I was sure they didn't want to kill me as well. They weren't someone I particularly wanted to meet at all, whatever their cause.

I trusted Kap, but had reason to suspect that his General was on the wrong side of things. That meant that Resistance as a collective existed in something of a grey area.

I didn't know if this meant that these Agents were the ones keeping me prisoner or if they were a unit sent to free me.

The men who had pinned me to the floor were Black Knights, so they could have been acting on Chaguartay's orders. I needed to look for the simplest explanation, which seemed to me that if accomplices of Chaguartay had captured me, the accomplices of Chaguartay must have been holding me captive.

I'd heard a woman's voice. That had to be Toshock.

The last piece of the jigsaw was falling into place. I looked down at the body on the bed. I couldn't make out her name tag from her fatigues, which were torn and burned in just the wrong places. But it could be her.

So I was free, thanks to person or persons unknown who, for whatever reason, wanted to keep themselves out of the picture. I should feel grateful, but it chilled me. Freed for what purpose?

Who was trying to get me to do what? This overriding sense that I was being manipulated was coldly familiar, like this wasn't the first time I'd come to this conclusion. If only I could remember what had been happening to me.

I looked around the tiny room. I needed to get out of there. Out of that room, out of the maze of the Research complex, ultimately out of Trinity, but I wasn't about to climb back out of the shaft into the Resistance bunker, even if I'd had any idea how to find it, so that meant I had to head back *into* Trinity.

Now that I knew the Mayor was out to get me, Trinity didn't seem to be the safest of places. But I needed to get out of this bunker and if that was going to take some uncharacteristically risky action from me, I was open-minded about that. This would leave me vulnerable, though. I needed to find a weapon. Also, shoes.

Phil Oddy

There was a small storage unit at the foot of the bed. The third draw I opened was full of guns. I took what seemed to be a medium-sized hand gun and raised it to see how it felt. It was heavy, solid, hard.

I felt simultaneously safer and more in danger than I ever had before in my life. There was no way I knew what I was doing. I pointed the gun at the far wall and tried squeezing the trigger. The trigger didn't budge.

I examined it a little better. Now I looked at it properly, I could see there was an obvious catch on the side. I slid it in the only direction that it seemed to want to move and then tried another shot at the wall.

This time the thing exploded in my hands with a deafening bang and lurched backwards, wrenching my shoulder as I battled to keep from falling over.

There was now a hole in the wall above the head of the bed. Plaster was raining down on the body lying on it.

My ears screeched with the aftershock of the noise of a firearm being discharged in such an enclosed space. My shoulder throbbed.

I wondered how much worse it was going to be if I had to fire it at a person.

However, I felt I'd figured out enough about how to fire a gun to be going on with, and it probably wasn't a good idea to hang around much longer given I'd just given out a very strong signal of my whereabouts to anyone who might be trying to find me. I slid the safety back on.

I did at least know that it was a loaded weapon, although how many bullets it held, and how many remained in the cartridge, and how to reload if I ran out were all things I parked for now.

There was a small cardboard box with more bullets in the drawer. I took this and stuffed it down into the deep pocket of my overall. I assumed they were the right bullets for the gun I'd taken. They were the only ones in the drawer.

I looked across at Begrandt. His feet looked the same size as mine.

Was I really prepared to do this? Could I take a dead man's boots from his dead man's feet? I was going to need some socks as well. His were significantly blood soaked.

My stomach was turning at the thought, but when hadn't it been doing that today? I took a step towards Begrandt's body and bent down to take hold of his left foot. The smell was overwhelming, and I turned my head away, instinctively, to protect myself even as my eyes stung.

My gaze fell on something sticking out from under the bed. It was a pair of boots. Not able to believe my luck, I scrambled across the floor, avoiding the legs of the second corpse hanging over the edge of the mattress.

I hooked them out. A pair of thick socks was stuffed inside which were inside out and worn. I didn't mind though, at least they weren't being worn by a dead person.

I pulled the socks on. It felt good to have my feet covered. The boots were too small, but I crammed my toes in. They would have to do.

I got to my feet and, ears still ringing, I left the room.

The next room I came across, at the end of the corridor, was some kind of hub, with other corridors radiating out from it at regular intervals. I checked the Echo map. I was on track.

The room itself was filled with banks of computers. Half-filled, rather... The far end of the room seemed to have exploded and whilst the machines still stood, they were ripped open and blackened.

Most of the rest of the consoles were dead, some of them had wisps of smoke coming from the back of them. Very few lights flashed on the panels of LEDs on the near wall.

There was, however, a plan of the complex, etched into the plaster, very analogue for a room so filled with tech. I ran to it, forgetting that I should be visually sweeping the area before running across it, just in case someone was using a bank of defunct computers as a convenient cover.

Someone like Agent Wright, bloodied and lame, who coughed as he raised his gun and pointed it at my back. I spun, waving my own gun wildly, first way too high and then straight at Wright's head, which was bruised and raw on the right-hand side.

Blood was drying on the base of the bank against which he slumped, and I surmised he'd collided with it with some force, probably when he'd been thrown through the air by whatever explosion had taken most of his legs off. Wright shook his head and pulled his trigger.

There was a click, but nothing more dramatic than that happened.

Wright sighed and dropped the weapon, slumping back against the cold metal. His whole body slid down, with no legs to brace himself, leaving his head propped up, the rest of his torso and what was left of his legs lying uselessly in a growing pool of blood.

'It went off, the bomb,' he mumbled. 'I couldn't stop it. You got what you wanted.'

I stared at the man who, hours ago, had captured me under suspicion of being Authority, but who now appeared to think that I'd planted an explosive device that had disabled him.

He didn't appear to be a threat, with an empty gun and very little of his blood remaining in his body, so I approached.

'What?' I dropped to my knees, the rasping gurgles of Wright's laboured breathing making my chest feel tight. 'Who do you think I am?'

Echoes

'Beck,' spat Wright, blood flooding his mouth and dribbling down his chin. 'I tried to stop you…'

This didn't compute. I had been locked in a room, tied to a chair. I had already been stopped. Why did Wright think I'd planted a bomb?

He should have known all of this. If he didn't know about what had happened to me, then maybe he wasn't working with Toshock. Perhaps I was seeing both sides of the battle after all, Toshock on one side and Wright on the other.

But if Wright came to free me, why did he now think I'd blown him up?

'I didn't do this,' I protested. 'Why would you think I did this? Weren't you..?'

But Wright said nothing else, and the next rattling exhalation was his last. I stared at the dead man, another body on top of everything else I'd seen in the last hour. It was strange how quickly I'd become accustomed to death.

I took out the Echo, trying not to get it smeared with Wright's blood, which had got all over my hands. Standing up, I went back across to the plan on the wall.

I found the hub on the Echo, then the same place on the wall, where a red letter R marked my current location. I could trace the route I'd taken through the corridor, around the bends, in and out of the sleeping quarters, all the way back to a white square, which was in an area of the map marked "Isolation".

Isolation was right.

I glanced back at the Echo, at the route mapped out for me all the way to the mouse. I double checked I had it orientated right, lining up the path I'd taken to get here.

Something wasn't right about one of them. They didn't match. From the hub, I was supposed to take a corridor that, on the Echo, ran down in a straight line. It wasn't marked on the plan.

I checked I was facing in the direction I thought I was, keeping the way I'd come in on my left. The way out should have been behind me.

I turned around. The wall was blank. A hidden door? I walked towards the wall, but I couldn't see anything to show that it was anything other than solid.

'Estrel,' said a voice, causing me to jump and my heart to pound. Pound harder. It had been pounding for a while. It was exhausting.

I turned, sweeping my gun around. The face was familiar, but it took me an extra couple of beats to process it.

Jo Jo, Clar's pilot, stood in the doorway, his hand half up in a way that suggested that he wasn't completely convinced that I was actually going to shoot, but not altogether certain that I wouldn't.

With relief, I lowered the gun.

With relief, he lowered his hand.

'Estrel, thank goodness.'

Now I wasn't pointing a weapon at him. Jo Jo came into the room, stepping around the smoking, destroyed equipment.

'What the fuck is going on?'

'How did you find me?' I asked, raising the gun again as my suspicions took hold.

It might be all too convenient, Jo Jo turning up to offer me help just at the moment I needed some.

'What the fuck, Estrel?' screamed Jo Jo, putting his hands back up. 'I don't know what's happened here but…'

'Where did you come from?' I demanded, stabbing forward my gun hand to highlight that I wasn't someone to underestimate. Although, that was exactly who I was.

'What?' Jo Jo's voice was getting quite high pitched. 'I was with Clar. We've spent the last couple of hours trying to hack the security in the Research complex. They've got some intense firewalls but… I got into the live feed and all I could see was you tearing around like a madman, waving a gun. What the hell happened here?'

I wiped my forehead with the back of my gun hand. Jo Jo flinched, even though it now wasn't pointing at him, but I understood why. I only hadn't shot myself yet because, as I had just realised, I still had the safety on.

My head was reeling. I didn't know what to make of anything. I carefully tucked the gun into a loop built into the waistband of my overall.

'You've been looking for me?' I realised that this made his sudden appearance less suspicious.

'Like I said, we were trying to hack Research,' he explained, 'but we didn't know where they had taken you. To be honest, I thought you'd be deep in a bunker in Authority right now. I was hoping we'd pick up a clue from a few hours ago, from when you got taken, which might have given us some idea where to look. I didn't imagine you'd still be down here.'

I shook my head. There was a lot of information to process. *A few hours ago?*

'So how long has it been?' I asked.

'Since you got captured? Hours, I don't know. Three, four… It's pushing six o'clock now. What did they do to you? Are you OK?'

'Yeah, nothing,' I said, although that wasn't true. 'I mean, nothing awful. They hypnotised me, tied me to a chair. There was a white room. I feel like there's more, but it's hard to remember.'

'A white room?' Jo Jo was looking around. 'I went past a white room on my way in… just before the dead Resistance

Agents.'

'Yeah. I saw those too. There's another one down there,' I said, gesturing at the row of banks where Wright had fallen. 'I woke up. The door was open, and they were all dead. All of them apart from Wright here. He was only nearly dead.'

Jo Jo leaned back and glanced down to where Wright's corpse was lying.

'So,' he said. 'Just that? They hypnotised you and left you there?'

'There was other stuff,' I said defensively.

Now it felt like Jo Jo was the one being suspicious. Like he thought I was making it up.

'They kept bringing me back up and talking to me...'

'Talking to you?'

This was irritating me.

'I was told they were trying to keep me there until I reset, I think. Someone said something about... like, wiping the slate clean? They took my Echo.'

I pulled the napkin out of my pocket.

'But you got it back?'

'Yeah, I found it. I think. Or someone left it for me. I don't know who let me out, if it was these guys, or if they were the ones who locked me in. There are a lot of dead people around here, maybe everyone's dead, on both sides. That guy, Wright, he said something about an explosion, before he died.'

'Yeah, Kap warned us about that,' nodded Jo Jo, peering at Wright's corpse. 'He got word that Research was going to be the next target, made sure we knew to stay away. I found a way through the firewall just after it went off. Might be that the blast took some security layers out. We need to get out of here, though. We don't know who's responsible and we don't know if they're still here.'

'Wright seemed to think I was responsible,' I said, as much

to gauge Jo Jo's reaction as anything else.

I wasn't sure what he was suspicious about, but he didn't seem to trust me. It would be interesting if my being the suspected bomber was something he'd consider as well.

To his credit, Jo Jo looked surprised.

'That's odd. Why would he think that?'

I said nothing, because I didn't know.

'Unless Resistance is being fed false information,' he suggested. 'Maybe they didn't lock you in, but didn't come here to get you out, either. Perhaps they were manipulated to come here to take you out. As in, kill you. Tell them there's another bomb and they come running to neutralise it. You're collateral damage, wandering around in a daze. They shoot you thinking you're the bomber and then suddenly you're out of the picture without whoever's got it in for you having to get their hands dirty.'

'Except there was actually a bomb,' I pointed out. 'It took Wright's legs off. Destroyed those computers.'

However, the mention of disinformation made me realise that the apparent mistake on my Echo could well be deliberate, designed to get me wandering around, lost, until either Resistance shot me or I got blown up by the bomb that got Wright. It's just that the timing was off.

'There is that,' mused Jo Jo thoughtfully. 'I think we need to check out these bodies.'

I really didn't want to, but the kid was right. Something wasn't making sense. Someone had shot those Agents, and being squeamish would not help me figure out who.

The smell of death hadn't receded, but I felt less affected by it the second time. It seemed that it lost its shock value with repeated exposure.

I wasn't sure I was happy about that, but I needed to be

here. Something didn't make sense, and we had to find out what we could.

'I don't like the fact that it seems to be deserted,' mused Jo Jo. 'It's possible a fire-fight scared everyone off, but this place is a labyrinth. Panicking civilians don't make smart decisions, don't find the exits first go. Yet we have four Resistance corpses and nothing else. No sign of another squad, no petrified scientists cowering in a cupboard…'

'To be fair, we haven't checked all the cupboards,' I noted.

Jo Jo shook his head.

'The security feed I tapped had a heat layer. I saw nothing with a signature except you and a bunch of lab equipment.'

Apparently satisfied with his inspection of the dead Agent Begrandt, he ventured deeper inside the room, approaching the bed gingerly.

'Holy fuck,' he breathed.

'You found something?'

I snapped to attention.

'I found someone,' Jo Jo gasped.

I followed him into the cramped room and peered over the remains of the unidentifiable dead body.

'This is General Toshock,' Jo Jo explained, confirming the suspicion I hadn't quite worked all the way through earlier. 'Was General Toshock. What the hell was she doing here? Leading a tactical squad is a little below her rank. And such a motley crew… Who's that in the corridor? Could you tell?'

'Jones,' I said, 'and Knott? Knip..?'

'Knope,' nodded Jo Jo. 'Agent Knope is an idiot. I've had the misfortune to get talking to him on more than one occasion. But Jones is smart. And wily. Begrandt, too. Agent Wright can barely shoot straight. It's such a bizarre group. All led by Toshock.'

'I wondered if it was two groups?' I said. 'One that

imprisoned me here, and one that came to rescue me. Perhaps Knope and Wright weren't as stupid as they were corrupt?'

'Maybe.' Jo Jo scratched his chin. 'But something doesn't add up. I don't like it.'

A shiver crept up my spine.

'I don't think we should stay here.'

Jo Jo shook his head in violent agreement.

'I don't trust what we're being told,' he said. 'Someone's trying to manipulate things here.'

'Of course, yes.' A memory came rushing in, something from a dream. 'Perhaps this all happened the way it was meant to. Maybe I'm meant to be confused. If I think I've learned anything I'll want to Echo it, so I won't forget next time. But if what I've learned is nonsense…'

'You have no reason not to trust it, once you've reset,' said Jo Jo. 'You wouldn't know any better, and who can you trust if you can't trust yourself?'

'That's effectively the principle I've been working on all day,' I said, 'but I'm doubting myself now. I'm often wrong. Why would I assume I'd got all of this right?'

I pulled the napkin out of my pocket and waved it at him.

'It's as good as wiping the slate clean,' I concluded. 'Potentially better. One piece of misinformation on the Echo pollutes the whole thing. If it leads me to make a wrong turn, thinking I can trust my experience, then everything I learn is potentially irrelevant, if not actively damaging. Look at this map! It's nonsense!'

Jo Jo took the Echo and inspected it, before handing it back.

'I don't know. That seems pretty obviously confusing,' he said. 'It's like you're meant to suspect something's not right.'

'That might be the point,' I said. 'I don't know, right now, what's true and what's not. I don't know if anything I've already echoed is true or not either. Maybe that's what they want. I'm second guessing all of it. '

'If you're worried about echoing nonsense, then you won't echo anything.' Jo Jo's eyes went wide. 'Oh, wow, that's clever...'

I stared at the napkin in my hand.

'So I just throw this away?' I asked. It seemed fairly obvious to me that the conclusion was staring me in the face. 'I can't trust anything. I can't trust this map, I can't trust the reset times...'

'...you can't trust Mouse,' finished Jo Jo. 'I think you need to question everything. Shit, this is bad.'

I fell back against the wall and slid down it until I sat crumpled on the floor. I screwed up the Echo and tossed it under the bed.

'That's it, then,' I muttered. 'I'm trapped. Forever.'

'Do you trust me?'

Jo Jo, sat next to me on the floor.

It reminded me of a similar heart to heart what seemed like an age ago, with Mouse in the tunnel. It wasn't just our physical proximity; it was the feeling of being lost and confused, and dragged along by events.

'Don't answer that, you barely know me. Do you trust Clar?'

I shrugged. I pondered the alternatives.

'Clar saved me. You're always there. This will be the second time you've taken me somewhere, the second time that you've helped me get out of a situation I didn't want to be in, just in the nick of time. That's really convenient. Really, suspiciously convenient. But...'

'But?'

'But there's something in my gut,' I admitted. 'Something in my heart, even. I've got no real reason to trust you, either of you, and probably more than a few reasons not to... but yes. I trust you. I can't afford not to. I'd be dead.'

'Great!'

Jo Jo leapt into action, and dived under the bed, fishing the Echo out from underneath it and stuffing it in my hand. He pinched my cheek and sprung up, grabbing me and hauling me back to my feet.

'You should trust me. I'm going to help you figure this out. You should keep that scrappy napkin. Find a pen, caveat it, but don't lose it, because it's all you've got, apart from me. And Clar.'

A thought struck me.

'Maybe, but maybe not.' I spoke slowly, allowing time and space for the thoughts to coalesce around a plan of action. 'Toshock's dead...'

'Yeah...' Jo Jo wasn't following me, yet.

'But we know she wanted me to find Mouse.' I held up the Echo. 'Whoever left this for me wanted me to find Mouse.'

'No, they wanted you to look for Mouse,' said Jo Jo. 'That map will not take you to Mouse.'

'Details,' I said. 'Hear me out. Toshock might be working with Chaguartay, bad. Toshock appears to have been staying in here, very close to the White Room, bad. Toshock appears to have been being guarded by Begrandt, who you, a person I have decided to trust, think is a good Agent, bad. Toshock appears to have been killed by whoever freed me, bad.'

'I accept all of this,' said Jo Jo, impatiently, 'what's you point?'

'Toshock wanted me to find Mouse,' I explained, 'but whoever freed me didn't. That makes me think I shouldn't trust Mouse.'

'I said that,' protested Jo Jo.

'Except that Clar does.'

'Clar does what?' asked Jo Jo, although I think I could see

the penny dropping again.

'Trusts Mouse,' I said, 'I think that destroys my hypothesis. Whatever I do or don't think about what Toshock has been up to, and now she's dead, it's all a bit besides the point, we're going to do what she said. Because you trust me and we both trust Clar and Clar trusts Mouse, we're going to FIND MOUSE. Again.'

'I didn't say *I* trusted *you*,' said Jo Jo, but I could see he didn't mean it.

CHAPTER 14

'Which way do we go?'

I'd thought I was already following a map to Mouse, which now I had to disregard, both because I now had to question the origin and motivations of every piece of information I held and because the route it wanted to take involved passing through a solid wall.

Jo Jo examined the wall at the foot of the bed. There was a plan of the complex etched there as well, identical to the one in the control room, apart from being smaller. The red letter R, to show our current location, was a few squares along from the hub.

'These are on the wall in every room,' said Jo Jo.

I kicked myself for not noticing. I could have saved myself some time.

'It's pretty simple from here.'

He swept his finger back through the hub, along a long corridor, through zones marked "Cybernetics" and "Genomics", around a corner, through what I assumed was the marking for some doors and off the right-hand side of the map.

'But we can check in after a while and make sure we're not

off track. It gets pretty confusing pretty quickly around here and it's easy to lose your bearings.'

I nodded. I realised that the map I had been trying to follow was only going to have taken me deeper into the complex, trying to find whatever was behind that wall. To what end, I wasn't going to spend too much time trying to imagine.

I would not be led down that path, not today. But if it was drawn on the Echo, then it was something I might find myself inclined to follow on a future iteration and if, as I now realised I was assuming, it led into a trap then it was a trap that could get me in any of my futures. *Clever.*

I needed that pen, needed to add those caveats. Or find a whole new way to echo. Again, I got a glimpse of a thought I'd had once before, a thread that I had an urge to pull, to try to unravel the fog that was still clouding my thinking even now I was free of the White Room.

'What was that?' asked Jo Jo, jolting me out of my thoughts.

I shook my head. I had heard nothing. Then I did. It was a loud clang, distant but unmistakable. A door had opened.

There was something else around the edge of my hearing. I strained to hear more.

'Is that a dog?'

'Something that barks.'

Jo Jo shivered. He pointed at the region to the top of the plan, marked in green.

'This is where they keep the animal subjects. Nobody exactly knows what they do down here, but there are rumours, stories. It might be something as benign as a vicious guard dog…'

'… dogs…' I corrected him.

The sound was getting closer and louder, and it became

easier to discern multiple voices in the mix.

'... dogs,' agreed Jo Jo. 'but I wouldn't want to chance it. We need to go, and fast.'

I didn't need telling twice. I was already at the doorway and looking out. The corridor was clear of dogs, vicious or otherwise, for now.

'We go left,' yelled Jo Jo, but I was already moving in that direction, away from the hub and back towards the White Room.

The barks, loudly reverberating from the walls now, were coming from the right and whilst escape was important, my reflexes prioritised not getting ripped to shreds.

Jo Jo was already at my shoulder and moving past me within a few strides. The noise was getting louder, sounding wetter. I could picture salivating jaws and lolling tongues.

I engaged my thighs and pumped as hard as I could, my heartbeat pulsing in my mouth, in my ears, stretching every under-used sinew to propel myself forward faster and faster, seeking to outpace the slavering horde behind me.

I gasped arrhythmically, all control lost, a desperate attempt to suck in enough oxygen to fuel my screaming muscles. The thumping in my head and the snarling from behind merged into one, a flood of white noise overwhelming my conscious mind, leaving me nothing but instinct with which to drive myself forward.

We thundered past the White Room and into what, for me, was uncharted territory. I tried to conjure up a picture of the wall map in my mind's eye, to get my bearings, figure out which way we were headed.

We had to be getting deeper into the complex, but by this stage I was blindly following Jo Jo as he whipped around bends and crashed through swinging doors. I had to keep pace to avoid getting hit by one rebounding in my face, but Jo Jo was swift. At least he seemed to know what he was doing and where he was going.

We ripped around another corner. I'd expected to find another hub around this bend, but instead there was a wall that we had to skid to the left to avoid crashing into headlong. We sprinted down the left-hand corridor, apparently not considering turning right.

Jo Jo had asked me if I trusted him. I seemed to be demonstrating implicit trust right now, following his every turn without question. In fact, I didn't want to get left behind to be savaged and didn't have the spare lung capacity to question anything.

Despite our random path, the barks and growls were getting louder. The pack - it sounded at a minimum to be a pack - was closing on us, presumably following and potentially spurred on by the scent trail of panic and fear that we left in our wake.

I didn't know how much longer I could keep this up. All that thought did was prompt more fear. It probably made me a tastier quarry.

Jo Jo pulled away and was now a few metres in front of me. He glanced behind us, over my shoulder, and a look of panic flashed across his face. I sincerely hoped that it was merely worry that I wasn't up to this, that I was flagging, which I clearly was, but I could smell them now.

The funk of thick sweat stuck to fur, a wave of raw, bloody meat, the stench of dread: I could almost feel the breath of the beasts at the head of the pack on the back of my neck.

Jo Jo paused, and turned, allowing me to barrel into his arms, the impact of my flailing body almost knocking the slight youth from his feet as he absorbed it.

'What are you doing?' I screamed as he wrapped his arms around me and pulled me sideways.

'In here,' he shouted in reply as, together, we fell through a conveniently open doorway I hadn't even seen.

The room spun as Jo Jo threw me to the floor, wrenching my shoulder as I fell on it, my legs crying in agony from the effort I'd pushed through them, my heart thudding audibly and refusing to slow down.

I lay in a heap, heaving painfully, first with every breath, and then with the bile that hit my throat and wrenched its way out of my mouth.

Jo Jo was searching for a close button. I could see it from where I lay, tried to point, tried to call out. I couldn't force out the words, couldn't control my arm, couldn't attract Jo Jo's attention so that I could show him what I could see.

Tears of anguish and terror and fear and pain, stung my eyes as I scrambled onto my feet. My legs were weak, my lurch for the door control panel ungainly and desperate.

Jo Jo heard the commotion and turned to see me, stained with tears and vomit, tumbling forward with the last ounce of strength that I could muster. He followed my trajectory with his eyes and then he saw it.

He moved quicker than me and, as my strength finally faded and I collapsed to the floor, he was at the panel, hammering at the largest, reddest button.

With fractions of seconds to spare, the door slid shut, snarls and barks and the scratch of sharp claws trapped on the other side.

Jo Jo stood with his back to the door, chest heaving, wincing with every thud of a bloodthirsty body throwing itself against the other side. His eyes were wide.

My world stopped spinning and, gingerly, I sat up.

'You OK?' asked Jo Jo.

'Yeah,' I nodded, before I thought better of it.

Phil Oddy

My head hurt, my chest hurt, my legs hurt and my shoulder hurt. I was feeling nauseous. It didn't help when, apparently reassured that I was OK, Jo Jo dropped his hands onto his knees and vomited too.

'You OK?' I checked.

Jo Jo held out his hand and nodded.

'That was lucky. Was that..?' I wasn't sure.

'Lucky?' Jo Jo asked, looking back at the door.

Right on cue, something banged into the other side, snarling.

'Yeah. Very convenient.'

'Too convenient?' I asked. 'We ran down a lot of corridors with zero open doors. Then, just as we're about to get caught…'

'I'm going to lean into lucky,' said Jo Jo. 'But we are now, effectively, trapped.'

I looked around the room, taking it in for the first time. The only door in or out was the one that we'd just sealed shut and were in no hurry to reopen. Jo Jo was correct. We were trapped.

The room was brightly lit. There were shining metal-topped benches, scattered with equipment that I couldn't identify, high stools randomly placed, as if the occupants of this lab had vacated in a hurry.

On the wall there was the expected plan of the underground Research complex. The red R showed we were in a section dedicated to "Consolidated Research", which was vague enough to mean anything.

There weren't any computers in this one. Instead, there was a shiny metallic pod with a curved glass front, behind which was a small control panel and a swivel chair.

'What's that?' I got up from the floor woozily and wandered over to check it out.

I leaned into the pod. The screen was off. Jo Jo stepped

away from the door, against which bodies thudded another couple of times as he did so. It seemed solid. At least Jo Jo seemed satisfied that it was going to hold, as he came across.

'I don't know,' he said, peering in from the other side.

He tapped at the screen. Nothing happened.

'Hold on.' He grabbed the arm of the seat and swung himself in.

He arched his back and pushed his feet into the floor. A familiar red R symbol appeared in the middle of the screen as it booted up.

'There you go,' he said, grinning. 'It's weight triggered. It went to sleep while the chair was empty. I'm evidently not heavy enough to bring it back on. I wonder who it's calibrated for.'

Symbols streamed across the screen, too fast to read, but I don't think they were words, anyway. Jo Jo tapped at the side and pulled up a menu. The options seemed strange.

'What have we got here?' asked Jo Jo, of nobody. '"Sandtimer", "Pachyderm", "Charges"… what is this?'

He tapped on "Pachyderm". The screen cleared and the words "PROJECT PACHYDERM" appeared at the top.

'Intriguing,' said Jo Jo, just as the words "CLASSIFIED" and "CONFIRM IRIS SCAN FOR AUTHORISATION" flashed further down. 'O… K…'

Jo Jo tapped the option to cancel.

'Pretty sure I don't have security clearance for that,' he grinned. 'But worth bearing in mind. I can't hack what I don't know exists.'

He tried the other menus. They all led to variations on the same screen. He cancelled them all.

'What are you looking for?'

'I don't know,' Jo Jo shook his head. 'Something that will help us out? A Com link with the surface would be outstanding. I'd quite like to talk to Clar right about now. Failing that, some surveillance on the corridor outside would be nice...'

Right on cue, two enormous bodies crashed against the other side of the door. I thought I saw it bow slightly.

'... maybe a kill switch, some kind of dog tranquilising siren..?'

'Is that a thing?'

'I don't know it's not a thing,' shrugged Jo Jo, 'but it doesn't look to be a thing that this computer's going to help me find. Got to do something, though. We can't just sit around and wait to get rescued, especially not since, I don't know if you've noticed...'

'That door will not hold forever.' I finished his sentence for him.

Correctly, it appeared, because Jo Jo just nodded and said nothing more. He tapped at the screen again, choosing different sections, menus and submenus, hitting dead ends and backing out, cancelling warnings, searching, searching.

His actions became increasingly frantic, his taps on the screen striking harder as more and more paths were closed. I watched his face cloud and darken. This did not look good.

The door creaked as more creatures threw themselves at it. I moved away from the pod and stood between it and the door.

I pulled the gun out of my waistband and carefully slid the safety off. I took the box of bullets from my pocket and rested it on a workbench.

Taking a deep breath, I planted my feet firmly, a shoulder's width apart, and took a deep breath. I raised my gun.

Two more bodies thudded against the door. The bulge as it bowed was noticeable now. I didn't know what they were made of, but it would not be enough.

Echoes

Bang! Bang!

Two more, the frequency of the impacts was increasing. It was as if they knew they were making progress, knew they were close to breaking through, with us, their prey, trapped beyond.

My gun hand was wobbling alarmingly. I adopted a two handed grip. It almost helped.

Bang! Bang!

A chink of light from the corridor shone through as the doors briefly came apart before closing. I panicked.

Bang! Bang!

I fired off two shots which struck the doors as randomly as I had loosed them. The clang of the bullets hitting to the door rang out.

'What the fuck?' shouted Jo Jo, and I turned to see him half out of his chair. 'I jumped out of my skin! What are you doing? Don't weaken them any more than they are already.'

'Sorry,' I said, shaking my head desperately. 'I panicked. But listen…'

The sounds of bodies hitting the door had stopped.

'Maybe you scared them off,' said Jo Jo, approvingly. 'Go easy though, try to avoid blowing a hole for them to climb through. I've got to reboot this screen.'

I turned back to the door. I could do this. They wouldn't be able to burst through. They might push the doors open enough to squeeze through but, while they were squeezing, that was my chance.

I could get off enough shots to get one of them in the head. I was sure I could.

I looked at the scuffed burn marks of my previous two attempts. I needed to narrow my odds. Two steps closer. I didn't dare go any further than that.

My world narrowed. There was just me, the gun in front

of me, the doors ahead of that. Tunnel vision blocked out everything else. I just had to wait. When the time came, I had to shoot. We had no other chance.

Bang! Bang!

The doors bulged, but held.

'... Jo...'

A speaker crackled to life. Jo Jo and I looked at each other with hope.

'Jo Jo,' came the voice again. 'Jo Jo, can you hear me?'

Jo Jo leaped out of the chair and ran across to the door. The screen on the pod's console flickered and went dark.

'Estrel, keep that screen live,' he shouted, as he searched the panel, running his finger along the rows of lights and buttons, reading their labels as he went.

He was reading silently, but I could see his lips move. I slid into the seat and the screen flickered back on. I, it seemed, was perfectly heavy enough.

'I can't see where I need to...'

Jo Jo pushed himself away from the wall and spun around on one foot, looking for some kind of microphone to speak into.

'I can hear you, Jo Jo,' said what was now clearly Clar's voice.

'Clar? Where are you?'

Jo Jo walked into the middle of the room and projected his voice upwards.

'I'm back at Eamer's, but help isn't far away,' said Clar.

Relief flooded me. Jo Jo's shoulders dropped as the tension left them.

'I'm glad you're safe. Someone left the security channels open. Was that you?'

Jo Jo grinned to himself.

'Thank fucking… Clar you are a lifesaver.'

'Not me,' said Clar, 'But I know a man who is. Quite literally, I think. Hold the line, caller…'

There was a sudden burst of laser fire on the other side of the door and the sound of half a dozen crazed canines silenced and dropping to the floor.

The door hissed and slid away, revealing the singed and sagging bodies of creatures that may have had some distant relation to a recognisable dog but had long since become estranged. Fangs curled out of their mouths and under their jaw-lines. Claws disappeared into razor points inches from the pads of their paws. Their hides were no longer covered in fur, but were leathery-thick, rippling over taut muscle.

I recoiled. *What the hell*?

'Kind of glad we didn't get caught by those,' said Jo Jo, gingerly stepping over the corpses.

I was waiting to check that none of them jumped up unexpectedly to devour my new friend, before risking the same manoeuvre myself.

Just ahead of us, knelt in the corridor behind a gigantic cannon mounted on a tripod, was a Resistance Agent that I didn't recognise. Behind him was a man in a wheelchair who was lowering some kind of grenade launcher.

'Say thank you to Agent Batt,' said Kap. 'You're lucky Clar spotted you when they did. And that you were so close to that lab. And that I figured out how to get the door open for you. And shut again. You are very lucky.'

Agent Batt? The name wasn't lost on me. Kap had managed to find him, then. I wondered if he'd ever really been lost.

Increasingly, I thought that everything happening to me seemed designed to confuse and disorientate me. I was about to ask, but the name "Agent Batt" meant nothing to Jo Jo and he jumped in first with more immediate concerns.

'What the fuck are they?' asked Jo Jo, pointing at the dead creatures that I found it very hard to still think of as dogs.

'Experiments,' Kap said. 'Maybe failed ones. Maybe successful ones. Hard to tell. You need to get out of here.'

'Kap, you should know... Toshock. We found her.' Jo Jo put a consoling hand on Kap's shoulder. 'She...'

'I know,' sighed Kap. 'It was always a risk. She knew that, I knew that...'

I couldn't quite believe what I was hearing.

'You knew?'

I couldn't hide the shock in my voice. Just when I had thought there was little left to shock me.

'I know a lot,' admitted Kap. 'I didn't think it was necessarily wise, or in fact necessary full stop, to share it all with three random strangers who pitched up on my doorstep.'

'She locked me in a room!' I protested.

'I don't believe that's true,' replied Kap. 'That wasn't part of the plan.'

I let it slide. I wasn't convinced, but I wasn't going to convince him. He was loyal to his General, after all.

'But Toshock wasn't missing?' I almost added "either".

Jo Jo glowered at me, shook his head slightly. I wasn't sure what it meant, but I shut up.

'Toshock's been trying to stop the bombs going off,' said Kap. 'Whoever's planting these devices has been a step ahead of us all day. You need to get out of here.'

'You think it's Authority,' said Jo Jo.

It wasn't a question, but Kap shook his head in answer.

'No, not Authority.'

'Then shouldn't Authority be the ones trying to stop the bombs?' Jo Jo asked.

This seemed very reasonable to me.

'We've been a step ahead of Authority all day,' shrugged Kap, 'which puts our bombers two steps ahead of them. Today we're on the same side. Resistance is fighting for Trinity. It would be nice if Trinity survived long enough for us to win it...'

I became aware of a thundering noise further down the tunnel.

'... and now, if you're done, as I've already said, you need to get out of here.'

The thundering got louder, resolving itself into something like hooves echoing down the tunnel. Hooves, snarls, I imagined I could feel a warm gust of musk rolling towards us.

Batt knelt back down to set up his cannon again. The hairs on the back of my neck pricked.

'There's more?' I asked.

'There's more,' agreed Kap, shouldering his weapon as Agent Batt swung the cannon around. 'You need to get out of here.'

We didn't need telling for a fifth time.

CHAPTER 15

The shaft that we climbed up to street level was much shorter, if no less dark, than the one I'd had to descend. I held it together for long enough to emerge at the other end, into a narrow alley with walls that towered above me.

It was dark here, too. Night had fallen, and the thick blanket of smog that hung moodily over the city blocked any light that might have come from the moon or stars. The shadows that the walls cast just added an extra layer of pitch.

I didn't have to wait long for Jo Jo to finish the climb, but I spent what time I had recoiling from the evil smell. It reminded me of the bodies of the Resistance Agents I'd found after I'd escaped from the White Room - fermenting death, but with an extra dash of excrement.

The walls appeared black, shiny in the dusk. I didn't want to get close enough to find out what was making them glisten.

Jo Jo scrambled from the hole and slid its cover back into place carefully.

'No need to attract attention unnecessarily,' he said in a whisper. 'Man, that's ripe, isn't it?'

'What is it?' I gagged. 'Is there an abattoir around here?'

Jo Jo shook his head.

'Probably best not to know. If you're lucky, it's nothing more than dead rats. If you're unlucky, it's something worse than that. These are The Alleys. Nothing good can come of asking questions around here.'

'The Alleys?'

I noted another example of a tendency in Trinity to take perfectly ordinary nouns and make them proper. I could hear the slight inflection in Jo Jo's voice when he did it.

'They're much like they sound,' explained Jo Jo. 'Alleys. We're close to Docklands here. It's all darkness and dead ends. Very useful if you're a criminal organisation looking for somewhere to conduct your business away from scrutiny. Very dangerous if you're an otherwise innocent party who accidentally finds themselves wandering through without a guide.'

'Like us?'

Out of the frying pan... We were supposed to be climbing to relative safety.

'No, not like *us*,' scoffed Jo Jo. 'Like you, if you didn't have me.'

'You're a guide?'

'I like to think I know my way around. I certainly know the rules of the road. The first of which is: when you smell a smell like that, walk in the opposite direction. Quickly.'

I wasn't sure that I could tell which direction the smell was coming from, which left me very little option other than to follow Jo Jo's lead and hope that his apparent confidence wasn't all bravado.

I patted my pocket to check that I still had my gun. Its firm presence made me feel more secure. I'd even fired it now.

However much Jo Jo claimed to know his way around these

Alleys, we hit many dead ends before I could feel confident that the stench was receding, or before we seemed to make any progress towards anything other than more Alleys.

Eventually we rounded a corner to find ourselves somewhere, if it were possible, even darker and grimier than where we'd come from. It wasn't so much a narrow courtyard as a slightly wider section of alley. A huddle of figures gathered halfway along, seven men facing the wall in a small semicircle.

Jo Jo immediately jumped backwards and flattened himself against the wall. He pushed me back into a similar position.

'Shit,' muttered Jo Jo. 'Mishka. I was hoping to avoid Mishka.'

'Who's Mishka?' I asked.

Jo Jo pointed at one of the men.

'Weasel face. The one buried by the leather trench coat.'

He was shaking something in cupped hands. His focus was intense as he stopped, opened his fist and blew on whatever was inside. Dice, I assumed.

'That's Mishka. Eamer's pet assassin. I don't think…'

'Oi, no spectators!' One of the huddle turned and spotted us.

'Double shit,' spat Jo Jo. 'That's the last thing we need.'

Most of the rest of the group had turned as well, by now, with Mishka standing at the front. They were all sizing us up. It didn't take long.

'Follow my lead,' hissed Jo Jo. 'I must have gone wrong somewhere. If they're gambling here, then we're deep in The Alleys.'

'How deep?'

'Deep enough that no one will find our corpses.'

'Wouldn't you like to join us, lads?' grinned Mishka.

It was the least welcoming smile I'd ever seen. I was pretty certain that no, we would not like to join them.

'We would love a game with you gentlemen,' lied Jo Jo, 'but alas. I don't have my Com.'

'You don't have your Com?' sneered Mishka, sucking his teeth. I was pretty sure that he had fangs. 'Are you a child?'

'Well, no, it's just that…'

'Are. You. A. Child?' repeated Mishka, more forcefully.

The air of menace was palpable. Danger made the air thick.

'I have credits,' I said, without thinking.

It was true, I did. I'd loaded up my Com yesterday, and I'd spent very little since I'd arrived in Trinity. I probably had several hundred at my disposal. Jo Jo's quick-fire glare told me in no uncertain terms that this was not information I should have volunteered.

'Excellent!'

Mishka turned as I felt an arm wrap around my shoulder and firmly guide me towards the game arena. I glanced to my left, into a leather face with brown teeth through which gusted breath of liquorice and tobacco.

I felt him reach into my pocket and extract my gun. As I watched it sail over the wall behind me, I sighed.

'I'm going to do you the courtesy of assuming that you are familiar with the game…' continued Mishka.

I was about to protest, but Jo Jo hissed again in my ear.

'Give me your Com,' he whispered. 'I'll place your bets. Watch him like a hawk. I'll try not to lose you too much money.'

Oh no, my Com… I patted down the pockets of the overall, desperately hoping against forlorn hope that either my captor or my liberator had slipped it back into one of my pockets. I didn't have my Com. Mishka's voice echoed in my head. *Are you a child?*

Echoes

'Jo Jo…'

It was as if he knew what I was going to say before I did. Jo Jo closed his eyes and breathed deeply. When he opened them, they were plated with steel.

'OK,' he said. 'Say nothing. Just know that when we die, it will be your fault.'

'Place your bets!' cried Mishka, scooping his hands in front of him once more.

The lights on six Com screens flashed in the darkness. Jo Jo turned away from the group and moved his hand in a way that suggested he, too, was placing his bet. Only I could see that his hand was empty.

Mishka blew hard into his clasped fists and shook them.

'I've got a good feeling about this, boys!'

He whooped and thrust his hands out in front of him. Unexpectedly, a small, plastic horse left the fist of the weasel-faced assassin, spun through the air, and rebounded off the dirty brick wall in front of him.

The spin was perfect, the flick of Mishka's wrist on-point, and the horse stopped dead and dropped, falling only an inch from the wall. There was a collective intake of breath, a momentary grumble, the beginning of protests.

To my surprise, Jo Jo stepped forward and trapped the horse under the toe of his boot. The grumbles turned into howls of complaint from the assembled gamblers. Given what Jo Jo had just said, I remained silent.

Mishka spun on his heel to face Jo Jo.

'You can't do that!' His snarl cut through the thick air.

In a moment, he was nose-to-nose with Jo Jo. Mishka was the smaller man, but he was coiled like a lethal spring. I didn't fancy Jo Jo's chances at all.

'I just did, though,' shrugged Jo Jo. 'We need to get to Eamer's. We don't have time to waste playing games.'

He stared into Mishka's face, which was fractions of inches from his now. I admired how he held his stare.

'But thank you for your gracious invitation.'

He seemed so relaxed, so cool. With what little knowledge I had of Mishka, I felt anything but cool. I felt like I was sweating inside, my breath short, every sense on high alert ready to run. It seemed like all eyes were on Jo Jo right now, but I would not risk even one still being on me. I remained stock still.

Mishka was baring his teeth now, showing off actual fangs, weapons that I could easily picture him using to gouge the flesh of his victims. His fists were clenching and unclenching. Sweat was popping out all over his brow and his eyes were wide and wild.

I calculated that Jo Jo had about twenty seconds left before he would have no choice but to move his foot.

'I don't know why you think I'm going to help you with that.'

Mishka flashed a grin, looking as much like a threat as any grimace.

'Just let us slip away.' Jo Jo's voice took on a soothing tone. I don't know how he managed it. 'None of these fine gentlemen,' and at this point he gestured to the huddle of gamblers who seemed to be anything but fine gentlemen, 'will think any the less of you. Mercy is an admirable quality in someone who so regularly dishes out death. Take a break, have a day off…'

There was a rumble from the group. They couldn't hear what Jo Jo was saying and were imagining a stitch up.

I had heard what Jo Jo had said, and I knew he wasn't attempting a stitch up, but I wasn't at all sure what he *was* trying to do and, regardless, I didn't see it working. However, I hadn't left us with many options and I couldn't be anything other than grateful for him taking his life in his hands to come and piss off a dangerous man.

There was hope in every second that passed in which we weren't getting stabbed.

Those could have been famous last words, as something flashed in Mishka's hand, a chink of reflected light. I saw the knife, but my voice stuck in my throat, my hand stayed stuck to my side.

Before I could react, there was a flurry of movement in the shadows and Clar materialised behind Mishka, with his wrist in their hand.

'What did I tell you last time?' they said. 'Play nicely.'

Mishka yelped, tried to pull his hand back, but Clar's grip was firm.

'Well, if it isn't Mouse's puppy dog. Does your Mistress know you're out on your own after dark?'

He leaned in and whispered something into Clar's ear. Clar's face gave little away, but I saw a shadow drift across their impassive features for a second.

'Come on,' said Clar, through slightly gritted teeth, 'there is no need for that. All we're asking is that you don't stab Jo Jo. That's not much to ask. He can owe you…'

Now it was Clar's turn to lean in and whisper something in Mishka's ear. Mishka's poker face was much weaker than Clar's. His eyes grew wide, visibly panicked. Clar leaned back, smiling.

'Nice throw, by the way.'

I looked down to where, in stepping back from Mishka's lunge, Jo Jo had removed his boot from over the horse. It sat upright on its hooves.

There was a yelp of delight from Mishka and a grumble of complaint from the rest of the crowd. Coms beeped as credits changed hands and Clar slipped away towards Jo Jo, into the far shadow. I scurried around the group to join them.

'Come on,' Clar urged. 'While his attention is elsewhere. Also, I ripped off fifty credits, so we need to be not here when he finds out.'

I glanced back. Mishka was frowning at his Com screen, apparently trying to do some complicated maths.

'Wasn't that excessively risky?' I asked.

'He owes me,' Clar said, with a shrug. 'At least that much. But we should go. You know, if we want to stay alive.'

Clar strode through The Alleys with a sense of purpose that had evaded Jo Jo. Jo Jo himself brought up the rear but that didn't stop me constantly looking over my shoulder to make sure that we weren't being followed by a newly impoverished hitman who wanted to punish us for his misfortune.

As if I wasn't twitchy enough at the thought of who or what else might lurk in the considerable shadows waiting for unsuspecting prey.

We approached Eamer's bar from the back. It loomed out of the darkness, three stories jutting out from between semi-derelict warehouses, a profoundly unwelcoming place.

The Alleys faded behind us and we made our way into a wide yard strewn with rubbish, rusting delivery vehicles and empty pallets. I would have described it as a delivery yard, except that it didn't seem that anyone had made any deliveries for some time.

Stepping over broken glass, I tried to pick out a doorway from the gloom, in case I had to make a run for it.

'Watch out for the corpse,' said Clar, nodding at what I had taken to be a pile of bin bags.

I jumped fully into the air in shock. Behind me, Jo Jo burst out laughing.

'You completely took off there! Both feet off the ground!

They're probably just drunk.'

The corpse groaned and brought up the contents of its stomach. I jumped sideways to avoid the ripe, fermented sludge.

'How do we get in?'

Clar motioned, of course, to the darkest corner of the yard, in which I was going to have to trust there was a door. Above their head, a light went on in a first-floor window, a violet bulb swaying in the middle of an empty pane.

'Back door's over there,' they said. 'We just…'

'Hey sweetheart!'

I looked up at the sound of the voice from the first-floor window. A barely clad blonde woman hung out, backlit with violet clouds of vapour enveloping her head from the pipe in her mouth, attached to a device out of sight in the room behind her. She was wearing her underwear, at least on her top half. It left little to the imagination.

'You couldn't stay away, huh?'

'Huh?' I repeated.

I'd heard what she'd said, but also thought that I couldn't have heard what she said because she seemed to think I was a client of hers. I felt the flush of my cheeks in the dark.

'Come up and see me, sweetheart! You know I keep the bed warm for you!'

The woman blew me a kiss and disappeared inside, pulling down the wooden blind. Jo Jo gave me a quizzical look through the gloom.

'I do not know who that is,' I protested.

Given that it was true, I couldn't have sounded less convincing. I was feeling very guilty about something I hadn't done. That I wasn't about to do.

'Laihla seems to know who you are,' Clar grinned. 'And Laihla never forgets a face. Or, so I'm told, a…'

'Yeah, I think she might have confused me with someone else,' I snapped, flashing another nervous glance up at the empty window.

'I think that's likely.' Clar suppressed a laugh.

I looked ahead and realised that they were holding a heavy metal door open. A grey light spilled out into the gloom of the yard, parting the darkness. It didn't, however, make the entrance appear any more welcoming.

'Through there?'

I very much hoped that the answer was going to be "no".

'Welcome to Eamer's,' said Clar. 'I know it doesn't look like much.'

They peered through the doorway.

'Actually, it looks like the worst place in the world and that wouldn't be entirely wrong... But, if anything, this is the more sophisticated way to enter this renowned establishment. Less chance of treading in pools of vomit, anyway. More chance of being catcalled by the working girls, to be fair.'

I noted that there was, in fact, a pool of vomit just behind us I had only recently narrowly avoided. I noted it silently, however. It must be grim around the front.

'Mouse is in there?' I checked.

'She is. Take a sharp right when you go through the door and head down the stairs into the basement,' warned Clar. 'If you carry on down the corridor, you'll find yourself in the bar. Don't go into the bar.'

'Don't go into the bar,' repeated Jo Jo.

'Don't go into the bar,' confirmed Clar. 'It's possible you'll be recognised. And it's certain we'll never be able to get you out again.'

I laughed, looking at Jo Jo.

'You? Given how unfazed you were by being chased by hordes of slavering dogs...'

'They weren't dogs…' said Jo Jo.

'… or you by breaking up an assassin's gambling ring,' I looked at Clar. 'Yet you don't think you could pull me out of a bar.'

Clar smiled knowingly and shook their head.

'Welcome to Eamer's!'

I proceeded through, ducking my head to avoid the dripping pipe above the doorway.

CHAPTER 16

As instructed, I took a sharp right as soon as I passed through the door. The staircase was made of winding iron, some of it painted red, much of it rusting, and descended into the stuffy darkness of a large cellar.

I expected a cellar under a bar to be filled with barrels and bottles, but this one had a large generator filling most of it, with a wide chimney taking up the rest. The generator was silent and cold. If it were running, I imagined that the room would be unbearably hot and loud.

I reached the bottom step and took several paces into the room. There was no one else there. As I turned, Clar's head appeared below ceiling level.

'So where's Mouse?' I asked.

I'd been promised that she was going to be here. Clar took a moment to look around before stating the obvious by way of a non-reply.

'Mouse is… not here. She told me she was going to be stuck here until she got the generator working. Eamer was less than pleased when she came back.'

'Less than pleased that she'd left or less than pleased that she'd come back?' I asked.

'Either. Both. Regardless, she said she needed to keep her head down and do what she was told.'

'So where is she?'

Clar seemed to be deliberately not answering my question, and I was feeling frustrated. Everything I'd gone through to get here was punching me in the back of the head, calling me an idiot, asking me why I'd ever thought I could rely on her.

'Maybe she got told something else,' Clar shrugged.

At least I thought they shrugged. It was hard to tell when I could only see their head.

'Stay there, I'm going up.'

'Wait but…' Before I could finish, Clar was gone.

I took a deep breath, pulled a face, and stuck my hands in my pockets. One of them hit something soft, and I pulled it back out, bringing the crumpled paper with it. I'd forgotten about the Echo, with the adrenaline of the last hour. Looking around for a flat surface, I smoothed it out on top of the generator.

So much for keeping faith with the Echo, so much for finding Mouse. So much for trusting Mouse. That was working out really well. Where was she?

Right now it seemed that Mouse had a talent for never quite being there when I needed her to be. The whole "of course I'm here to help but let's fence this Com first" saga was feeling even more disingenuous now.

Perhaps she'd never been there for me, had no intention of being there for me. Perhaps the world didn't revolve around me and perhaps I was overthinking this.

Except I was stuck in a time loop. Literally, everything was revolving around me. I stayed still while the world kept going. Around me.

I stared at the words FIND MOUSE again, the crude map

that led to nowhere. Left for me by someone I didn't trust.

Someone who had kept me prisoner. Unless they were the ones who released me?

Someone who had tried to help me. Unless they were the ones who tried to warn me?

Why did I need to find Mouse? What was Mouse to me?

Caveats, I thought. *I need to hurry.* I looked at the list of times, the reassurance that I still had hours left before I reset.

What if all the times were wrong? What if I looped now? I would have no way of knowing that they were wrong on the next loop, either. Maybe that had happened before. I was assuming the loop was the same length every time. What if it wasn't?

What if the reset time was random? Or it could be predictable, but adhering to a pattern I hadn't yet identified. I scrutinised the later times; the ones written in red crayon. They looked like I wrote them, but to be honest, how could I tell? The digits were thick and chunky, poorly formed in an attempt to stop the tissue from tearing.

The more I stared at it, the less I believed it was real. I screwed it up in my hand, raised my fist to throw it away. But my arm wouldn't move, my hand wouldn't release.

I lowered my arm and opened my hand. Slowly, it unfurled in my palm. I couldn't bring myself to do it.

It was all I had. *I definitely wrote most of it.* If I couldn't trust myself, then I couldn't trust anyone. I threw my head back and silently screamed.

Why hadn't I written FIND MOUSE? At no stage, in no iteration, had I felt comfortable enough to tell my future selves that Mouse was trustworthy, that she could help me. Was I wracked with these doubts, these uncertainties, every time?

I made a decision and climbed the stairs.

Without really thinking about it, I found myself in the corridor, heading towards the bar. I had been told not to go there and yet my feet kept moving.

To my left there was a staircase guarded by a burly bouncer in a black fedora who made pointed eye contact with me, wordlessly interrogating me about my intentions. I looked down, avoiding eye-contact, by way of a non-answer.

I had nothing specific in mind. It definitely didn't involve going up the stairs. Not if I could help it. Laihla would be up the stairs and whilst I was sure it would be an interesting diversion to dig into whatever misconceptions she had about who I was, I didn't think it was one I had time for. She also scared me a little.

I pressed on. The doors to the toilets hung precariously on their hinges, insufficient to contain the waves of chemicals and warm piss that flowed from beyond them. I held my breath, gagging as I'd left it too late, and quickened my pace.

The bar was so quiet that I wasn't certain that it *was* the bar I was approaching until I reached the threshold. This was not the den of iniquity that I had been warned so strongly about. There were empty booths along two of the walls, the counter itself running along the third, at which two hunched figures sat at opposite ends with a large screen on the other wall playing to their shoulders.

There was no sign of Clar, or Jo Jo, but Mouse stood polishing a glass behind the bar. She saw me as soon as I stepped in, and I saw her catch her breath as she did.

'Fuck's sake…'

She was too far away for me to hear, but I could read her lips.

It wasn't as if I had expected her to be pleased to see me. I approached, and to my surprise Mouse put down her glass and cloth and leaned over the bar, throwing her arms out.

Echoes

I leaned forward and let her grasp me awkwardly around the back of my neck, while the edge of the counter top dug in just below my ribs. I could feel my shirt getting damp around the middle as it soaked up the lake of spilled drinks.

'You keep doing this, you dick.' Her breath was warm against my face. 'This is exactly how I remember it.'

She pulled back and let me go. I thought I saw a tear in her eye. This was not the reception that I'd expected, and not one that I'd prepared myself for.

I saw something vulnerable and tender where previously I'd only seen something cold and evasive. She seemed to be fond of me. Once again, I didn't know how I felt about her.

'I… how did you find me? How did you get out?' she asked.

Without checking what I wanted, she grabbed a tankard and filled it with beer. She could have been reading my mind. I almost salivated at the sight.

'Long story.'

I picked up the drink. I didn't want to get into it. Didn't want to get into what I'd been through to get here, or how conflicted I was about whether it was a good idea.

'Jo Jo helped, and Clar. They brought me here. I was looking for Clar. Just now, they came to find you.'

'Funny, they didn't mention it,' said Mouse, lifting a section of the bar and stepping out to my side.

I turned in the direction she was inclining her head, to see Jo Jo lurking in the shadows of a booth.

'Clar slipped out.'

I got the impression that sliding in and out was very much how Clar moved through people's lives. Their absence made me feel a little less secure.

Jo Jo had been nothing but helpful, but Clar made me feel like everything was going to be OK in a way that I really needed now that I was back around Mouse. Because Mouse was having the opposite effect.

'Take a seat. I'll join you in a minute,' she said, clearing some glasses from a nearby table.

I raised my beer to my lips with one hand and raised the other to acknowledge Jo Jo. He waved back and I walked across the sticky vinyl floor to the booth.

Jo Jo and I waited ten minutes, silently nursing our drinks. We felt the impact of the events of the last few hours; there was no need for us to dissect them.

For me, at least, the lull of the quiet bar was like a balm on the raw wounds left by the escape from Research and the trek through The Alleys. We sat, and breathed, and drank, and enjoyed not needing to talk.

I would have described it as time to think, except it wasn't. I didn't think, at least not any more deeply than to acknowledge the series of lurid images that elbowed their way into my mind's eye.

I acknowledged them, sipped my beer, and let them go.

Then Mouse slid into the booth, but at least she brought drinks, which was helpful as I had almost finished my ale by the time she sat down.

'What's this?' Jo Jo held a wide-brimmed glass up to the light. 'It's green.'

'It's Green,' repeated Mouse. 'I thought that's what you were drinking at the moment.'

Jo Jo pulled a face. This wasn't what we were drinking at the moment, either of us, and there was no way that Mouse thought it was.

I couldn't tell if she was trying to be funny or get us drunk. Mouse waved a hand in the air and behind her head, without looking away from us. A server I hadn't previously noticed arrived at the table with a tray.

I drained my glass, tasting apple. I'd expected mint.

'This is the sort of service I could become accustomed to.'

'This is Kashka,' said Jo Jo, meaningfully, although I didn't know what the meaning was.

He turned his head to Kashka and smiled. Kashka looked nervous, like she didn't know whether to acknowledge the familiarity. Smart girl, I thought, uninvited familiarity is probably dangerous around here.

'It's OK,' Jo Jo reassured her. 'He's with us. He's had a bad day.'

Kashka smiled, relaxing, and a look came into her eye that matched the one that Jo Jo had in his. I got the impression that they knew each other well.

'Are you on your own?' she asked, picking up our empty glasses, without taking her eyes off Jo Jo.

The presence of me and Mouse didn't seem to count. Jo Jo laughed.

'Clar's gone to check something out,' he said. 'But don't worry, they'll be back. I'll make sure they know you were asking after them.'

'Thank you,' giggled Kashka. 'And I was asking after both of you…'

She quickly reached out and touched Jo Jo's cheek. Now I really felt like I was intruding on something. I also realised that I hadn't asked where Clar was.

Mouse had said Clar had "slipped out to check on something". I felt like that was reassuring. I don't know why I assumed that what they were checking out was related to me and my situation, but I did, and I felt better knowing that Clar was on the case.

It sounded like they'd be back soon.

'I'll have another…'

I was apparently buzzed enough from alcohol not to worry about interrupting whatever it was that was happening.

'…and whatever my friend actually wants.'

I gestured at the Green.

'You can probably take that away.'

'I didn't say that,' said Jo Jo, picking it up, 'but I will also take a vodka. Straight.'

Kashka turned, with a flick of her hips and a half-blown kiss, and went to get the drinks.

'So what now?' asked Mouse.

I'd been certain that I knew how I was going to play things when I found her again. Now I wasn't sure what was going on. The way she'd greeted me, expletives and a hug, seemed emblematic of the confusion that set in whenever I was with her.

I thought I should be on my guard. I wasn't, and it wasn't just the alcohol. It went back to the sincere, but awkward, hug. I realised that however much I was trying to be sensible, part of me liked being around Mouse. Quite a big part of me, if I was honest.

'You tell us,' said Jo Jo. 'You're the one with the memories.'

'Of dreams I thought I'd had,' protested Mouse.

She hadn't brought herself a glass of Green and sipped at a red wine. I wondered if she was indeed trying to get us both drunk, and if so, why? There was no consistency. I couldn't get a handle on her.

Was that what I was enjoying? That didn't sound like me.

'I'm not sure they count as memories. They're not exactly detailed. And I don't even know if trying to retrace those steps is a good idea.'

'How do you mean?' I asked, although I thought I agreed.

'Well,' Mouse said, 'I'm not sure we got anywhere. You wrote nothing on your Echo. From this point we've got what, about six hours? We could well have frittered that away, learning nothing.'

'I've learned that I don't like this green stuff,' said Jo Jo, shaking his head.

'That was part of it,' said Mouse, glancing at me. 'That's what you were drinking, last time. You got through two bottles of Green. I thought if I triggered a sense memory or something… I don't know. This is stupid…'

'I've learned that you don't like my idea of reuniting you two to see what happens…' said Jo Jo.

'Didn't say that,' said Mouse, 'but I don't know where we go from here. Estrel? What do you think?'

I hadn't had a chance to think about that. Not to say that there wasn't a lot going on in my head, but I hadn't processed most of it yet. I wasn't entirely sure that I trusted most of what I'd processed up to now, either.

'I…' I threw up my hands in lieu of actual words.

A squeak by my shoulder told me that Kashka had brought our drinks. She looked taken aback. I apologised.

'Don't mind him, he's excitable.' Jo Jo dumped the vodka into the glass of Green.

Kashka said nothing and scuttled away.

'So what do we do?' I asked.

'I think that's up to you,' replied Mouse. 'I mean, you're the one currently without a tomorrow. I'll try anything. Both of us are here for you. We'll do anything, go anywhere…'

Jo Jo necked the vodka and Green, raising the glass in the air.

'Wherever the wind takes me,' he toasted.

I looked from Jo Jo to Mouse and back again. Jo Jo was looking flushed, and I could tell his attention wasn't with us. His eyes kept flicking back to the bar where Kashka was loading the dishwasher.

I thought that coming back here, reuniting with Mouse, was going to give me some answers. The only thing I could see myself getting at the moment was a hangover. Except I'd reset before it kicked in.

I could think of worse plans. I needed to be more proactive than that, though.

'I think I want to get out of here.'

Was that a surprise? I hadn't expected that it was going to come out of my mouth.

It made some sense, though, at least to me, at least at this moment. Everything else seemed impossible. Finding my bag, retrieving my tablet from the rubble of the Administration building, constructing a new, elaborate web of Echoes. Maybe I didn't have to do any of it though. Maybe I could try walking away. If it didn't work, I wasn't going to lose anything I hadn't lost already.

'Makes sense, this place is a dive,' laughed Jo Jo, as Mouse punched him firmly in the arm.

He hadn't understood.

'No, I mean out of Trinity,' I explained. The more I said it, the more I meant it. 'I want to go home.'

Jo Jo's grin settled into something more serious. Maybe he wasn't that drunk after all.

'You know you might just end up here again?' he pointed out. 'When you reset.'

I hadn't thought of that. For some reason, I'd definitely felt that leaving Trinity behind would also leave the time loop behind. But, of course, Jo Jo was right. There was every chance I'd just end up back on the train this morning, heading into the city, ready to do it all again.

'I know,' I said, to cover myself.

At least, for the first time today, I felt like I was leading, directing events, and in a direction that actually felt comfortable to me. Even if I hadn't quite got all the details down.

'But it's worth a try. I don't feel safe here and I still don't know what happens if I die.'

That was something else. Even sitting here in a quiet bar there was every chance that, within minutes, something would have plunged me straight back into danger. I could live without that, even if it was only for a few hours.

'You might die trying to leave,' said Mouse. 'It's not necessarily straightforward.'

Which was another excellent point. It was almost as if there were no good options open to me, which was no surprise.

'But you can help, right?' I asked.

She'd got me out once, she could do it again. Mouse nodded.

'Sure. I think I can…'

In that pause, everything came rushing towards me, like a flood. That was it, then. I was going to leave. I was going to go home. Relief filled me. The tension and anxiety that had been so ever present were flushed out. My eyes moistened.

'Tha…'

My voice cracked. I didn't say it.

'What about Eamer?' asked Jo Jo. 'You've only just come back. Isn't it risky for you? Leaving the city again?'

'Don't worry about Eamer,' grinned Mouse. 'I know what I…'

There was a loud bang, followed by a clatter and a muffled pop.

'Fuck's sake…'

Mouse stood up and turned towards the corridor back to the generator room. But then she paused, and something passed across her eyes.

'I… Estrel, come with me,' she said.

Phil Oddy

She didn't give me time to question it. Looking back, I didn't have to do what she said. Only moments earlier I decided I was done with following, following Mouse especially, and yet here I was doing just that.

Mouse was out of the booth and marching across the room to the corridor. I trotted behind.

'Is something wrong?' I asked.

There had definitely been an explosion, which on a day of bombings was not a good thing, but Mouse's reaction hadn't suggested fear, or even unease. If anything, she seemed perturbed.

'We'll see.'

Mouse swept out of the bar and into the corridor, past the stinking toilets and the heavy guarding the stairs. She nodded at him, and he tipped his hat, deferentially.

That was weird, I thought. Mouse obviously held some status. Was she really in the doghouse with Eamer? This just fed into the reasons that I couldn't get a handle on her. More ambiguity, more confusion.

She vanished down the spiral stairs at the end of the corridor. I followed, again avoiding eye contact with the guy in the fedora. I was only halfway down to the cellar before I choked on the toxic cloud of fumes.

'Mouse?' I called into the fog.

There were a series of bangs and the grinding of some gears that were not keen on cooperating. I heard a yelp. Mouse emerged pulling a surly boy who was sucking the base of his thumb. She had him by the elbow.

'Estrel,' said Mouse. 'Meet Miguel.'

'Hi Miguel.'

''Strel,' mumbled Miguel, his hand in the way of anything clearer. He took it out of his mouth and waved it at me.

'Burned my hand. That thing gets hot.'

Another bang and a puff of smoke exploded out of the murk.

'Miguel helps around here,' explained Mouse, 'while his mum is working. Upstairs.'

I got her meaning.

'Ah right,' I said.

Poor kid.

'What was wrong with it?' asked Mouse, looking at the generator as it belched more smoke.

The stench in the enclosed space was making me feel ill. I thought that a more pertinent question was what was wrong with it now.

'I thought it was the genhead…' sighed Miguel, putting his hands on his hips and staring at the machine.

I got the sense that he was trying to give the impression that he understood far more about the workings of a generator than I suspected he did.

'…but I'm doubting it now. I gave it a thump and it kind of started up again. But… you know. It doesn't seem exactly healthy.'

The kid had a gift with an understatement. The grinding noise went up a couple of semitones.

'The… genhead,' nodded Mouse.

The fumes were making me feel light-headed now. I giggled. There was something about the way she said it. Maybe the Green was getting to me as well.

'Yeah.' Miguel smirked a little. 'The genhead. That's a thing. A thing that this generator has, probably. It's not genning much right now, but that might be the fault of the regulator over… regulating or…'

'Switch it off Miguel,' said Mouse.

Miguel disappeared into the smoke. After a prolonged

pause, during which Mouse and I stared at each other, eyebrows raised, the generator fell silent with a final grinding roar. Miguel reappeared as the smoke receded, sucked up through the chimney, and funnelled away. The smell, however, lingered.

'We're going to leave you,' Mouse put her foot on the bottom step, 'to think about whether the noxious atmosphere in here might signal some sort of combustion-slash-exhaust problem or whether the problem is one of…'

'Of…?' asked Miguel,

'…of lack of expertise on your part. I'm sorry, Estrel, I thought there was something here you needed to see, but it turns out that I might have just given you a headache.'

She had given me a headache. My head was pounding, but I didn't quite understand what she meant. I seemed to have surrendered control, reduced back to chasing around after Mouse.

I had wanted to leave. I'd forgotten that, it seemed, very quickly.

'It was here, wasn't it?' I asked.

'Where you disappeared? Yes, it was here. Not now though. It was…'

She screwed up her face. I could see her trying to summon a memory that was evading her.

'… later,' she finished, weakly.

'OK,' I said, slowly. 'But there was something else, something you thought was happening now. After the explosion..?'

'After the explosion, yeah.' Mouse ran her hand through her hair. 'It's gone. I thought the generator starting up was going to show us something, give us some sort of clue, but…'

She shot a look at Miguel.

'Fix it properly!' she shouted, coming up the stairs.

A funny look came across her face, another shadow. She raised her head to look me in the eye.

'I've got a feeling we should be back in the bar right now. That you should be back in the bar.'

'I want to go home,' I said, trying not to sound too pathetic.

'You need to be in the bar,' she insisted.

Despite myself, I went.

When we got back to the bar, Jo Jo was staring across at the giant screen, which was filled with images of smoke, rolling in grey clouds. It looked a lot like a feed from the cellar might have done a few minutes earlier.

In the foreground, a reporter was commentating with his finger in his ear, trying to block out the background noise, while vague shapes materialised and dematerialised through the haze behind him.

'Another bomb?'

Mouse slid back into the booth. Jo Jo nodded, without taking his eyes off the screen.

'They've hit the Citadel, again. Or nearby, anyway. One of the tram stops, it sounds like. Smothson Place, or Tyndyll Wheel. This guy…' Jo Jo gestured at the reporter on the screen, 'seems to have been there when it went off. Following the White convoy…'

'They bombed Jack White?'

From the look on her face, I could tell that Mouse was genuinely shocked.

'He's missing,' Jo Jo nodded, 'but it's not looking good. It ripped apart his Pod. Evie was in the vehicle behind. They just interviewed her. She didn't say it, but I don't think she thinks that he's still alive. Seems like your hypothesis might need revising in light of new information.'

'Hypothesis?' I asked. 'What hypothesis?'

'I assumed it was Resistance planting the bombs,' explained Mouse, rubbing her chin thoughtfully. 'It seemed to make sense. Administration, Authority, the Dome, the Devoted, Chaguartay all seemed to be targets. They have thrown the city into chaos. It seemed like the sort of thing they'd be into...'

'But Kap didn't...' I began.

'Kap's crafty,' said Mouse. 'That could all have been for our benefit...'

I thought about what Kap had said to us when he rescued us back in Research. He hadn't been telling us the whole truth in the bunker, but not in the way Mouse had assumed. Not that she was to know that, mind you.

'But hitting Opposition?' she continued. 'Taking out the one chance anyone has of deposing Chaguartay without all-out civil war? That doesn't seem smart. It doesn't feel like it makes sense. They're meant to be on the same side...'

'Well, I don't think I'd go as far as to put it that way,' said Jo Jo. 'But they're both *against* the same side.'

'Which usually means the same thing...'

Something occurred to me.

'The Resistance squad we found in Research was trying to stop a bomb,' I said. 'And Kap said they knew it was going to go off. It sounds like they had an idea who was behind it.'

'Wait, what Resistance squad?' asked Mouse, interested. 'You saw Kap again?'

'Clar was going to tell you,' said Jo Jo. 'But then they didn't.'

This comment, which was both true and hinted at something else bubbling under the surface, puzzled me. I wondered, again, where Clar was, exactly, and what had caused them to disappear so suddenly. Mouse didn't seem fazed, though.

'And they were trying to find a bomb?' asked Mouse. 'Or a bomber?'

'Possibly both,' said Jo Jo. 'They were dead before I could ask them any questions.'

'One of them thought I'd planted it,' I added. I thought that was helpful.

Mouse's brow wrinkled. Apparently it wasn't helpful, it was confusing.

'I thought you said they were dead,' she accused.

This took me aback. I knew I had nothing to hide, but still felt worried about crumbling under her scrutiny.

'He died fairly soon after he accused me of that,' I said, 'before Jo Jo arrived.'

Mouse could have looked more convinced, I thought, but she didn't press any harder.

The indistinct undertones of the voices coming from the screen changed in cadence and pitch. A woman with a fierce wound above her eye was being interviewed.

The screen drew my attention. In the corner of my eye, Mouse threw her hands up, looking at Jo Jo.

'This might have been important information!'

I didn't catch what she said next. Something about the woman on the screen seemed familiar to me.

I'd seen her earlier today, back in the reception at Administration, but that wasn't it.

Something was nagging at me, like an itch down my back, hard to reach, hard to scratch, but I felt like I didn't just recognise her. I *knew* her.

I hadn't felt that before, but I really felt it now. Maybe that was because now I could hear her voice. I felt drawn to her.

It was like she was trying to tell me something. Her eyes, through the Com screen, locked with mine and I knew she could see me. Even though I knew she couldn't.

I turned my attention back to Mouse and Jo Jo, who seemed to be arguing now. Mouse, in particular, seemed put out.

It was apparently Jo Jo's turn to throw his hands in the air.

'I don't see that it matters,' he insisted. 'I got Estrel out. Now we need to get him out of here and then we can worry about it.'

'I'm worrying about it now,' spat Mouse. 'If Chaguartay and White are both targets, then this isn't what we're used to. This is a whole new threat. Someone's actually trying to destabilise the city.'

'And it's working,' Jo Jo agreed. 'But Estrel wants out, and it's not his fight!'

At least he was in my corner.

'Maybe it is, maybe…' Mouse didn't seem convinced. 'Maybe it does have something to do with him. Maybe this does relate to this… this time loop or whatever. Maybe it is his fight and maybe he doesn't get to walk away…'

I heard the words, but I didn't really process them. I had stopped listening.

I knew what I found so familiar, so compelling, about the woman projected in front of me.

'Who's that?' I asked, pointing, although deep down I already knew.

Jo Jo and Mouse both turned in their seats.

'That's Evie White,' said Jo Jo. 'Potentially grieving widow. Probably grieving. Miss Evandra Chaguartay, as was. Why?'

I knew who she was. I knew what I needed to do.

I needed to change direction, yet again, but at least this time it was my decision to do so.

'I don't want to leave Trinity,' I said.

Jo Jo's face fell. I felt bad. He'd been sticking up for me. I also saw the look that Mouse shot him across the table. I wasn't keen on giving her the satisfaction, but I knew I had little choice. Not now. I thought there was no way I was going to get any answers, not on this loop. But here was my last hope.

'I need to talk to her. Can you find her? Tonight?'

Mouse sat back in her seat, folded her arms and looked me up and down.

'Don't need to find her,' said Mouse, glancing up at the screen as a tear rolled down Evie White's face. 'She's right there, at the Citadel. Why do you need to talk to her? What's going on, Estrel?'

'I don't know,' I admitted, and I didn't really, 'not until I get to talk to her. But she knows something, something about why I'm here.'

'How do you know that?' asked Jo Jo. 'You only just found out who she is.'

I took a deep breath.

'I know her voice,' I said.

It was her. I knew it was her. She was the voice in the White Room, the one with the ambiguous story.

"I can't tell you what to do," she'd said. "You're going to have to figure this out for yourself, Estrel."

I was figuring it out. I'd found her. No one had told me what to do, but I knew this was right.

I hadn't yet worked out what it was going to take, but it was time for me to pour my water on the ground.

CHAPTER 17

The miniTram rattled its way through the streets of Trinity, taking us towards the Citadel. It wasn't busy, and we sat near the back, with me taking the double seat in front of Mouse.

Rain freckled the window lightly, smearing the streetlights and the neon signs of dubious night-time entertainments. We were leaving Docklands, which left everything a little less grimy and a little more bright, the contrast turned up on the tram window as we headed towards the centre.

I turned around to talk to Mouse.

'So you know her?' I asked. 'Evie White. How?'

'I know many people.' Mouse waved a hand dismissively. 'Maybe even most people.'

'But you? Miss Underworld? I would have thought your connections were... of a different nature. She's one of the most influential people in the city and...'

I thought they must move in very different circles.

'And I'm a bartender to dubious characters?' asked Mouse with a slight smile. 'It's OK, I get why you find it weird. We were at school together. My beginnings weren't as humble as you're assuming.'

She folded her arms and stared at nothing out of the window.

'We weren't friends. But I can get you into the meeting in the Citadel. I can give you an in. The rest is up to you. You can tell her your story…'

'I don't need to tell her my story,' I said. 'I need her to explain hers. It was her, I know it. When I was deep under, in the White Room. She told me a story, brought me round, showed me the way. I didn't realise it until now, until I heard her voice again. I need to break the cycle. To "pour my water on the ground".'

I had told Mouse and Jo Jo the story. This wasn't as bizarre a reference to throw in as it might have otherwise been.

'And she's going to tell you how to do that?'

Mouse carried on staring out of the window, didn't look at me. I wondered if I'd said something wrong. She seemed so hard-edged it took me by surprise that I'd offended her, that I even could.

I nodded, folded my own arms.

There were two other people on the tram. I glanced across at the woman sat on the other side of the aisle from me. From her overladen bags, loosened clothing and slumped stare, she appeared to be on her way home from her day. She wore the grey uniform I recognised from the factory workers I'd encountered that morning. It seemed like a lifetime ago.

I wondered if it was always like this, if the impact of living this day of all days, over and over again, had any lasting impact on me, whether the effort echoed back with me, even if the detail did not. How could I perceive time in the same way, even just knowing that it didn't work the way I'd assumed?

The phrase "wearing a bit thin" floated up from somewhere deep in my mind. Right now, that was exactly how I felt.

Echoes

I thrust my hands deep into my pockets and slid forward in my seat until I had jammed my knees firmly, if painfully, under the guardrail in front of me. My spine felt like it had to bend at right angles in the middle of my back, it wasn't at all comfortable but like that, with my chin tucked into my chest, my head didn't roll around with the lurching of the Tram and I had a chance of closing my eyes to think.

We were headed to the Citadel. That's where the White convoy had been going before it was attacked. Despite the risk, people seemed to be flocking to the site, to find out what was going on, to mourn, to take in the full gruesome spectacle I wasn't sure what drew people to something like that.

The original crisis meeting about the events of the day, the one that the Whites had been secretly travelling to, was still due to take place, although the nature of the discussion had shifted somewhat. It was also no longer a secret. That was the meeting that Mouse was going to get me into.

There was no plan past that, but at least being in the same room as Evie White would be a start. I assumed she'd recognise me, that she'd pull me aside, grant me a private audience…

I didn't know. I was making plans on the fly. Getting in was step one, the rest I could figure out afterwards.

Jo Jo hadn't volunteered to come with us. He'd said something about having things to catch up on whilst exchanging loaded glances with Kashka. I could imagine what they had to catch up on. It didn't seem that they were going to wait for Clar, after all.

I wondered again where Clar was, what they were doing, why they'd left without saying goodbye. I was so close now, I knew it. So close to an answer, both an explanation and a solution, I hoped, although I'd settle for either.

And then I'd write it down in bold capital letters on an

Echo to remove any last trace of doubt. I would have liked Clar to be there for that. It would also have been reassuring to have their significant presence around. Just in case.

I breathed out. I needed to figure out what I wanted to ask Evie White, how to get the answers I needed.

The tram lurched to a halt to let a crowd of new passengers on. I kept my eyes stubbornly shut, so I didn't realise at first but, after a minute, I noticed a musty presence on my left-hand side.

Ignoring whoever it was, I tried to breathe more deeply, mimicking sleep, but I gradually noticed a damp pressure against my arm as they leant into me. I managed only a further fifteen seconds of pretending before I felt a blast of warm air in my left ear.

'Would you like a biscuit?' The voice rasped and bubbled like a half blocked drain.

Disgusted, I slid myself back up, hands still trapped in pockets, shaking my head, looking shocked and trying to appear as if I'd actually just woken. I wasn't sure why it was important, but I felt like I didn't want the stranger to know I'd been trying to ignore him. I got the impression he was volatile, and I was keen to avoid unnecessary danger.

'Wha..?' I asked.

I noticed that Mouse had moved seats to the other side of the aisle, and was now glancing across at me nervously. This didn't seem like a promising sign.

I was tying to figure out what her frantic eyebrows and subtle inclines of the head signified, but all I got was a distinct impression that I should switch seats as well. The moment for me to do that safely had passed, while I'd been pretending to sleep.

'Biscuit?' the man asked, holding up a packet of what I could swear were hog-biscuits.

Echoes

They had "Hog Biscuits" written clearly on the packet.

I grunted, hoping that they would accept this for the universal signal of "no, leave me alone". This would have been the perfect time to pull out my Com and bury my mind in scrolling through the channels. *That* was the universal sign of "no, leave me alone" but, of course, I didn't have my Com.

The stranger seemed to get the hint, for now at least, and leaned the other way. I inspected my fingernails, drummed my fingers on the window, fiddled with my right ear, hoping that he might think I was listening to my non-existent Com on an earpiece that wasn't visible in my reflection. If he could carry on not noticing that for another stop, that would be incredibly helpful.

A sign, reading "Barley Omen, for Tunnel Terminus" flashed past the window and Mouse stood up behind me and made a motion towards the door with her arm.

'This is as close as we're going to get,' she called. 'The cordon's just down there. We'll have to get off here and walk.'

I got to my feet, digging the biscuit guy with my elbow somewhat harder than was strictly necessary as I stood. He got the message, sliding out of his seat and into the one on the other side, next to the woman with the loaded bags. He made a big show of offering her a hog-biscuit as well.

'Thanks for leaving me.'

I looked over my shoulder. The biscuit guy was now on his feet as well. Mouse nodded to him.

'Deakin,' she said.

Deakin smiled, revealing a pair of chiselled fangs, not unlike Mishka's. They were, if anything, even creepier. My head snapped back to Mouse.

'You know each other?' I asked, outraged.

She could have said something. Was that what the eyebrows, and the head tilts, had meant? She could have been clearer.

'Do we?' cackled Deakin, pushing past both of us and clapping Mouse firmly on the shoulder.

Mouse shuddered. This back-story was something I wanted to know. I was also always going to be too scared to ask.

'I'll see you at the meeting. I assume that's where you're going.'

Mouse rested her hand on my chest to slow me down and allow a gap to open up between us and Deakin as he stepped onto the street and turned right towards the walls of the Citadel.

'I'll stick with you,' muttered Mouse as we disembarked the Tram.

She seemed genuinely rattled. I wondered what we were headed into, and whether this brand new plan of mine was such a good idea.

The crowd was thick as we, too, turned towards the Citadel. I had to dart to keep up with Mouse as she disappeared into the throng. Good idea or not, we were doing this now.

I needed Clar. Everything would feel better if Clar were there.

I caught up with Mouse just in time to follow her down a narrow alley, little more than a gap between two ancient buildings. You could tell this part of the city was older, the Citadel being the sunken old centre that they had built the modern Trinity around.

Apparently, at least according to Mouse, it was originally elevated from the plain, providing a perfect base to be defended from invaders who, sailing in from the sea, coming down from the mountains or crossing the Northern Exposure, would have been clearly visible before they could even think about getting within firing range. That was before the foundations of the Citadel, built as they were on top of what was effectively an even older plague pit, gave way, creating the unplanned labyrinth of The Catacombs below and the precarious slant on the towers above.

'We're going to need to play this carefully,' explained Mouse, as we squeezed ourselves to the end of the narrow ginnel. 'They arranged this meeting on the SubCom, secure Coms only, at short notice. No one should know about it.'

'You know about it,' I pointed out. 'There are many people in the street who seem to know about it too.'

'Oh yes, of course I know things. And most of these people don't know about the meeting. They're here for the disaster porn. I'm surprised more weren't scared off. You know, by the bomb… Feelings are really running deep. It's a shame about Jack. I really think he might have had a chance. Except that Chaguartay is going to steal the election anyway, of course. And Jack himself might now be dead, I guess. That's a disadvantage. Anyway, it wouldn't surprise me if they carried on and had the rally, anyway. It's a shame to waste a crowd if you've got one, however sad the circumstances…'

The way Mouse was oscillating between extreme pessimism and macabre realism was not filling me with confidence. To be honest, I didn't care about the undercurrent of unrest, or particularly what came next. I just wanted to talk to Evie White.

I realised Mouse was still talking.

'… but at one point this was a highly secret meeting of significant Opposition persons which no one outside that very select group should have known about. Whoever is planting these bombs managed to plant one on one of the most significant Opposition persons while they were on their way here. And they definitely shouldn't know about it. Not unless they're embedded very deep.'

Mouse stopped by a narrow wooden door, painted black. There didn't appear to be any visible way to open it.

'We can't trust anyone.'

She put her shoulder against the door.

'Fortunately I rarely do.'

The door conceded and Mouse slipped through. I breathed in and followed. We seemed to have broken into a small galley kitchen.

'We're slipping in the back?' I asked.

'We are slipping in the back,' confirmed Mouse.

'How do you know about it? The meeting? Are you a significant Opposition person?'

'Absolutely not!' swore Mouse. 'I have my ear to the ground.'

She laughed, put her hand inside her jacket and pulled out a grey-green box.

'I also have my ear to this field Com I found in a Resistance bunker I visited, up on the Northern Exposure, earlier today.'

I recognised the device that Kap had given her that morning. It hadn't helped us in Research, but it had helped bring me here and that gave me confidence.

Perhaps this was it, how it was meant to happen. Perhaps I'd done everything right after all.

I looked around at hot water urns and rows of poorly washed mugs stacked in front of a wide, shuttered window. Mouse had cracked another door at her end of the kitchen and was peering out.

'We're in the refreshments booth?' I asked.

There was a mini fridge full of canned fermented milk drinks by my feet. I thought about opening some cupboards, to check if a previous me had left any Echoes, but I didn't. I didn't think I needed them anymore. I was so close.

Mouse put her finger to her lips and opened the door a little further. Apparently satisfied, she squeezed through and I followed.

We found ourselves at the back of a large conference hall, banked rows of seats filling up in front of us, descending towards a stage with microphones and empty chairs. There was a gentle hum of subdued conversation, rustles of shuffling papers, and the intermittent chink of teacups on saucers. For a top secret political meeting, it had quite strong philosophy lecture vibes.

'Evie's not here yet,' said Mouse. 'But it's worth you knowing who is who around here.'

She pointed at a crow-faced man with the physique of a starving rake, moving across the stage, shooting a scowl at someone in the audience.

'That's one of Ort'a's students. Rumston, maybe? They all look the same to me, inbred streaks of privileged piss. You know the type?'

I didn't, but I nodded. Ort'a I'd heard of. He'd been Opposition leader at the last election, had his arse handed back to him on a plate, legitimately or otherwise, by Chaguartay, who had taken some eighty per cent of the vote.

'Does he still hold much influence?' I asked. 'Having lost the last election so badly?'

'There's no shame in losing to Chaguartay. It's almost a badge of honour. Besides, half the party, albeit the more snivelling, creepier half, are only here because of him. He still holds considerable sway. Many people wanted him to run again. He probably will again, now. That might explain why so many of them are here so early. Putting in the groundwork.'

I looked around the auditorium, and spotted the guy from the tram, Deakin, talking to an old man in a hood, near the front row. He turned and pointed at me, and then at Mouse. The old man looked in the direction of the point.

'Ort'a's scowl is better than his acolyte's,' observed Mouse. 'Ignore him. He probably can't even see us from there.'

I wasn't so sure, but Mouse seemed relaxed. Ort'a turned back to his conversation with Deakin. I saw him accept a biscuit.

'We should split up,' said Mouse. 'it's kind of obvious we sneaked in with us lurking around here at the back. I'm going down there to see what I can find out, whether Evie's even here yet. You go... somewhere else?'

'OK.'

I wandered right. Mouse descended some steps and appeared to catch the eye of someone at the end of a row. I wasn't certain it was for real.

The guy at the end of the row seemed to fixate on his Com, but she pulled it off with conviction. She at least looked like someone who was meant to be there. Conscious that I probably didn't, I drifted toward a table bearing coffee.

A woman stood by a giant chrome jug, carefully pouring a worryingly light brown liquid into a cracked mug. I spotted the gold Ashuanan elephant hanging from the charm bracelet on her wrist.

'That looks undrinkable,' I ventured, letting my accent come out a bit as I approached the woman from the side.

She looked up and smiled, bright and earnest. Her eyes sparkled at me, and I realised I wouldn't be able to describe what colour they were. I stuck out my hand.

'Estrel Beck,' I said, before I had time to remember that I was supposed to be keeping a low profile and that using my real name might not be wise.

She had to put the jug down and swap her mug to the other hand to take it, all of which left me standing with my hand stuck out long enough for it to feel awkward.

'Sara Chaguartay,' she said, without a trace of an accent, eventually taking my hand and shaking it once.

Chaguartay. Interesting. Potentially useful, potentially dangerous? Too late to do anything about it now, either way. But confusing. Here, at this meeting, and wearing an Ashuanan elephant. Must be a distant relative, though. Evie wasn't from Ashuana, she was from... what had she said? "Beyond Ashuana, the Eastern Deserts". I wasn't even sure where that was.

'Hello Sara.' I ploughed on, with a smile that I hoped was warm and welcoming, but I worried might be creepy and insincere. 'Chaguartay is a, erm, distinctive name. Any relation?'

'No, I...' she paused, seemed to think for a moment. 'It's a common name where I come from.'

That made sense. Not related.

'Ashuana?' I nodded at the charm on her bracelet, lest she thought I was making assumptions based on the colour of her skin.

'Lots of people think that,' she said, holding up her wrist and shaking it so that the elephant danced on the end of its chain, 'but look, no fiery halo, no trident tail...'

Not sure where to take this next, I just nodded. I would say nothing, but I knew an Ashuanan elephant, like any good Ashuanan boy, even one that had had its halo and its tail snapped off.

I poured myself a mug of atrocious looking coffee, raising it as if to toast Sara. It was atrocious *smelling* coffee too, like rotting leaves. Interesting that she hadn't picked up on the accent, though, maybe she wasn't from Ashuana after all.

Sara raised her mug in jokey response and stepped past me as I took a swig. If anything, it tasted worse than promised.

'I'm kidding,' whispered Sara as she passed. 'He's my dad.

She's my sister. No flies on you, Ashuanan boy...'

I span around, watching her sashay away.

'Wait, I...,' I began, questions bubbling up like lava.

Something was wrong, something didn't fit. Someone wasn't telling me the truth. I needed to follow her, to ask her more questions, but a firm hand grabbed my spare arm, pulling me in the other direction.

'Estrel,' hissed Clar, 'you need to get out of here.'

This was a shock to me. I hadn't really questioned what Clar had gone to check out, had only briefly considered that it might be anything to do with me, yet here they were, in the place that I had, suddenly and unbeknownst to them, decided that I needed to be.

A chill hit me. The last two times that Clar had suddenly appeared today, it had been to rescue me from mortal danger. And yet I'd thought, several times, how much more reassuring it would be if they were with me. What was I feeling now?

'What?' I asked, squashing this unpleasant thought down. 'Where did you come from?'

'I needed to check some things out,' said Clar. 'Didn't take long. Then I had to find you. And that wasn't a simple task, to say the least. Mouse took an... an interesting route to get here. You realise that there was no reason for you to come in through the kitchen?'

'What do you mean?'

I was even more confused than I'd been a moment ago. That chill wasn't going away, either.

'I don't know that you can trust Mouse,' said Clar, unbelievably.

'Can't trust Mouse?'

I stared at them. It seemed a bit late in the day for this.

'You took me to Mouse. You left me with Mouse. I thought

you said…'

'I was wrong,' Clar looked pained, 'and I think I've put you in danger. You need to get out of here. It's not safe. We need to go now. Come with me and then I can explain.'

I pulled my hand away. Clar's pleas were bouncing off me, without leaving an impression. I knew I should be listening, but I wanted to drown them out with a screamed "No!"

I wasn't standing for this. If there was something that I needed to know, then I needed to know it now. I would not disappear off, once again, with someone who thought they knew what was best for me.

I was standing my ground. Clar could tell me what was going on or Clar could do one.

'Why now?' I asked, instead of giving that speech. 'What's happened?'

'It's complicated, but please.'

Clar seemed to be begging, now. I wavered. Clar hadn't let me down so far. Maybe I should take this seriously.

I looked around. The theatre was filling with people, but they looked like academics and students and activists and debaters. There were people wearing cardigans. I thought I'd spotted a pair of sandals. I couldn't be in much danger here, could I?

'There isn't a lot of time,' said Clar. 'But tell me why you want to meet Evie White?'

'I recognised her voice.'

Clar wasn't there for that part. It was a fair question.

'I think she was the one who let me out.'

'You told Jo Jo that she told you a story. What was it about?' Clar asked.

So they had talked to Jo Jo. But that was the question, the whole thing, to find out what the story was about. I played it straight.

'It was about her childhood.'

It wasn't wrong, but also wasn't the part I needed explaining.

'In Ashuana?'

This confused me. I knew she wasn't from Ashuana, whatever trinkets her sister appropriated. Clar must know this, too.

'No, beyond Ashuana…' I stumbled. 'But I think it was allegorical. I don't know. Does this matter? When I get to talk to her, I'll ask. Mouse said she'd be able to…'

'She won't be able to tell you,' said Clar, bluntly. 'It's not allegorical. But it's not her story either.'

'Not her..?'

Now I was confused.

'Not her story,' said Clar, again. 'As in, it didn't happen to her, and as in, she didn't tell it. It's Toshock's story. She grew up in the desert. She poured her water on the ground. You're chasing the wrong answer to the wrong question. And, more importantly, right now more critical to your personal safety, is that you're chasing the wrong person.'

'Toshock…' I stopped.

My heart sunk to my stomach. I realised I might have made a very significant mistake. Two voices, both female, but from very different parts of the world. I'd been out of it, though. Had I really mixed them up?

'But Toshock was trying to kill me. She thought I was planting the bombs. She locked me up and then came after me when she thought I'd escaped. She…'

'She knew much more about this than any of us,' said Clar.

Their eyes were kind. It was painful to look at their empathy.

'I think she died trying to rescue you. You heard two voices in the White Room. You said so yourself. Are you so certain you have the right one?'

'I don't believe you,' I said, stepping backwards.

This wasn't strictly true, but my defences were shooting up. I was trying to protect myself, trying to make sense of the mistake that I'd made. Clar shook their head, but did not follow as I turned and pushed through the crowd.

If I was wrong about this then... Mouse, I had to find Mouse. I had to prove that I'd made the right choice in trusting her.

Clar was wrong, and I had to prove it. I couldn't afford to be wrong.

I pushed through a knot of people. My elbows caused a mug to spill, I trod on several toes, a murmur of discontent was following me. I chose not to hear it.

I found myself at the top of the steps. There was only one way I could go. Everyone behind me was too annoyed at me, so I started down, looking each way along the rows, head flicking back and forth.

Mouse had gone down. I just needed to find Mouse.

'Stop right there, young man.'

Ort'a's hand on my chest brought me to a stop. The old man, much shorter than me, looked up into my face. He looked puzzled.

'Have we met?' he asked.

'No, no, I don't think so,' I stammered.

His face was a fossil scraped out of sedimentary rock. His breath was even older than that. There was an air of vague familiarity about him.

It was entirely possible that we had met, but that should only be in a forgotten timeline, not anything he should remember.

'Odd,' mused Ort'a. 'I could swear your face was familiar. Or your...'

He tailed off, removed his hand.

'Never mind. You may go. Watch your step.'

I wasn't sure if he meant literally or figuratively, but I continued downwards, still visually sweeping the rows, more and more frantically, for a familiar face.

Without a sign of Mouse, I reached the bottom of the steps. I turned to face the way I had come, my back to the stage, and surveyed the rows of seats again, this time from below.

She seemed to have disappeared. I realised I was still holding a mug. At the end of the front row, there was a door leading out of the auditorium and, next to that, a small table. I walked to the end of the row and placed my mug down on the table.

Maybe the door? Maybe Mouse had left? Seen something, followed someone? I turned for one last look up at the rowed seating.

There, at the top, off to the left, I glimpsed something familiar, a gesture, a turn of the head. It was her; I was certain.

I needed to get back up to the top. I couldn't see her anymore as the crowded balcony was filling up faster than people were taking their seats. I had to get up there.

Keeping my gaze on the point where I was sure I'd seen Mouse, I ran to the bottom step and climbed back up. My toe caught on the second step and I stumbled, splayed out my hands to break my fall, while people jumped out of the way, throwing tuts and glares at me.

I found my way back to my feet and had to push, twisting and turning to squeeze past the disgruntled delegates on their way in the opposite direction.

I passed Ort'a again, who gave me a severe look before grinding his heel into my toes. I was certain that it wasn't accidental. I didn't understand what the old man had against me, but neither did I have time to challenge him on it. I continued upwards, dragging my now injured foot, taking the weight on the other.

Faster and thicker, the audience poured down the aisle, buffeting me as I, head down now, absorbed their shoves and focused on nothing but reaching the top.

There must be fewer people up there now. It must be easier to see. She must be able to see me trying to fight my way back.

I was too visible, too exposed. Evie White, if she was even there, was secluded off-stage, in a green room. This was a dangerous waste of time. I shouldn't have asked Mouse to bring me there.

I hit the top step, raised my head. Mouse was dead ahead of me, in conversation with two thickset men in black jackets.

I stopped in my tracks. Surely not, not here? How were there Black Knights here?

Mouse looked up, saw me and pointed a finger. On instinct, I made to dart to my right, but found my way blocked by Sara Chaguartay, flanked by two more black jacketed Knights. My heart sank.

I looked around in desperation. I was betrayed. I was trapped. Clar, the last chance I could think of, was nowhere to be seen.

I turned, helplessly, on the spot. I felt a gentle hand on my shoulder.

'Come on, Estrel,' said Mouse, in a tone that cut deep into me. 'We need to get you out of here. There's someone who wants to meet you.'

The words sank in, and I knew exactly what they meant. It was exactly what I'd asked for, exactly what I'd said I wanted. An audience with Evie White.

Inside, I crumbled.

CHAPTER 18

Despite the presence of at least four Black Knights, it was two of the Devoted who grabbed me by the shoulders, pinning my arms behind my back and dragging me backwards.

They did not try to lift me when we reached the stairs and my heels bounced painfully and helplessly off each step as we descended.

The crowd parted, of course they did for this, then regrouped once we'd passed, staring at the spectacle as it, we, continued down to the bottom.

I tried to cry out, to plead with Mouse, who followed in our wake, but the words wouldn't come. It was like the blow she'd struck with her betrayal was too much, too hard, and had knocked the wind from me.

'You don't need to do this,' I tried to say, but it didn't come out at all.

Mouse's face, with its laser-guided pity, its stare devoid of compassion, plunged a knife and then twisted it. I tried to look again, helplessly, once more, for Clar, even for Jo Jo, for anyone who might help me.

All I saw was the rock-steady scorn of Ort'a, the bared

fangs of Deakin, the undisguised disgust of every third face I searched. I was on my own. I had no one left on my side.

At the bottom of the steps, the Clerics dragged me to the right, across the front of the stage, towards the door I'd approached earlier. They crashed through it, leaving it to swing back and catch my legs on its rebound.

I didn't cry out in pain. There didn't seem to be any point. Mouse appeared in the doorway, which receded rapidly as they dragged me down the stone corridor.

'You don't need to do this!'

I finally found the breath to shout.

'I want to see her, I would have gone willingly…'

I found more strength, struggled against the arms that held me as I felt myself tipped and dragged down stone steps.

'I do need to do this,' she said, without emotion, 'and you don't want to see her. I know you've realised your mistake.'

She remained in the doorway and the Clerics stopped for a moment. I stared at Mouse, the strain of keeping my head up, while they tilted me back at such an angle, burning my neck.

'What happened, Mouse?' I asked. 'I thought you were trying to help me. When did you decide to turn against me?'

Mouse laughed, but there was no humour there. The sound was bitter, taunting.

'No decision was necessary. And no turning against you. I wasn't here to help. I'm not here to betray you either. You should know that. It's not personal. I just did whatever I needed to. For me. For Mouse.'

'That's not true!'

I refused to believe what I was hearing. I desperately scrambled to find reasons Mouse was wrong, reasons she shouldn't believe her own words.

'You helped! You believed me. We talked at the top of the shaft. I felt something. You said…'

Echoes

'You helped me find something it was useful for me to know,' said Mouse. 'Credit where credit is due. But don't mistake that credit for loyalty.'

'No,' I insisted. 'Toshock told me to find you. I doubted it because I thought Toshock was out to get me, but Toshock was trying to help. I know that now. Why would Toshock tell me to find you if you can't be trusted?'

'I have no idea.'

Mouse took some steps down the corridor towards where I was still being held, suspended over a stone staircase.

'You're not making sense right now, Estrel. When you didn't trust Toshock, you were perfectly willing to overlook that and follow me, anyway. Now you've found out that Toshock is on your side. Why does that have to mean that I am too?'

'But *FIND MOUSE*,' I said.

My last throw of the dice.

'Why would she write that? I know you wanted to help me. What changed?'

Mouse reached me. She raised her hand and touched me on the cheek. As caresses went, it was hard. Her thumb nail dragged on my skin, she pinched until it pricked. I felt a trickle of blood escape and run down my face. I flinched.

'Maybe Toshock doesn't know me any better than you do.' She inclined her head. 'Maybe she thinks I have answers I know I don't. It doesn't really make any difference to me. But it doesn't matter, does it? It became your mission anyway. You're so lost, so clueless, that you jumped to attention to the first instruction you read. You didn't even stop to question it. Everything you *know* is wrong, Estrel. We live in two different worlds. Yours is based on a lie. You never saw that. I don't think you could, even if you'd wanted to. You occupy the same space as me, but you just don't know. You can't know, you don't have the frame of reference. I can't help you, Estrel. You're on your own.'

I felt like someone had punched me in the gut. I was pretty sure that was coming later once they had taken me to wherever I was being dragged.

Once again they bumped me down the stairs, leaving Mouse stood at the top. I went to scream, but the cries choked me, the tears stinging my eyes blurred her to a silhouette, waving patronisingly at me as I receded into the darkness of The Catacombs.

I finally got to meet Evie White. She was sitting behind a broad wooden desk in a small, low-ceilinged room. The desktop was empty. This seemed to be an impromptu office space.

Her face was stone, her hair smartly tied back. Her eyes were the same indescribable colour as her sister's. But they were empty and cold.

I don't know how long the two Clerics pulled me through The Catacombs. Every corner was an impact, a fresh shot of pain, a crunching blow that knocked another level of resistance out of me.

Ceilings soared above, then dropped low, oppressively bearing down. Corridors widened and then narrowed to where my two guards had to drop to single file to make it through.

They made no accommodation for me. They squeezed and yanked me through every bottleneck, my joints giving way where the rock would not.

'Sit down, Mr Beck.'

Evie sat with her arms spread wide. Her manner, however, was less welcoming than the undecorated stone walls.

I found my battered body manhandled into a metal chair. Shackles clipped shut, straps were applied. A metal ring held my neck to the back of the seat. All I could do was to stare straight forward.

'I don't have a lot of choice, do I?'

My restraints were a step up from the White Room. I really wasn't going anywhere this time.

'No, you don't.'

Evie smiled a cold, humourless smile.

'As I think I explained before, the last time I had you in this position, I very much want you to stay in one place. Just until you're no longer a problem for me, or what I am hoping to achieve. Last time we tried this, you weren't very good at it. You'll forgive me if I take extra precautions this time around.'

Evie White stood up from behind the desk and walked around it to stand at the front and lean back. She rested, half sat on the empty desktop, arms folded and ankles crossed.

She viewed me with apparent interest but, past that, I couldn't tell what she was thinking. I held onto the hope that I took from the fact that she seemed more interested in keeping me prisoner than in killing me off.

'What are you trying to achieve?' I asked.

I thought I might as well. I had nothing, really, to lose anymore.

'And how was I stopping you? You think I'm planting the bombs as well?'

'Ha!' Evie laughed, but with the same icy demeanour and dead-eyed stare as before.

She didn't move apart from that, didn't uncross her arms, didn't uncross her legs.

'No, I don't think you're planting the bombs. In fact, I know you're not planting the bombs. I'm planting the bombs. There you go, mystery solved.'

This was a relief, and an answer, the sort of thing I'd been looking for all day. I was worried, however, that despite the lack of immediate peril, I was staring into the eyes of a psychopath. No flicker of emotion had appeared when she'd said it. That couldn't be right.

'You're planting the bombs?' I asked.

Just to check I'd heard right. No, not that. If she had asked, I would have told her it was to check I'd heard right. Actually, I think I was just trying to keep her talking.

'But I thought that your husband…' I realised that she also didn't have the head wound she'd sported on the news broadcast earlier.

'Yes, you were meant to.' Evie cut me off with a wave of her hand. She pushed herself up off the desk and paced the room in circles that took her behind the chair I was secured to. I couldn't move my head because of the ring around it. I didn't like it when she was out of my field of vision. It reminded me of the White Room. It sounded like, despite what she'd been saying on the Com Channels, she didn't think he was dead after all.

'So where is he?' I asked.

'I don't know, to be completely honest with you,' Evie said, wandering back into view. 'Jack White was not the man everyone thought he was. He wasn't a leader. He wasn't about to save the city. He wasn't about to save anything, or anyone. Least of all himself.'

'So you blew him up?'

I couldn't quite believe what I was hearing. Not that the Emperor had no clothes, but that she'd just bombed him because he wasn't up to scratch.

Evie passed back in front of me. She stopped and turned to look.

'I created a diversion,' she said. 'I gave him a chance to slip into the shadows, to shirk the responsibility that he didn't want. He bit my hand off. He's probably rolling drunk round

The Alleys right now. That or tucked under some trade he's taken a fancy to.'

She spat this last line, the first flicker of emotion she'd given away since they had brought me in. She started to walk again, but I saw a slight tremor in her lip as she turned away.

I assumed it was anger. Maybe she wasn't a psychopath. Maybe she was the opposite. She wasn't faking emotion, rather faking indifference. I would have shaken my head if I'd been able to.

'One bomb nearly blew up your father,' I said.

That morning seemed like a different universe. But Chaguartay's escape had been very slick. Clar had specifically said so. I had a horrible feeling.

'Daddy knew what was happening,' Evie confirmed. 'He was never in any danger. He got out well before there was any risk. Unlike some people I could mention?'

'Was it his idea?' I asked, ignoring the dig.

For someone who just wanted to keep me contained, she'd done a damned good job of nearly blowing me up. Twice.

'No!' snapped Evie. 'There's a transition of power occurring here, Mr Beck, the beauty of which will pass most of the citizens of Trinity by. It's my plan, my creation, my idea. My father was a great man. It takes greatness to replace him. Jack White could never. He wasn't a leader. I'm a leader.'

'Like father like daughter?' I hazarded.

'Oh, you don't even know the half of it,' she laughed.

I felt hot breath on my ear.

'I have such plans. Trinity will be a force to be reckoned with. The baton will be handed from father to daughter. The people will be so happy.'

'People hate Mayor Chaguartay,' I said. 'Why would they accept his anointed successor? I don't think you're going to get the coronation you're looking for.'

'No one will see it that way, let me assure you,' hissed Evie. 'Once the dust settles, once it becomes known that Jack White is dead…'

'Dead?' I asked. 'You said that he wasn't dead.'

'He isn't, but he might as well be,' Evie scoffed, coming back around and leaning in.

I could feel the flecks of spit on my cheek as she dashed out her hard, staccato words.

'I'm pretty sure that no one is ever going to see him again. Once he's had his fun, I suspect he'll vanish as suddenly as you will at the end of tonight. Only he won't be going back to the beginning.'

'More like meeting an end?'

I got what she meant. She wasn't being subtle.

'Shut up,' Evie snapped, standing up straight. 'The people will be scared. They'll rise up, depose the hated Mayor and turn to a reluctant, grieving widow who will save them.'

I saw. I saw what she wanted, what she'd planned and, what was worse, I saw it all working.

'So you're bombing them into submission?'

'The bombs are the start, yes,' she agreed. 'It will take more than bombs to spur the sedated masses of Trinity into action.'

Evie passed in front of me again. She stopped and looked at me, face on.

'But I have more. And I will make them turn.'

A thought struck me.

'Resistance. They thought it was me,' I said. 'Down in Research. One of them directly accused me of blowing his legs off. How did you do that?'

For the first time since I'd been shackled to a chair in front of her, Evie White seemed lost for words.

'That wasn't you,' I said. 'You don't know who planted that one.'

It wasn't a question. It was my turn to chuckle. There was something else going on. Something she didn't know about. Something beyond her control.

I didn't really know anything about it either, to be fair, but she didn't need to know that. I could use this.

'Maybe your father isn't going to go as quietly as you thought?'

'No,' she backed away, shaking her head. 'It wasn't him. He's…'

'He's..?' I waited for her to finish.

'He's dying,' she admitted.

I didn't know why she was telling me so much. She didn't need to take me into her confidence.

'He probably hasn't got more than six months. He's got nothing to gain by fighting me. And so much to lose.'

'Not so much if he's dead, surely?'

I wasn't ruling out the petty revenge of a dying man. But I was interested in what he had to lose.

'Not him.' A sneer spread across Evie's face. 'But his precious Sara…'

'Ah,' I thought I understood. 'The favourite daughter?'

'The weaker daughter,' Evie spat. 'She wouldn't have survived this long without daddy dearest. She won't survive any further without me.'

'So it wasn't your dad, then?'

It was my turn to be confused, but I was, at least, enjoying the discomfort I could see on my captor's face.

'No. Not him.' She paused, thoughtfully, looking at me in a way I didn't quite understand.

I didn't know what to think. I didn't know what to believe. I had spent an entire day listening to the wrong people, following the wrong leads. I was very, very bad at this game I had been forced to play.

All the stress, all the anxiety, the constant, sweating nausea... All for a goal that I had no interest in achieving.

Evie looked up as if someone had appeared in the doorway. Her face dissolved into a mask of horror. I guessed that someone had, and she wasn't pleased to see them. I hoped it was Clar. I desperately needed Clar, but I'd settle for Jo Jo, or a repentant Mouse come to absolve herself from her double-crossing sins.

Once again, I wanted to turn my head, but I couldn't. All I could do was watch the confusion and fear flicker in Evie's eyes, before a muffled thud and whistle briefly preceded her crumpling to the floor.

There wasn't a lot of blood, I thought. It was over quickly.

'Is she dead?' I asked.

I wasn't in a lot of doubt.

'Unfortunately, yes,' said a voice behind me.

It was a voice that was vaguely familiar to me. I tried in vain to place it. It had an air of detachment about it. Like this was someone I was used to hearing on the Com, now present in the same room as me for the first time.

Familiar, but uncannily different.

'Are you here to rescue me?' I asked.

It did occur to me that someone who could walk into a room and shoot somebody dead without saying a word might not necessarily be someone with my best interests at heart. It paid to check.

'In a manner of speaking,' said the voice.

I could hear him moving around the room. As the man slowly appeared in my line of sight, a bulky gun held out in front of him, my eyes widened. He was familiar, after all. I knew exactly who he was. I was finding it very hard to believe, though.

'I planted the bomb, by the way,' said the man. 'The one in

Research. I was trying to draw Resistance in, to get them there so they could get you out. It didn't quite work out the way I planned.'

'You couldn't just have come and let me out yourself?' I asked. 'You killed a lot of people.'

'I only killed one person,' the man pointed out. 'The Researchers did the rest. You know, by now, that they weren't really Researchers, don't you?'

I had figured that much out. I hadn't seen so much as a lab coat the whole time I'd been underground.

'Black Knights?' I checked.

He nodded.

'But you don't have to worry about them anymore. Or Evie White, for that matter.'

He prodded at Evie's crumpled body with his toe.

'Although that's not, at this stage of the game, a particularly good thing.'

Satisfied that she was, in fact, properly dead, he turned to face me. He was my height and wore a grey hooded top under a long black leather coat. I would have known him anywhere.

I stared back at myself. An older version of myself, granted, but unmistakably myself.

'Hello Estrel,' he said to me in a voice that sounded like an echo. 'You're probably wondering what I've got you into here?'

CHAPTER 19

I let the silence hang between us for as long as I could. Unsurprisingly, we broke at the same time.

'What..?' I said.

'Come...' he said, before we both stopped. 'No, you go ahead.'

'What the hell? Who are you?'

I finished my sentence. I had to address this. Even though I could clearly see who he was, meaning me, I continued to refuse to believe the quite startling evidence before my eyes.

The older me rolled his eyes and sighed, but did at least set about releasing me.

'That's a stupid question, Estrel,' he said, rather harshly, I thought. 'But we don't have time to argue. We can walk and talk. Or run and talk. Whatever, we need to get you out of here.'

'But you're me, right?' I flexed my free wrist. 'I have got that right? Somehow?'

'Somehow, yes,' he... I agreed.

The restraint around my other wrist snapped open. I flexed that one too..

'Are you going to tell me how?'

'Eventually,' said the other me, unclasping the ring which was restraining my neck.

It surprised me to find that he had already released my ankles. I stood up, wobbled, and braced myself on my older self.

'Let's go,' he said.

'Go where?' I asked. 'With you? With me? With…'

I trailed off. I was failing to process this.

'With me,' said the other me, 'like I said, run and talk. And you can call me Estrel. Everyone else does.'

I pulled a face, but that was a potentially helpful offer. Estrel took off down the corridor through the door he'd appeared at, the same one I'd been dragged through earlier.

I took one more look at the crumpled body of Evie White, and followed him, limping as my crushed toes complained.

'I know you've got questions,' shouted Estrel over his shoulder. 'I would, and I'm you.'

We turned right, ducked under several low lintels and through a half collapsed archway onto a narrow ledge. Estrel jumped from it to the walkway below. He landed lightly and set off to the far side.

It looked high to me, but he'd managed the jump easily and he was me, so… I jumped down, landing on my good foot, and broke into a jog behind Estrel.

'Do you remember this?'

I was panting, catching up to Estrel, but when we fell into stride I found it was comfortable keeping pace with myself. This shouldn't have been a surprise.

'Good question,' said Estrel. 'But no, I don't. This didn't happen to me.'

He took some downward steps two at a time. I did the same.

'How does that work?'

It didn't make any sense.

'That's another one…'

Estrel seemed to disappear into the wall. I stopped in my tracks, noticed the spiral staircase to our left, checked my direction and followed him downwards. Estrel's voice drifted up.

'…and that's actually a *very* good one. But look, it would be easier if you stopped asking questions and just let me explain. Keep running, though. Unless you see someone with a gun. Then you want to hide. I can't afford for you to die. I mean, you can't afford for you to die, but I really can't. Think of the paradox.'

I almost stopped on the stairs. This was something, something real, something I'd wanted to know.

Dying was dying. It created a paradox. I had so many questions.

'Yes!' I exclaimed. 'A paradox. Don't I need to know the rules or something? How do I avoid creating a paradox? What shouldn't I do?'

'You shouldn't die.'

Estrel motioned for me to slow down as we neared the bottom of the staircase.

'Also, you should stop asking questions. I think I already said that. I'm not very good at listening, am I?'

'What?'

I was confused. This was confusing. And it turned out I wasn't the best at explaining things.

'You. You're not very good at listening.' He turned and grinned at me. 'It was a joke. Come on, coast's clear.'

Estrel scuttled across what appeared to be a wine cellar. It was cold and yeasty and full of racks of bottles. At the far end was a metal ring attached to the floor which he pulled, lifting a stone trap door with surprising ease.

'Ladder…' He nodded at the wooden rungs which disappeared into the darkness. 'I know you're not a fan.'

I shuddered.

'Why are we going down?' I asked. 'Aren't we trying to get out of here?'

'Slow on the uptake. I thought I'd always been this sharp,' said Estrel. 'You've got to pay attention to the micro-details. We've been going down this whole time. We need to get into Research. We need to get to my lab.'

'Your lab?'

'My lab,' confirmed Estrel. 'Come on.'

The ladder took me down to another cellar, smaller, darker, dustier and with less wine. I stood to one side as Estrel descended to join me, and we stood shoulder to shoulder in the cramped space.

'You OK?' asked Estrel.

'Uh-huh,' I grunted.

That wasn't true. My breathing was shallow, my armpits damp. I could hear my pulse.

'You didn't open the door,' said Estrel, kicking the wall in front of him.

The wall swung open and light and air flooded in.

'That's better,' he said, stepping over the small step, out into the light. 'I don't like it any more that you do, you know.'

That would stand to reason, with him being me.

'It's just that I've had to do it enough that I've come to realise it doesn't make any difference how I feel about it.'

'This corridor looks very familiar,' I observed, climbing out after him into what, I was certain, was a section of Research I had only recently left.

'It should,' said Estrel. 'We cleaned up the bodies.'

People or dogs? I wondered.

'It's down here.'

Estrel ducked through a doorway. I followed him into another familiar location. It was the lab where Jo Jo and I had hidden out. *Dogs.* The door still bore the pock marked evidence of my attack on it.

'Welcome to my lab,' said Estrel, swinging himself into the seat of the pod.

The screen immediately lit up, and he began hammering login credentials into the terminal.

'Your lab?' I looked at him.

This was some kind of enormous coincidence.

'I was here.'

Estrel looked up at me.

'Yes, yes you were,' he nodded. 'I was watching. I...'

He pointed to several cameras hidden in the corners of the ceiling. I hadn't noticed them before. To be fair, I'd had other things on my mind.

'I'm sorry.'

'You're sorry?' I didn't understand what he meant.

'I could have done something. I definitely could have got you out...' Estrel said. 'I didn't think I could get involved. Not then. Not until I realised what Evie was up to.'

'What was she up to?' I still didn't really understand that.

'She wanted you stopped. That's why she imprisoned you near the bomb I planted. She didn't know why it was there but she sure as hell meant for it to take you out.'

'But...' I had so many questions. 'So you... I... we... set that bomb?'

'We set that one, yes,' Estrel nodded. 'None of the others, but I wanted to sneak it in unnoticed. Seemed like the day for it.'

'You killed people,' I protested.

'Lots of people die, Estrel,' said Estrel. 'From here on in, lots and lots of people die. Focus on the right details.'

'What are the right details?' I screamed. I was losing my patience.

'She wanted you dead, Estrel,' said Estrel. 'How did she know she needed you dead?'

'She needed me dead?' This was mind-bendingly difficult for me to process. 'I don't know why she needed me dead? I thought she was just trying to reset me. She didn't know about the bomb…'

'Didn't she?' asked Estrel.

I didn't know. I hadn't thought she did. But if I'd proven anything through the course of the day, it was my lack of ability to read people.

'Shit,' he said.

'What?'

'I think I'm getting ahead of myself here. This was better when you weren't asking questions.'

He climbed out of the pod and stood in front of me. He put his hands on my shoulders and looked me directly in the eye, which was disconcerting. It's peculiar to be face to face with someone who looks exactly like you.

'We are rapidly, *rapidly,* running out of time here. But you deserve to know. Maybe you even need to know, although you can't take that knowledge with you. But let's start with some context. Evie Chaguartay is a cancer that this city will never beat. Today is the start of a terminal decline. You were supposed to stop it. That's why you're here. That's why you loop. You're supposed to change things so that she can't.'

'Didn't you just kill her?' I asked, no less confused.

'I did,' nodded Estrel, hanging his head for a moment, 'but it won't count. You want to know about rules? Rule number one, to avoid the most inevitable paradox, people from the future can't kill people from the past.'

'You're from the future?' I asked.

'Yes, I…' Estrel raised his head and stared at me again. 'No, you're right. This is a lot. I'm from the future, your future. I've come back because it was the only way to stop what was happening. Because I could have stopped it, before, but I didn't. Now, you're the one that has to stop it. But I can't get involved, not directly.'

'So what happens? Now that you did?' I asked.

'Oh, this is all going to unravel soon.' Estrel chuckled. 'I well and truly fucked the timeline to save you.'

'Thank you?' I said.

I felt like I was wading through treacle to get anywhere.

'But you had to, didn't you?'

Estrel pulled a face I couldn't interpret. I wasn't used to recognising my own facial expressions.

'Well, yes, in some ways,' he admitted, 'I had to save you to save myself. If you died back there, then I wouldn't be here now.'

'Right. So…'

No, that made no sense.

'But you said this never happened to you.'

Surely for there to be an older version of me here, who travelled back into my timeline, they had to have lived my life already?

Estrel took his hand off my shoulder and tapped his finger against his forehead, hard. It made a knocking sound.

'I know! It's a mind-fuck,' he cackled, 'if you stop to think about it. Which is why I tend not to.'

He spun back around and climbed back into his chair, bending over the terminal again.

'Maybe it happened. Maybe you forgot. I don't know…'

'I don't think you had a lot of choice,' I said to the top of my older self's head. 'Killing her.'

'No,' said Estrel, between bouts of frantic typing. 'But that's just the thing. I don't think I had a choice, but I'm going to be honest: I don't think I helped.'

'Don't think you helped?' It was my turn to laugh. 'I'm still alive. So you're still alive. I think that has to help.'

'No, no, no… this is why it hurts to think too hard about it,' said Estrel, through gritted teeth. 'That doesn't stand up to examination for long, does it? I'm only here because of what she did… what she's going to do. So if I kill her, then I shouldn't be here. And if I shouldn't be here, then I can't be the one who kills her, and if I don't kill her, then she kills you…'

'And you don't exist? It seems to be that from a continuity of time, anti-paradox point of view, that's kind of how things were supposed to work out?'

'Yes, but…' Estrel paused his typing and rubbed his face with his hands. 'I shouldn't be here. You're supposed to fix things so that I never need to come back. That's why I can't help you directly. That's why me planting a bomb made things go skewiff. And then killing her has messed things up even worse. You're supposed to figure it out for yourself, Estrel. But you're so bad at it.'

'Whatever, you're the expert,' I snapped, frustrated. 'What are you doing, anyway?'

'Bringing forward the reset.' Estrel tapped a few more keys and then spun round again.

'Bringing forward the… What?' I gaped. 'You can do that?'

'I can do that,' confirmed Estrel. 'I set it up. I can change the parameters.'

His words echoed around my head. "I set it up." Was he really saying what I thought he was saying?

'You… you did this?'

I took a step towards my older self in anger. *To do what?* I wasn't sure.

'You trapped me, you trapped yourself? You trapped us in this loop? Why?'

'Yes!' cried Estrel. 'I'm sure I already said that. Yes, I created the loop, with a bit of help, but... I did it to save her. To save us all, really, but mostly to save her.'

'Right, too many questions.' Just when I thought I was getting somewhere, I realised I was still struggling to keep up.

'There are,' agreed Estrel, 'and not a lot of time to answer them. You're missing an important one, however.'

I stared at him.

'What? What question.'

'Well,' said Estrel. 'I'm you, right? Older, but not that much older. And you know you. Do you think you know how to put yourself in a time loop?'

'No, not really,' I said. 'But you just said you did it.'

'I said I did it,' said Estrel, 'but I didn't come up with the idea. Who's lab do you think this is?'

'You just said it was yours.'

Estrel's brow wrinkled reflexively.

'They said this might happen.'

'Who said what might happen?' I doubted my future self's sanity.

'They, the... the people...' A shadow passed across his face. 'Science guys. Shit, this was fast. We need to get you out of here. The timeline is deteriorating quickly.'

'The timeline is what?'

That sounded terrible.

'Deteriorating, collapsing.'

Estrel stared at me. It was unsettlingly intense.

'It's like... it's like it's been expending so much energy trying to hold itself together in the face of the paradox we created that it's exhausted itself and now it's just, kind of, collapsing.'

'And what happens when it collapses?' I was almost afraid to ask.

'Nothing,' replied Estrel.

'Oh, right, so, that's OK then?'

It sounded fine.

'No,' Estrel corrected himself, 'I mean, there's going to be nothing. No timeline, no nothing. Not anything. You know what I mean.'

I kind of did. He wasn't making much sense, but he was still me, after everything.

'I think so,' I said reassuringly. 'You need me to reset early, so that I don't collapse with everything else.'

'Yes!'

I could hear him sigh with relief. He raised his eyebrows, hopefully.

'I'm winging it now, though. All on my own. I hope it works.'

'I wondered what would happen if I died,' I said. 'At one point, I thought about trying to find out. Felt like I had little to lose at that point. Good job I didn't go through with it.'

'Oh, you dying wouldn't have been a problem, per se,' replied Estrel. 'It's all about how you die. An accident caused by your own actions, that would be fine. Like, I don't know, *letting go of a ladder and falling down a very long shaft..?* Once the time came to reset, you would have jumped back to the start of the loop, right as rain. Murdered by Evie Chaguartay? You'd probably have a horrible time but ultimately you'd be OK. You're a little bit invincible, to be honest with you. That's nice isn't it? As long as it's not your last loop, as long as Evie doesn't die the same day, you can survive pretty much anything...'

I wasn't sure I'd define "survive" in the same way but I

understood . It wasn't nice, though. It confirmed that I was trapped. It was almost impossible for me to break the loop without committing murder. And whilst Evie White wasn't my favourite person, I wasn't sure I was capable of that.

'...But that's not what's happening here. The problem with the current situation is that the time for you to reset probably won't come. This timeline is about to end. No more timeline, no more time. Now shut up while I make sure that you get out of here.'

'Oh, right,' I mumbled, chagrined. 'I'll...'

I was aware of voices shouting and footsteps running from the corridor.

'The door!' Estrel called, focussed again on the screen.

He waved his right hand toward the panel that Jo Jo had struggled to operate. I had the advantage of knowing where the close button was. I hit it and the door of the lab hissed shut.

Above the panel, a small monitor screen flickered to life. I wasn't sure if it would have been useful for this to be working earlier, when Jo Jo and I were under siege, or whether we'd been better off being left in the dark.

'Monitor them,' said Estrel, still staring at his own screen.

His fingers flew around the touchscreen and the keyboard. I glanced back at the monitor. A grey, murky image of the length of the corridor outside took shape. A group of five men were thundering down it, shouting, although now I couldn't hear them, I just watched their mouths flap and their arms flail. They were panicking, that much I could tell.

'Black Knights,' I said to Estrel. 'They're running from something.'

Estrel grunted and kept on typing.

'Will the doors be strong enough to keep them..?' I asked.

Suddenly, there were only three of them. I could have sworn that the two at the back had just popped out of existence. My question stopped on my lips. *What happened there?*

It happened again. Now there were only two men running. They didn't seem to have noticed that their companions had disappeared. Maybe they didn't remember that they'd had companions.

I doubted that I'd ever seen them myself. It was an odd notion that other people could exist in the world other than me and… older me. I rubbed my eyes, then looked back at the monitor. The corridor remained empty.

'Coast is still clear,' I called out to the other me.

Estrel finished his work and stood up. He took my hands in his and stared into my eyes.

'Focus, Estrel,' he said. 'Look at me. You need to hold it together. I've brought the reset forwards, but things could get very weird before you jump back.'

'Jump back? What? When?'

'I don't know. Soon.' Estrel paused. 'It's not a very precise process. But the timeline's collapsing. Things are being erased. You need to focus. I need you to remember. I need to know.'

'Need to know what?'

My head was feeling fuzzy, but in the line of my own gaze, I felt clarity washing in.

'I… yes, you're right. There were people in the corridor.'

I looked back at the monitor.

'Is it just me or is there less corridor than there was a minute ago?'

'Possibly,' agreed Estrel, distractedly. 'Very possibly. Just hang on a little longer. We'll get you back.'

'How long was I supposed to go for?' I asked. 'When was the reset originally?'

'Don't you know?' Estrel looked worried. 'Is this… does it even work?'

'I think it does.' I nodded. 'I think I've looped many times. Tens, definitely. Maybe hundreds.'

'But you don't know?'

He seemed panicked. I thought he'd know.

'What, you don't remember? When you loop, you don't remember?'

'No, I've got no idea,' I said. 'I just wake up on a train on my way into Trinity…'

'At six fifty-four?'

'What?'

I hadn't paid that much attention but…

'Yes, I guess so. I…'

'That's the way I remember it,' nodded Estrel. 'It's a nice sequence, six-five-four. So I set you up to reset at twelve thirty-four tomorrow morning. One-two-three-four, you see? But if you don't remember…'

He dropped my hands and paced back and forth, agitated.

'What's the matter?' I asked.

'If you don't remember, then how do you even know it worked?' demanded Estrel. 'How do you even know you looped? What if this is your first time around and…? I've messed with the timeline too much! I tried to just nudge you in the right direction but… I'm so stupid. I thought you were a looped version but what if you're just me? What if it doesn't work?'

'If it doesn't work?' I asked.

Now it was my turn to panic.

'You said nothing about there being a chance it wouldn't work. Don't you know? Don't you remember? All those loops, all those lives?'

'No, I told you, I don't remember,' he said. 'I don't think I ever will. Not until you get it right. Then that reality will click into place and I'll never know any different. Because it won't have been any different. In the meantime, I'm just passing through, Estrel, all of your loops at once, same as Mouse, same as Clar, same as Evie Chaguartay...'

He ran his hands through his hair.

'Or so I assumed! And now I've collapsed the timeline, and we've achieved nothing. This could be it. Maybe we failed. Maybe I failed.'

Estrel placed his head in his hands and let out a small moan.

'No!' I cried.

I knew I'd looped. I could prove it. One more time, I thrust my hand into my pocket. I pulled out a scrappy piece of napkin and held it up in front of me.

'No, it worked. I know it worked. I have this!'

'What is it?' asked Estrel, taking the tatty paper from my hand and smoothing it out to read against the wall in front of him. 'It's got jam on it.'

I smiled.

'It's my Echo,' I said, simply.

We sat down on stools. The danger had passed. I couldn't actually remember what the danger had been. A lot of fuss about nothing.

Something happening outside this room, but that made little sense because there wasn't anything outside this room. I was even vague about the room itself. The walls seemed fuzzy.

Estrel still had the Echo in his hand. He was turning it over and over, inspecting it from all angles.

'It's...' Estrel stopped. I could tell that he wasn't impressed. 'It's something. It's ingenious. But scrappy. All these times...'

'It's not a very precise process?' I repeated back to him.

'I guess not.' Estrel rubbed his chin. 'You must have been

confused.'

'A little...' I admitted. 'I don't remember anything. This is all I have to go on. The past me's... the past us's... they weren't great at leaving clues.'

'You forget everything?' he asked.

'Everything,' I confirmed. 'If I don't Echo it, then I don't know about it.'

'Shit,' breathed Estrel.

I realised that I'd forgotten what I was thinking about earlier. Something about walls, whatever they were. Estrel was still talking.

'... I don't remember any of this happening, but that means nothing. We just collapsed the timeline. But I don't recognise any of this, either. And look at this!' He pointed at the Echo. 'Did you? Did you find her?'

'Mouse?' I laughed. 'Yes, I did, for all the good it did me. I still don't know what Toshock wanted me to...'

'Toshock?' Estrel seemed confused.

'Yes, Toshock,' I pointed. 'That's her handwriting.'

'No, it isn't,' said Estrel. 'It's hers. Mouse's. She wrote that.'

'No... I...'

I remembered how Mouse had reacted to the words the first time she'd seen them, like she'd seen a ghost, then how she'd been so quick to confirm the similarity between them and Toshock's writing.

'I've been set up. I can't believe I trusted her.'

'Toshock?' asked Estrel.

'No, Mouse,' I growled. 'She's been playing me the whole time.'

'Mouse?' Estrel seemed shocked.

'Yes, Mouse, she betrayed me to Evie White, she...'

'Mouse betrayed you?' Estrel was shaking his head.

'Yes, why is this so hard for..?'

Estrel cut me off.

'Mouse wouldn't do that,' he insisted. 'Mouse loves you!'

'What?' The world stopped. There was silence in the room. This didn't seem likely, or possible, and yet it made so much sense.

Estrel stared at me in disbelief.

'She loved me,' he said quietly. 'I loved her. You must have really screwed things up. I'm kind of glad that this reality isn't the one where we won.'

My mind reeled. My heart surged. Images flashed in my mind, memories resurfacing, something I'd lost but was following me.

This wasn't the first time I'd seen this. A face, a woman's face. *The White Room. Lek.* I'd seen this dream before. It was... *It was her. She was there when I looped.*

'I think I can answer your question,' I said.

'What question?' He didn't know what I was talking about.

'Evie White. *Evie Chaguartay*. How did she know?'

'I don't see...' he argued, before giving up. 'Tell me.'

'She was an Echo. Evie White was an Echo...' I said. 'It was my fault. I messed this up. She must have known, got to Mouse before I even found her. You didn't screw the timeline up. I did. Mouse wasn't an Echo. She only knew what Evie told her. Evie was the Echo, my final Echo.'

'Well...' Estrel paused for thought. 'You screwed it up first, I guess. I screwed it up worse. Maybe you could have carried on without Mouse, maybe you still could have...'

There were tears in his eyes now.

'You...' I didn't know what to say.

I didn't know what to say because I knew exactly how he felt.

'You said that you did this for her?'

Estrel gave a dry chuckle.

'I did this for her,' he repeated. 'Today was the day we met, the day I arrived in Trinity. I lost my luggage, after a misunderstanding…'

'… with a Face behind a window?' I asked.

'With a Face behind a window!' agreed Estrel. 'I left my tablet in the bag. I didn't realise until I'd been waiting in Administration reception for five minutes, so I had to ask the reception guy…'

'Ahji?'

It hit home that this was me, that we'd lived the same day, making different choices. And now he regretted his and wanted me to make different ones. But only certain different ones.

'… maybe. I don't remember his name. I had to ask him to let Mr Toun know I'd been delayed and run back over to the terminal building. When I got there, they informed me they had already sent my luggage on to Bridge and there was nothing I could do. That's when the Administration office blew up. It was chaos, and I didn't know what to do. I wandered for a bit, in what seemed to be a downtown direction, until my Com reception came back. That's when I realised I'd spent two hours walking the wrong way and that Tunnel Terminus was back the way I came. My feet were about to give out, so I went into the nearest bar for a drink. It was Eamer's, and Mouse was behind the bar, and that was it. I didn't want to leave after that.'

'Yeah, that definitely wasn't how it happened for us,' I said. 'She seemed suspicious of me from the off. Said she'd dreamed about me and it spooked her.'

'Dreamed of you? So she remembered a previous loop?'

'Maybe, or maybe that was what Evie told her to say.' I looked at him. 'Although from what she said, maybe she dreamed you two actually meeting. Maybe those parts were genuine. Maybe the Echoes don't work in quite the way I thought.'

Estrel smiled, softly.

'Maybe what we had was special,' he said. 'I miss her.'

'She's probably right out…' I began, before I looked up.

The monitor was dark and, beyond that, there was a fuzziness creeping in that made anything else hard to see. Hard to imagine, even. I had to really concentrate on seeing the door. The door that I knew was there. Had been there. That I'd shot at.

What was a door?

'It's closing in,' said Estrel. 'She doesn't exist anymore, not in what's left of this reality.'

'So you stayed for her?' I was trying to distract him, but I also wanted to know.

Maybe I wouldn't remember any of this, but I had a chance to find out. I needed to know.

'I did. We were happy for a while. I mean, I'd been here for days when Chaguartay stepped down and Evie took over. There was optimism, joy even. It felt, briefly, like a shadow had lifted. It didn't take long for the lights to go back off again. There was a lot of support for the raids to start with, even though it was Black Knight gangs carrying them out. They'd swoop in at night and detain anyone deemed to have abused their power under the old regime, which turned out to be everyone other than the big man himself. Then they took down the heads of Authority, then Administration. I saw the streams of Ernold Toun being dragged out in his nightshirt. It seemed a lot, but everyone was being told that they'd caused the problems. They'd been on the take, lining their pockets, keeping everyone else down. To be fair, the economy was booming. The Factories had never been so productive.

Problem was, it was on the back of workers who were being tweaked through their water supply. She doubled the dose…'

'The meat guy!' I shouted.

'The what?'

Estrel was thrown.

'The guy. In the cafe. Konoz? Koron? Something like that. He told me the people were being drugged. I thought he was crazy.'

'Just because he was right doesn't mean he's not crazy. And never eat anything he serves you. I made that mistake, nearly wrecked my first night with Mouse…'

'Sorry,' I said, 'I interrupted.'

'Then she pardoned her father,' continued Estrel. '*Then* it got really bad. They had arrested so many people, but no one knew what happened to them, where they were being held. Rumours started, horrible stories of underground prisons and human experimentation. Opposition leaders asked questions, distanced themselves from Evie White. Opposition leaders found they were raided next. Loyal comrades who she'd used to get where she was all vanished in one night. They called it the Night of the Vapours.'

I looked over my older self's shoulder. There was definitely no longer a wall. The floor just ended a few feet in front of where I thought it had been.

Beyond that, there was nothing. Not darkness, not vague, swirling mists. Nothing.

Nothing existed beyond that very short horizon. I couldn't see it, because it didn't exist. Estrel glanced in the same direction, and visibly flinched.

'I don't know how much longer we've got,' he said.

'Am I going to reset soon?' I asked him.

'Probably,' he said, 'but it's too late to do anything about it anymore.' He nodded at the console on the wall. There were no longer any visible buttons on it.

'OK, I guess we wait and see,' I said, sounding far more casual than I felt. 'Night of the Vapours?'

'She gassed them. Right here in the Citadel, in that auditorium you were in tonight. Decimated the Clerics as a side benefit. After that, there was no opposition left. She could do what she wanted.'

'And what did she want?'

'I never got to see that,' said Estrel. 'Mouse was there at the meeting. The Night of…'

'Damn.'

I could see the pain on his face. I felt it too.

'The people who own this lab, they found me soon after. They knew Mouse. She always was well connected. They gave me hope. They gave me a purpose. They sent me here.'

'To today?' I asked.

'Weeks ago,' Estrel clarified. 'I've been working up to today. Putting things in place, preparing for the big day. The day I… you fix things so that none of it has to happen.'

I thought about the images we found on Toshock's devices. I was being manipulated, after all. But apparently only by myself.

'Why?' I asked, finally. The bench behind Estrel was fading, beyond that was the nothing.

It scared me, but I had to know.

'What is your purpose? Why did you put me in a loop? How do I get out of it? You said I have to stop Evie. Stop her how?'

'Kill her,' said Estrel, simply. 'Stop her, finally, definitively. I want you to kill her.'

'But you already did that, and the timeline collapsed,' I objected.

'That's because of the paradox,' explained Estrel. 'That's

why you have to do it, not me. Independently, with no coercion or direction from me. You have to kill her. You'll go round and round the loop until you do.'

'What if I never do?' I protested.

'Eventually you will. Infinite monkeys and all that. It seems like you found a way to learn, anyway.' Estrel held up the Echo. 'I mean, it's rubbish. Literally…'

He screwed up the Echo and tossed it behind me. I whipped my head around in time to see it disappear into nothing.

'You're smart. We're smart. We'll find a way. You've got forever.'

That triggered something in the back of my mind. I didn't think that was true. I went to say something, but Estrel stood up and wrapped his arms around me in an enormous bear hug.

'I shouldn't have told you any of this, mind you. But at the end of time, it probably doesn't matter anymore. You're going back, Estrel. No Echoes this time. But this is all still in you. I know it is. This was a dead end. I need you to try again. *It lies within you.* It's ironic, because it's what Evie said she was trying to do, but I need you to go back to square…'

CHAPTER 20

'We will shortly arrive in Trinity, Bridge Terminus, our final destination for mainline passengers. We would like to thank you for travelling with Trinity Rail and hope that your journey has been a pleasant and comfortable one. Please ensure that you take all your belongings with you when you disembark the train. For security reasons, any unattended baggage will be considered to be a security risk and may be destroyed…'

I glanced at my watch. It said six fifty-four. That was an appealing series of numbers, I thought. The moment I thought it, a strange feeling came over me.

My heart started pounding. I felt at a distance from everything, fractionally out of sync with the world. I glanced at my coffee cup. I'd probably drunk enough to stimulate an elephant. That would explain the palpitations, if not the déjà vu.

The carriage was busy. I thought I'd bagged two comfortable leather seats to myself when I boarded in Ashuana City but the person who had booked the seat next to me, an elderly man who hadn't taken his hat off all journey, had got onto the train at the last minute. I'd had to move my bag to the table in front of me, having left it too late to nab luggage-rack space. My knees kept bumping into those of the woman opposite me, so I'd spent a fair proportion of the journey apologising until she got completely fed up and moved when a seat became available in the next carriage.

The fourth member of our table was a Cleric, he said, from the Citadel in Trinity. I'd come across the Devoted before, preaching serenity in parks and shopping malls back home.

Outside of Trinity, they were an amusing oddity, an anachronistic religious cult, proponents of mysticism in an age of reason. I knew some people who were religious, of course, but they were generally older, or from immigrant families, and usually kept their beliefs low key.

This Cleric kept himself to himself and, in particular, didn't seem to have much with him, which meant that I'd been able to push my bag into the departed woman's quarter of the table to make room for breakfast.

The breakfast things had been cleared away now, but my plate had left a greasy ring on the shiny tabletop. I picked up a napkin from the pile to my right and wiped it away.

Again, my heart was racing, the world rushing backwards. *Weird.* I stared at the napkin, but the thought threatening to break through wouldn't come.

I yawned and stretched. There was plenty of room for my legs and behind my head was an actual cushion. Despite everything, it was very comfortable. Shame I didn't have time for a nap before we got in.

'… hope you have a great stay in Trinity and look forward to welcoming you back onboard in the near future.'

The announcement finished.

I looked out of the misted window. We were travelling over a bridge, a viaduct across a vast valley, the slopes thick with trees. Something wound through the bottom of the canyon, but from this height, it was hard to tell if it was a river

Echoes

or a road.

I knew it to be a river, though; the Triton winding its way down from its source in the Proctean Mountains before it flowed through the city ahead and on into the Middle Sea. I hadn't been to Trinity before, but I'd done my research. At least, I'd looked it up on my Com and could remember some details. I hadn't had long. I'd only found out that I was coming yesterday.

The thing was, I really didn't want to be here. This was the big one, the trip for me to make the sale that would get me the ultimate promotion, to the senior sales team. But I didn't want to be on the senior sales team. I hated the senior sales team - seven Crispy Burton clones and one actual Crispy Burton. They were everything I dreaded becoming.

I hadn't even meant to take this job. It had been a natural progression from the last natural progression from the last natural progression from the post room at my dad's company, a stop-gap that I'd taken to tide me over when I'd run out of money after college.

I had drifted into a career I didn't want and had no respect for. And now I was in danger of drifting into the next stage, at which point I really couldn't deny that I was a salesman. I really didn't want to be a salesman. My dad wanted me to be a salesman.

I loosened my necktie, ran a finger around my collar. I felt clammy. It was making my breakfast stir in my stomach unpleasantly. I tried to sigh out a wave of nausea but gagged, almost bringing up my breakfast anyway.

I'd had time to catch the metro home to shower and change before the car came to take me to the station for the overnight to Trinity. I thought I'd read on the train, but the book I'd taken from the lounge sat unopened on the table in front of me. I'd been trying to conserve my Com battery for the big presentation, but I should have just brought a spare pack and watched streams to pass the time instead. It was a long journey. I'd been bored.

The brown leather bag was open in front of me, and I rummaged through it. I wasn't really looking for anything; it was just something to do.

I found an apple and some wax-paper wrapped sandwiches I'd bought before I got on the train in a hurry, filling undetermined. I decided not to unwrap them as it looked like they were mayonnaise based and already leaking out.

My tablet had worked its way to the bottom of the bag. I took it out and wiped some mayonnaise off it with another napkin. Wouldn't do to turn up for an important presentation with mayonnaise stains on the equipment.

Was it an important presentation, though? This couldn't be an important contract for TrakcD. Not if they'd sent me. And I didn't care if it went well or not, did I? I didn't even want to be a salesman.

Except I kind of did care. I didn't like the idea of doing a poor job. That was annoying. I annoyed myself. I checked the pockets on the front and found my toothbrush and a change of underwear. Just in case I didn't make it back tonight. Why, exactly, was I doing this?

The train reached the end of the bridge and crossed into the city. Trinity. I closed my eyes and blew out. It was going to be fine. Cutting through the city walls, there was a ten metre tunnel. We were plunged into momentary darkness, before the train burst through the other side.

The carriage lights clicked back off, but the light was different on this side of the wall. The train remained high above street level, which was cast deep in shadow by the high-rise blocks that sprouted from the ground, shooting up to the top of the city walls, as if even they needed to find some cleaner air.

Around me, people started standing and gathering their things together. The old man got up and took his hat off, holding it against his chest, eyes closed. I wasn't sure what he was doing, but he was in my way, so I stayed seated.

The Cleric didn't move. He smiled at me. I tried to smile back, but I think I did it weird. I didn't feel comfortable. I turned my head, making a show of looking for someone or something that didn't exist to cover my embarrassment.

I filled in the gaps in the stories I would never know: a young couple, weighed down with baggage and a small baby, him struggling up and down the busy aisle ferrying bags, her struggling to soothe their restless child, on their way to visit his parents for a week of judgement and emotional blackmail; a business executive in crumpled pinstripes, his face red and bloated from the whisky he'd used to lull himself to sleep, his shirt stained with a coffee spill, scrabbled in the overhead rack for his briefcase which I could see was several seats further down the carriage, ill prepared for striking deals and driving bargains; a teenaged couple with eyes for no one but each other, still entwined, still dressed in last night's clothes which, given that they boarded this train the night before, would actually be the night before's clothes, keen to slink back to his place where they could be more naked and less conscious of the need to hide where their hands were; the old man in front of me finishing his prayer for the wife and family he'd left behind to come here, and shuffling down the aisle towards the carriage door, where he'd make his pilgrimage to the graveyard, to pay his respects to the only girl he'd ever loved.

I stood up as the train crawled into the station. The Cleric remained seated opposite. Past this station, Bridge Terminus, the train would switch tracks and carry on into the Trinity transport network. It was, I had discovered during my brief research, free for residents of the city.

The Citadel, in the centre, was where the Devoted lived and worshipped, and was several stops along the line. I walked down the aisle to the doors, heavy old-fashioned things that, once the platform had slid into view and the train had hissed to a pneumatic stop, the harassed-looking father had to stick his arm out of, through the window, to open from the outside.

The platform was busy, and he struggled to get the baby's carriage out and unfolded before he could lift their other bags and allow his partner to get off the train. I was last in line, behind the teenagers and the old man. I glanced behind me. The executive was still looking for his case.

I could have said something. I felt guilty that I didn't.

By the time I stepped off the train, most of the crowd had funnelled down the steps at the far end of the platform. But I had a strange sense of being observed. I looked around me. There was no one around.

The train's engines coughed out a noxious gust of exhaust and the train pulled out as I looked up and down the platform.

There was a coffee booth, a bored-looking youth reading his Com behind the counter. A "Vote Chaguartay" billboard towered over the opposite platform, casting a long shadow over the spot where I stood.

There was something that might have been a public toilet at the far end of the incredibly long platform, and a repeated pattern of high lampposts and metal benches, painted green, running along its length. Nothing else.

I pulled my Com out of my jacket pocket and flicked the screen on. The reminder of my appointment flashed. I had a little under two hours.

I'd checked earlier, so I knew that the Administration

building was a short walk from the train terminus, which gave me some time to kill, but that was the way I preferred it. I hated to be late, hated to be rushed.

There was time for coffee, if not a second breakfast. Maybe I could review my notes. Maybe I wouldn't bother because I didn't really care.

I could make out a wide flight of concrete steps leading down underneath the platform. The last of the other passengers was disappearing down it. All I seemed to do was follow the crowd, but there was nowhere else to go. Maybe on this occasion, it was fine.

I descended into a wide, gleaming lobby. Surfaces shone back at me, marbled, but whether they really were marble was something I wouldn't claim to have any expertise to determine.

As with the platform above, there was little in the way of ornament or decoration - sheer walls and clean angles surrounded me, apart from immediately opposite, where large, ornate gold gates, carved with vines and gargoyles and other bendy but, to me at least, unidentifiable things, stood towering over a narrow entrance. And exit, judging by the stream of people leaving. I recognised the old man, now shuffling at the back of the throng.

A cackle came from a figure huddled under a pile of blankets next to the bottom step.

'Piggens get yer?' the figure asked.

'Mm-hm,' I nodded.

What I really meant was "What?" but I was wary of getting into a conversation I was going to struggle to get out of.

'They runs amok, thems do.'

Oh, I think he meant pigeons.

'No,' I said, despite myself. 'No pigeons.'

I struggled to make out much more about them. The voice suggested they were old, but that's all I was getting. As far as I could see, they were a bundle of rags. There was a stench, which I didn't want to think about for long enough to even try to describe.

'Few come to Trinity anymore,' said the rags. 'Even fewer leave.' They cackled again.

It sounded like he was suggesting the pigeons came to Trinity on the train. It was like I was listening to him have a conversation with someone else, like the gaps he was leaving between his statements were not for me to fill.

There was another cackle. Once more, I had a tingle of something I'd experienced before. Not a clear memory, though, like the echo of a dream.

'Welcome to Trinity,' muttered the rags, settling down again under his blankets.

In the wall to my right there was a window cut into the marble, with a small counter in front of it. Below that was a logo I recognised, the insignia of Trinity Administration.

My appointment was with Trinity Administration, so that seemed to be a reassuring sign that I was in the right place. Behind the window there was a face. I approached, bending my neck to see inside.

'Good morning,' said The Face.

'Hi. I'm looking for information?'

'Welcome to Trinity,' said The Face.

'Thank you,' I replied, stepping up to the counter.

The Face swept a pile of papers, which seemed to include a comic and his breakfast of, apparently, rice and fried fish, out of the way and tapped furiously at a keyboard in front of him.

'We, at Trinity Administration, hope that your stay will be pleasant and mutually profitable.'

I should have been hoping for similar things, but I

definitely didn't. Pleasant would be OK. I wasn't bothered about the potential for profit. The Face nodded and smiled again, so I assumed he didn't read that much into my half hearted reaction.

'I just need to ask a few questions. Administrative questions, if you like.'

He smiled once more, as if he'd made a joke. I didn't feel that he had, so I didn't feel the need to respond. The Face looked a bit annoyed, but ploughed on.

'Name?'

'Estrel,' I said. 'Estrel Beck.'

'Purpose of visit?'

'Ah…'

I knew why I was there, but this was a question that suddenly felt like it had a million possible answers. One of which was the truth, but I also had a sudden doubt that the truth was the one I thought it was.

'I'm here from TrakcD Solutions. I have an appointment with…'

I realised that I'd forgotten the name of the person I had an appointment with.

'… with your transport department. It won't be in my name though, it's probably booked for a Crispy Burton. My name is Estrel Beck…'

'You said that,' said The Face, deadpan. 'What's a Crispy… Burton?'

'Oh, no.'

I could feel my face flush. It was way too much information. I needed to precis this thing right down.

'Crispy Burton is a sales manager. I'm here instead of him. I'm sorry for the confusion.'

'Ah,' said The Face, in a way that suggested he understood whilst continuing to look baffled. 'It's OK, I just need Business or Leisure. I'm not trying to pry.'

'Oh,' I said.

I realised the logo had thrown me. My appointment was with Trinity Administration, but Trinity Administration, which I understood to be some kind of publicly owned utility-provider-cum-public-transport-operator, also ran the railways.

What I'd assumed to be some kind of reception desk was nothing more than a ticket office. Or left luggage. Which meant that this guy didn't care. And if he didn't care…

I had a strange sense that I was about to do something significant here.

On the face of it, I was about to bunk off work for the day, but deeper inside me I felt, no, I *knew,* that it meant more than that.

I was about to sacrifice a career I'd never wanted, but that wasn't it either.

Words ran through my head. They sounded like song lyrics, but they didn't have a tune. Maybe it was a poem. I didn't think I knew any poems.

> *Have you poured your water on the ground?*
> *Or do you still see the sky when you look up?*
> *Are you ready to walk away?*

'Leisure,' I said.

The Face looked momentarily confused at how this answer seemed to bear no relation to anything else I had said up to now. Recovering, he adjusted his expression, nodded, and tapped at his screen.

'And will you be staying long?'

'I… don't know,' I said. 'I have a train back home booked but…'

Echoes

I looked around the terminal lobby. Everything was unfamiliar and yet I felt I belonged here, that I cared about what happened here. Like this was somewhere I was a part of, even though I'd only just arrived.

The Face nodded again, tapped at his screen, then pulled a lever under the desk, which caused a deep drawer to slide out of the wall next to me.

'Do you have any baggage that you'd like me to look after for you? You may place any items in the drawer and I will ensure that they are ready for you on departure.'

Departure. The word hurt. I considered my bag. I'd packed for the meeting. Sandwiches, tablet… the emergency toothbrush might be useful, but who walked around with a spare toothbrush in their pocket?

It would be good to lighten the load. I slid the strap of the bag over my head and placed it in the drawer. I could always come back. I knew I wouldn't.

'Thank you,' said The Face. 'If you place your Com on the contact pad, I will upload your receipt...'

I placed my Com on the pad, waited for the beep, and then turned. The Face was saying something to me about receipts and about another terminus and about hours of opening and I wasn't interested in any of it.

I didn't need that information. I wasn't going to leave.

I walked towards the ornately carved exit and pushed my way out into the light. The Trinity Administration building, a windowless concrete block, was indeed opposite the Bridge station entrance.

It towered over the multi-lane carriageway, the TransWay, which was criss-crossed with roads and tramlines, TransPods streaming past at alarming speed.

I felt like I would have recognised it even if it didn't have the *Trinity Administration* logo stamped across its middle. It gave it the look of a tombstone.

The passing traffic temporarily mesmerised me. I shook myself out of my daze. The world was my oyster. This world was my oyster.

A gull swooped up to my right, cawing and calling. That must be the direction of the port, I thought. The gull turned and flew in the direction it had come, all the time calling. Calling me?

I turned right and walked along the road. I quickened my pace.

Left-right. Left-right.
Left-right. Left-right.

Find-Mouse. Find-Mouse.
Find-Mouse. Find-Mouse.

It looks like you've finished reading ECHOES…

Thank you!

I really hope you enjoyed it, and if you did it would be great if you could leave a review somewhere… Amazon, Goodreads, Social Media, just tell a friend - any of those would be fantastic and make all the difference for me, struggling little indie author that I am.

Next, if you'd like to stay up to date with what I'm writing and when you can read it, pop along to https://philoddy.com where you can find links to my own socials, and you can sign up for my monthly newsletter.

Finally, there are other books I've written and contributed to, so if you're not sure what to read next, check out:

ENTANGLEMENT SERIES
   Entrapment (coming late 2024)
   Enlightenment (coming early 2025)
   Exodus (coming late 2025)
FOR CHILDREN
   The Man In The Moon
AS CONTRIBUTOR
   Royston and District Writers' Circle 40th Anniversary Anthology
   There Are Many Ways Of Getting Lost: The Royston Writers' Circle Lockdown Anthology

About the Author

Phil Oddy lives in North Hertfordshire and writes stories about how to cope in a confusing world, cleverly disguised as sci-fi/fantasy adventures. Find his website at https://philoddy.com - everything he's currently up to should be on there.

He is happily married with two sons, and has promised everyone lavish gifts if he ever writes a bestseller, so if you've bought one of his books then they all thank you.

Despite a long and successful career as an IT analyst in both the public and private sectors, writing is something he seems to be unable to prevent himself doing which means that by encouraging him you're either feeding an addiction or providing therapy. You can pick which.

When his fingers are too tired to carry on typing, Phil likes to relax by reading something by David Mitchell (either one is fine) or binge-watching Drag Race.

Acknowledgements

This book would not have been published if I hadn't finished it. And I wouldn't have finished it without the support and love of a whole load of people. Thanks are due to…

Everyone at the Royston (and District) Writers' Circle for all the stories you've shared, and for your feedback on mine. It's an honour to be part of such a local institution.

Julie Dore for being my first beta reader and giving me the confidence that I had written something worthwhile.

Everyone involved in The Bestseller Experiment podcast - especially the two Marks and everyone on the BXP Team Facebook group - whose willingness to share their experiences and successes have been an inspiration and a how-to guide.

Anyone who ever liked a post of mine on social media, especially the really boring word count ones, or the ones where I was moaning about how much I hate editing.

"Juliana Frink" who came up with the series title, "Entanglement".

Jon and Tom at The Failing Writers podcast who read out a whole chunk of an early draft and then said some really nice things about it.

My family for their support and their tolerance and their love.

To Alex, who was the first person I told the plot of Echoes to. He said that it sounded really cool.

To Sam, who is the only person, to my knowledge, who has read The Man In The Moon twice. I'm not sure he's ever read any other book twice. If that's not a glowing review I don't know what is.

To Susan, for everything. I couldn't do this (or anything else) without you. Thank you x

Printed in Great Britain
by Amazon